Praise for

Introducing Vivien Leigh Reid:
Daughter of the Diva

"Read it afte_____igh's
on-set adver_____e.com

"Collins and_____d in-
teresting ch_____rican
teen discove_____iings
Irish. Reade_____bug
and cheer he_____

_____oklist

"The story i_____set-
ting and lika_____IATT

"A humorou_____ature

"Collins and_____vien
Leigh Reid. _____he's
real. . . . A_____ut a
smile on you_____

_____.com

"A snappy, b_____n an
adolescent s_____de."
_____com

"A wonderful new book for your summer reading."   —*BellaOnline*

"Readers who enjoy Meg Cabot's 'The Princess Diaries' and Louise Rennison's 'Georgia Nicolson' will want to know what Leigh does next."
     —*School Library Journal*

Also by Yvonne Collins and Sandy Rideout

Introducing Vivien Leigh Reid:
Daughter of the Diva

Now Starring Vivien Leigh Reid

Diva in Training

Yvonne Collins **and** Sandy Rideout

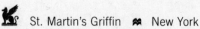 St. Martin's Griffin ✠ New York

www.stmartins.com

ISBN 0-312-33839-2
EAN 978-0-312-33839-8

First Edition: January 2006

10 9 8 7 6 5 4 3 2 1

For our nieces, honorary and otherwise:

Elizabeth and Jayne, and Michelle,

who got us started

acknowledgments

Thanks to Jenny Bent, Elizabeth Bewley, and Michelle Kroes for their belief in our divas.

Thanks also to: our friends in Hollywood North who shared their knowledge of acting, particularly Belynda Blyth and Michelle Michals; and the Los Angeles contingent, who showed us around their city one very damp week.

Finally, we're grateful as always to our usual supporting cast, especially Dave.

Now Starring
Vivien Leigh Reid

one

I am trapped in a moving vehicle with a madwoman—a madwoman who claims to be my mother, although it's never been proven through genetic testing. We are tearing up the 405 at breakneck speed and her eyes seem to be everywhere but on the road ahead. She jets past a lumbering Hummer and cuts off a Porsche without even signaling.

"Are you crazy?" I squawk, as the guy in the Porsche flips her the bird.

"Oh, chill," she says, either to Porsche Guy or me. She yanks down her visor, admires herself in the tiny mirror, and reapplies her lipstick with a flourish.

I stomp nervously on an imaginary brake as she crowds a BMW. "Watch out!"

"Darling, you're so uptight." This time I know she's speaking to me. What's more, I know she's silently adding "just like your father." It's only silent because this is Hour One of my visit to Los Angeles and we have to last eight weeks in the ring.

If I'd known she was deranged, rather than merely flighty, I wouldn't have agreed to spend a second summer with her. Last year, Dad didn't give me a choice before sending me to get to know her on her film set in Ireland, but this time I practically volunteered. Obviously, I should have demanded danger pay.

When the Porsche pulls up alongside us, I rap on the window and shout, "Help! I've been taken hostage!"

Instead of being embarrassed, Mom giggles and gives Porsche Guy a flirty wave. He smiles and waves back, continuing to keep pace with her. Many have fallen under Annika Anderson's spell before, but few at this velocity.

"I'm serious, Annika. If you don't slow down, I am calling the cops." I shake my cell phone at her. "And turn your lights on, it's nearly dark."

She flicks on the lights with an exaggerated sigh that's worthy of me.

"Why look at that," I say, pointing to the illuminated speedometer. "We've broken the sound barrier. I'll have a story to tell in Physics next fall."

"Whatever," she says in a tone also worthy of me, reaching for her cigarettes. I snatch them out of her hand and stow them in my purse. "Granny," she mutters.

I turn to stare at her perfect profile. "Pardon me?"

"I said you're a granny—a little old lady in a fifteen-year-old's body."

"Sixteen. And I am not uptight. I just want to make it back to Seattle alive. I can't believe this wreck even goes this fast."

"Wreck! This car is in pristine condition. I just had it custom-painted claret."

That would be maroon to anyone else. Mom could afford a nice car, but she chooses to drive this vintage Volkswagen Beetle because it reminds her of the first car she ever owned. In other words, she's clinging to her lost youth. I wish she'd cling to it in something with more legroom.

Screeching to a stop in front of a restaurant, Mom switches off the ignition. The attitude immediately disappears and she recovers her normal personality. I use the term "normal" loosely: Annika hasn't seen normal in a very long time, if ever. She is a Grade-A diva stuck in a B-movie career and that discrepancy has caused tectonic shifts all over the Earth.

"You're going to love this place," she says, tucking her long blond curls into a tweed newsboy cap and putting on her sunglasses.

"What's with the disguise?" I ask. "Are the police after you for piloting a rocket without a license?"

She surrenders the keys to the valet and leads me inside. "I just want to have a quiet dinner. I hate being pestered by fans."

If Mom really wanted a quiet dinner, I expect we'd be at her house in the Valley rather than at Kate Mantilini's in Beverly Hills. And if she valued her privacy, she'd have asked for a darkened booth along the wall rather than a table in the center of the room. No, the disguise is actually a desperate bid for attention. One of us has matured this year, and it isn't Annika.

Even the soundtrack is the same: "Being over forty in Hollywood is a full-time job," she whines. "Thank god I have so much support." Team Annika consists of an agent, a publicist, a therapist, a psychic, a yogi, a nutritionist, a personal trainer, a masseuse, a cosmetician, and a plastic surgeon. It takes a village to keep an aging actress afloat. "Darling, are you listening to me?"

"Yes, I'm listening to you, Annika," I say, although I tuned out long ago. "It's not like there's anything here to distract me." I asked to eat at Spago, where the stars hang out, but she said lots of "faces" come to this high-end diner. I highly doubt that.

"We talked about this, Vivien," she says. "You agreed to call me Mom."

I did, too, after many heated battles. And she agreed to call me "Leigh," which is my middle name, but she never does. It is one of many things we fight over. In fact, we fight over almost everything. That's how we deal with the big gap in our back story. Mom left for Hollywood when I was three and faded out of my life until she was little more than a name over the title of crappy TV movies like *Three Times a Devil* or *Love on the Dark Side*. Dad would tape them and watch them over and over, laughing his ass off. They aren't comedies.

Our big reunion in Ireland last summer didn't exactly rock

the box office, but with patience and persistence, I managed to turn her parenting performance around. She called me weekly throughout the winter and visited three times, including a special trip she made to see me in my school play. No one could blame me for thinking I had the upper hand in this relationship, but her behavior in the car shows we have a ways to go. I've come to L.A. to expand my horizons, and for that to happen, my mother needs to know her place. That smug smile on her face suggests she doesn't. It must be erased, and quickly.

"I still think of you as Annika," I say, watching the smug smile contract slightly. "But I'll offer you one 'Mom' for every 'Leigh.' " I look around at the half-empty restaurant. "Where is everybody?"

"It's late," she says. "In L.A., people go to bed early and get up early. Most restaurants close by eleven."

The lifestyles of the rich and famous come with a curfew? So much for my expectations about Hollywood. There is nothing for it but to order a chocolate sundae and regroup.

"Not without dinner first," Annika says, tapping one glossy red fingernail on the main course section of the menu. I open my mouth to protest and she adds, "Don't tell me there isn't anything you like because there are fifty options."

The arrival of a cute guy at the next table gives me an excuse to stall. I crane around to get a good look at him. "Oh my god!" I whisper to Mom. "It's Adam Brody."

Gawking openly, she asks, "Who?"

"Don't stare. He plays Seth on *The OC*."

"Oh right, that soap opera."

"Quiet, he'll hear you. *The OC* is a drama. Or maybe a dramedy. But it's definitely not a soap opera."

"Darling, that wasn't derogatory. I have nothing against a well-crafted soap, you know that. Would you like to meet him?"

I squint menacingly at her. "Don't even think about it."

"He's cute. I'll just—"

"No! I'm not a groupie. My interest in Adam is purely professional. We're both in the business, that's all."

Annika snorts into her wine.

I bristle. "I have a movie credit, you know."

She knows. I had a small role in *Danny Boy,* the movie she filmed in Ireland. The director encouraged me to explore acting further, which is why Mom has enrolled me in a hot acting program here in L.A. That and her guilty conscience. As if she could make up for twelve years of neglect in two summers.

The waitress returns and I order the seafood linguini. I don't really like seafood, especially things in crusty shells, but if expanding my horizons includes eating slimy mollusks, so be it. That Adam happens to be eating the same thing is a mere coincidence.

Scene 1: Leigh Plays Hard to Get

INTERIOR L.A. RESTAURANT, DAY

A young actress is dining at a Beverly Hills restaurant with her aging but beautiful mother. At the next table, a famous actor looks up from his linguini, intrigued by the girl's cool demeanor. Why hasn't she noticed him? Has he finally found a girl who isn't fazed by his fame?

The famous actor deliberately knocks his script off the table and kicks it toward the girl's table.

LEIGH
Excuse me, I think you dropped this.

ADAM
Did I? Lucky you noticed because I haven't memorized my lines for tomorrow.

LEIGH
I know how it is, so good luck.

                    ADAM
        Are you an actor?

                    LEIGH
        Yeah, my first movie premieres here next
        month. I'm in L.A. to take some acting
        classes, do a little surfing.

                    ADAM
        Maybe we could catch a wave together
        sometime.

                    LEIGH
        Maybe.

                    ADAM
        How about I call you at your hotel?

                    LEIGH
        I'm crashing at my mother's place. It's
        more comfortable than a hotel and she
        gives me my space. Anyway, it was nice
        meeting you...?

                    ADAM
        Adam. Adam Brody. I'm on *The OC*.

                    LEIGH
        I'm Leigh. I've never seen your show but
        I've heard it's good.

                    ADAM
                [sliding Leigh his card]
        I'd love to take you to your movie pre-
        miere. Call me.

```
                    LEIGH
        I'll think about it.
```

Adam inhales a final whiff of Leigh's Liquid Sugar perfume and pushes his plate aside. How can he think about food when he's just met the girl of his dreams?

Annika's voice drags me back to reality. "Snap out of it and eat your dinner."

I poke gingerly at a mussel. "Have you ever looked inside one of these things? It's disgusting."

"Then why did you order it?"

"I'm giving bivalves a chance."

Glancing over at Adam, she sees that he's eating the same dish. "Oh, for heaven's sake," she says. Removing her hat, she shakes out her curls and reaches out to tap Adam's arm. "Excuse me," she says. "My daughter is a huge fan of yours."

"I am not!" I say. Adam looks taken aback so I quickly add, "I mean, I'm a fan of the show. And of your acting."

"Thanks," he says. He smiles at me and a spotlight suddenly appears overhead that captures only Adam and me in its beam. My mother, outside the circle of light, no longer matters.

Then a voice emanates from the shadows offstage: "My daughter is an actor, too, Seth." The spotlight jerks away from me to shine on Annika. "You should have seen her in her school's production of *A Midsummer Night's Dream*. She had to play half the parts because no one else even auditioned. That school focuses entirely on academics and her father refuses to transfer her to a school for the performing arts." I glare at her helplessly as she continues. "Vivien—I named her after Vivien Leigh, the famous actress—bravely took on the roles not just of Titania and Hermia, but also—"

Don't say it, please don't say it. . . .

"—Bottom."

Adam's eyes widen slightly. "The donkey?"

Nodding, Annika continues, "At any rate, Vivien did very well and things will get easier for her after our movie comes out this summer."

He looks more interested. "What movie?"

"It's called *Danny Boy*. I'm the headliner but Vivien had a small role, too."

I excuse myself and go to the rest room. Annika can share my whole life story if she wants, but I don't have to stand by and listen. From the cubicle, I text message my best friend Abby, who lives in New York City:

```
Abby,
I h8 hr. I h8 hr. I h8 hr.
Annika jst humiliated
me n frnt of Adam Brody.
Pls. snd airfare. ther must
B a Dcent acting skul n nu York.
L
```

★   ★   ★

Ten unblinking eyes stare down at me from a shelf when I turn the light on in my bedroom. More Madame Alexander dolls. Over the years, Mom has given me at least a dozen and they've always creeped me out. Fortunately, they fetch a good price on eBay. Last month, I sold enough of them to buy a Puma bag, an outlay that would have required many grueling hours at the Pita Pit where I work part-time.

Standing on a chair, I grab the dolls and toss them onto the canopied bed. This room is embarrassing enough even without the dolls. Mom redecorated in honor of my visit, and judging by the "fairy princess" theme, she's still coming to terms with my age. In Ireland, she actually tried to pass me off as her sister.

I unpack my suitcase and place two alarm clocks on the bedside table. One has a shamrock sticker and is always set to Irish time. Right now it says 7:00 A.M. If I text Rory now, he can read my message when he wakes up. Flopping onto the pink ruffled comforter, I punch the keys on my cell phone:

```
Rory,
Landed n California DIS morn.
Can't BlEv we're goin 2 b 2geder
again n less thN 800 hrz ☺ L%k
4ward 2 CN yu. Christmas fElz
lIk it wz two yr.z ago. Miss U loads.
Yor devoted gf,
Leigh XOXOXO
```

My finger hesitates over the SEND button. The message is over the top because I feel guilty about getting so excited over Adam Brody. It's not like I have any serious interest in him or anything. Adam is a fantasy whereas Rory, my boyfriend of almost a year, is a hundred percent real. He'll be staying with us for a few days when his family visits San Francisco. Better to declare my undying love in person. I hit delete and type:

```
Rory,
Made it to California.
Mom iz stil a major pain.
She tinkz I'm 5 yr.z old.
More l8r.
Leigh
```

"Are you pestering that boy already?"

Startled, I sit up. "How about knocking next time? And I'm not pestering him. He's my boyfriend and he likes hearing from me."

"Boyfriend? Isn't that rushing things a little?"

I give her the eye roll. "We've been going out for a year."

"As I recall, you had one date in Ireland and two at Christmas when he visited his aunt in Seattle."

"With that memory, it's amazing that you keep forgetting I'm sixteen. My point is, Rory and I are in love."

"For someone so smitten, you were awfully interested in that Seth fellow earlier."

"Adam. And that's different."

"Last year you also thought you were in love with Sean Finlay."

I did have a major crush on Sean, the twenty-one-year-old Irish star of *Danny Boy*. Unfortunately, he had a major crush on my mother, which proves that he has terrible taste and would have been totally wrong for me. Still, I was furious that she led him on and I worked hard to keep the grudge fresh all winter.

"He might have come around if you hadn't flirted with him," I say. "I hope you'll control yourself when Rory's here."

I dump the contents of my makeup bag onto the dresser and line up my concealers from lightest to darkest, to match my evolving tan. I use them to cover the hideous mole on my left cheek. Mom has the same one on hers, but she calls it a beauty mark. It isn't.

Noticing the empty shelf above the desk, she asks, "Where are your dolls?"

"Last seen under the bed making fun of the décor. I'm too old for dolls, Mom. And I'm too old for this room."

"But pink is your favorite color."

"Purple is my favorite color. Even Dad knows that." He doesn't but I can't overlook an opportunity to make her feel guilty. "It's time you accepted that I am grown up. I'm old enough to get married, you know."

"Not without my consent—and don't even think about it."

"Just because it didn't work out for you and Dad doesn't mean the rest of us can't live happily ever after. Rory and I are absolutely, perfectly in sync."

As if on cue, my cell phone vibrates.

```
Leigh,
If U C Cameron Diaz, cn
U gt me hr autograph?
R
```

Okay, so the distance isn't helping our synchronicity, but when he gets here, we'll make up for lost time. Even bitter, cynical Annika will be forced to admit that Rory Quinn and I are meant for each other.

two

Gray T-shirt, green army pants, Adidas sneakers, powder blue Guess hoodie.

I stare at the mirror and frown. It works but there's no sparkle. Today I need to sparkle, even if only I see it.

Mom calls from the hall, "Let's go, Vivien! A professional is always on time."

Purple rugby shirt, Gap jeans, Adidas sneakers, black French Connection hoodie. Almost there. I exchange the purple shirt for a pink Abercrombie and Fitch T-shirt. That's it.

My low-slung jeans reveal a hint of the tattoo at the base of my spine. It's a small shamrock, a memento of my trip to Ireland last summer. Annika has one too. Convincing her that getting matching tattoos was a hip mother-daughter bonding ritual was the only way I could get parental permission.

I managed to hide mine from Dad and Grandma Reid for the longest time, but I finally slipped up. While reaching for a serving platter, I flashed it and Gran screeched as if she'd seen the mark of the devil upon me. I dropped the platter and when Dad ran into the kitchen he cut his foot on the shards. Now Gran brings up the tattoo every time she sees me, reminding me how sorry I will be on my wedding night when my husband sees it for the first time (I don't think she's joking). Dad prefers to pretend it never happened—unless we see someone else with a tattoo, at which point he puckers up in silent disapproval.

Mom hollers again from the hallway. Hastily gathering my hair into a ponytail, I run down the hall where Mom is standing, hands on hips. To preempt her smart remark, I say, "If I am wracked by insecurities, whose fault is that?"

"Mine, of course," she says. "To save time in the mornings, let's just assume everything is."

★ ★ ★

"Run the yellow," I urge Mom. "It's almost ten o'clock."

"What happened to your invisible brake? Last night you were the picture of *prudence*." Emphasis on the "prude."

"That's when I was trying to convince you to let me drive myself to class. I didn't realize you'd cast yourself in the role of chauffeur."

"If you're in the habit of running lights, I made the right decision."

"I'm more cautious than you are, Annika. You'd never catch me flipping the lipstick at a Porsche."

She fiddles with the side mirror to hide a furtive road-warrior smile. Today, in the bright morning sunshine, it's even more obvious that she's got a weird car thing going on. It can't be a coincidence that she's wearing maroon driving gloves.

I got my driver's license months ago, on the first try and without any help from Dad. He took me for one short spin and totally freaked when I grazed a Porta-Potty at a nearby construction site. It didn't even tip over! That man is wound tighter than a Slinky. So, I joined Driver's Ed, where the instructor was very supportive. Even now Dad refuses to let me drive his midlife crisis sports car. If I want to go anywhere, I have to borrow Gran's old beater. Sometimes she shadows me in Stan's car. As if I wouldn't notice a huge white Chrysler 300—the Moby Dick of cars—tailing me. Independence is a foreign concept in my family.

Today, Mom says, "I'm not running any lights to get you to class on time when you could have stopped at three changes of clothes instead of going for four."

The only way she could know this is true is if the mirror in my room is two-way glass. Either that or it takes her precisely four tries to get ready for a big day, but I refuse to believe that we're that much alike.

She pulls up in front of the Academy of Dramatic Arts and asks, "Do you want me to help you find the classroom?"

"Sure," I say, rolling my eyes. "Grab my stroller and let's go."

"Lose the sarcasm," she says, as I climb out of the car. "And fix your ponytail, it's scrunched."

Now she tells me.

★ ★ ★

I freeze in the open doorway, staring at my new classmates. There are fewer attractive students in the entire student body at my school in Seattle than there are in this room. Not that that's saying much. At J. D. Sandford Academy, brains are valued over beauty and brawn, so there is no incentive to care about personal presentation. The school uniform is designed to discourage students from wasting energy on their appearance that would be better channeled into algebra.

Here in L.A., my cool quotient, never that high, is already in a nosedive. I can't quite put my finger on why. Superficially, my clothes seem fine but something is lacking. The only thing I feel good about is my Puma bag, which is as nice as any of the designer bags parked under the girls' chairs.

The old man standing in the doorway says, "In or out?"

"In, I guess."

"Miss Reid, I presume? I am Duncan Kirk, professor of Reality Method 101."

Carbon dating would probably place Professor Kirk at about five hundred years of age. The man is a living fossil and a battered one at that. His gray hair is disheveled, his black jacket faded, and there's a circle of white flesh peeking through what appears to be a cigarette hole in his pant leg.

"You're late," he says. "You won't survive in this business if you aren't punctual."

"Sorry, sir," I say, to ingratiate myself. Roger Knelman, the director of *Danny Boy,* always insisted on "sir."

Peering at my bag through half-moon glasses, he asks, "I suppose that's a dog?"

"Actually, sir, it's a bag." Maybe it's time for bifocals. The class titters, making me wonder if I am missing something. "Oh, you mean the *logo.* That's a puma, sir, which is a cat. It's endangered now, unfortunately." When I'm nervous, I sometimes dredge up little-known facts from *National Geographic* just to fill the void.

Professor Kirk raises bushy gray eyebrows at me and the class titters again. "Thank you for the natural history lesson," he says, "but I was asking if you're carrying a dog in the bag."

"A dog?" He's already senile. "Why would I bring a dog to class, sir?"

He stares around the classroom. "My point exactly. But people your age want to take those silly little dogs everywhere these days."

"Only the girls, sir," offers a buff guy slouched in a chair. His sun-bleached hair sticks up in ten different directions but on the scale of cute, he surpasses Adam Brody.

Professor Kirk gestures to a chair. "Sit, Miss Reid. Let us begin."

A pretty blonde who could pass for Hilary Duff leans over to me and says, "We'd almost convinced him to allow the dogs. Now you've ruined it for everyone."

The exotic-looking girl beside her nods indignantly before tossing her long, shiny black hair. "Thanks, loser."

Another girl on my immediate left pats my arm kindly. She has green eyes, red, shoulder-length dreadlocks and a T-shirt that reads *Rip the Wave.* "Don't listen to them," she says.

Professor Kirk says, "Stand and state your name, the reason you're here, and describe your previous acting experience."

Here's my chance to redeem myself. Annika may not be a star, but she has appeared in over twenty movies, some of which people have actually seen. Plus, Sean Finlay is becoming a name and being his costar should mean something. Thanks to *Danny Boy,* I may have more insider knowledge of the film business than anyone here.

Scene 2: Leigh Reid Knocks 'Em Dead

INTERIOR CLASSROOM, DAY

Professor Jerk nods at Leigh to begin.

LEIGH
I'm Leigh Reid. I got interested in acting
last summer when I visited my mother on
the set of her movie, *Danny Boy.*

CUTE GUY
Your mother's an actor?

DUFF-ALIKE
Wicked!

RED DREADS
I read about *Danny Boy* in *Premiere* magazine. Wasn't it shot in Ireland?

LEIGH
Yeah, I spent six weeks there, shopping
in Dublin, hanging out in pubs....I even
got a tattoo.

DUFF-ALIKE
Wow, you're so lucky! My mom won't let me
have a tattoo.

LEIGH
My mom got one too.

Duff-alike hauls her chair closer to Leigh's.

CUTE GUY
So, you were on a real movie set?

LEIGH
How else could I have delivered my lines?

ENTIRE CLASS
You're in a major motion picture?

The students crowd around to quiz Leigh about her exciting life.

PROFESSOR JERK
I apologize if I was curt earlier, Miss Reid. With your credentials, I'm not sure there's much you can learn here. Would you do me the honor of helping to teach instead?

LEIGH
I'd be happy to share some pointers, Professor, but a good actor never stops learning. Sean Finlay, my friend and costar, taught me that.

DUFF-ALIKE
Oh my god! You worked with Sean Finlay? *The* Sean Finlay? He's SO gorgeous!

LEIGH
Yeah, I played his sister in *Danny Boy* and we hung out a lot. I'm afraid I broke his heart.

Duff-alike faints.

EXOTIC GIRL
[fanning Duff-alike]
Leigh, you're the greatest.

★ ★ ★

Eager to improve my social standing without delay, I wave my hand in the air. Professor Jerk ignores me and points to the Duff-alike.

"I'm Asia Pearl and I'm a dancer," she says. "You might recognize me from music videos. I'm taking both acting and singing lessons this summer to train for a career on Broadway. My goal is to become a triple threat."

I drop my hand and sink lower in my seat.

The dark-haired girl stands and says, "I'm Blake Burrows, daughter of Marlena Diaz, the supermodel from the eighties. I started modeling when I was two and got interested in acting last year after shooting a commercial for Revlon."

My new pal is next. "I'm Karis Tate and I practically grew up on film sets. My father is a director and my mother is an actor. They really want me to choose another profession, but I finally convinced them to let me take a class."

As we go around the circle, each student seems to have more impressive credentials than the last. Gray Cowley, the cute guy, is the son of Geoff Cowley, the Academy Award–winning actor. Gray himself has done tons of commercials. A year ago, he landed a lead role on a TV series, and when it didn't get picked up, he spent a year in Europe licking his wounds. Now he's brushing up his acting skills to try again.

When my turn comes, I clear my throat nervously. "I'm Leigh Reid."

"You're registered as *Vivien* Reid," the professor says.

Annika strikes again. "I've always gone by Leigh, my middle name."

Blake says, "Wasn't Vivien Leigh some actor from, like, the ice age?"

"She starred in *Gone with the Wind* in 1939," I say. "It's a classic."

"Lame," says Blake.

"Totally," Asia agrees.

"No lamer than being named after a continent," I tell Asia. "Or a nineteenth-century poet," I add for Blake's benefit. "Or did you know that?"

I glance at Karis and she gives me the thumbs-up. Across the room, Gray leans forward with more interest. Everyone loves a catfight.

Everyone except Professor Kirk. "Enough, ladies," he says. "Please continue, Miss Reid."

I tell the class about Annika Anderson, glossing over her B-movie history. It's obvious from their blank expressions that no one has heard of her.

"What films has she done?" Blake asks.

Reluctantly, I reel off some titles: *"Three Times a Devil . . . One Grave Too Many . . ."* Laughter ripples through the room and I reach hastily for my ace in the hole. "I got interested in acting after playing a small part in a feature film."

Blake snorts. "*You* were in a feature? Which one?"

"Danny Boy."

Gray slumps back in his chair. "Never heard of it. Must have tanked."

"It did not tank! It hasn't even been released!" My voice is shrill. Gray chuckles and the guy beside him gives him a high five. "We shot it in Ireland last summer."

"Ireland?" Asia says. "Boring."

This is not going at all as I'd hoped. And Professor Kirk, far from trying to defend me, is leaning back in his chair with his eyes closed.

Finally, giving it one last shot, I say, "It's much easier to get a tattoo over there."

"You've got a tattoo?" Blake asks.

I nod, relieved to be making an impression at last.

Asia scrunches her pretty face. "Why would you mutilate your body like that? Henna is way cooler."

Professor Kirk finally rouses himself. "Could someone wake me when the party is over?"

★ ★ ★

"Hi, Sprout," Dad says. "What could possibly be wrong already?"

He thinks he knows me so well. "Nothing's wrong. I'm just calling to say hi."

"Tell me you're not calling to whine about acting school already."

If there's one thing Dad hates, it's whining. He usually responds by delivering one of his *"When I was your age we were so poor we roasted rats on a spit for dinner and felt lucky to get them"* stories. This is probably my only major regret about being raised by my father alone. If Abby has a rough day, her mother is standing by with ice cream and sympathy, maybe a trip to the mall. Dad is more likely to assign extra chores to help me shake it off.

Since I clearly won't be getting any sympathy, I can at least deny him the pleasure of telling me to suck it up. "Acting school is great," I say. "The professor is great, the students are great, and I couldn't be happier."

Not having Mom's ear for sarcasm, he promptly lowers his whine detector: "Atta girl. I knew you'd fit right in."

three

My mother greets the Starbucks barista as a long-lost friend. For all I know, he could be; plenty of baristas are out-of-work actors, especially here in L.A. Besides, Mom doesn't seem to have many real friends. Maybe she's only comfortable with people when there's an espresso machine between them.

"Excuse me," I say, interrupting their celebrity-sighting update. "I'll take those car keys, Mom. Last night, you said I could drive."

She turns to me and laughs incredulously. "I said no such thing."

What she actually said was "We'll see" in the tone that means *"It's late and I don't want to argue but you don't stand a chance in hell."* Being an optimist by nature, however, I always try to see the possibilities even with someone as negative as Annika.

I order a white hot chocolate, extra whip, and a scone.

"Your eating habits are atrocious," Annika says.

"At least I eat," I say, flaunting my whipped cream mustache. It bugs Mom that I can eat anything I want and not gain weight. She subsists on scraps of vegetable matter and pale bits of grilled protein. It's the Aging Diva Diet that's so popular in Hollywood circles. "Would you prefer that I live on caffeine and smokes like you?"

"No, but you're still growing."

I sincerely hope not. Earlier this year, Dad measured me as he does on every birthday and carved a little notch on my bedroom door frame. I was five foot ten. The next day, I found some sandpaper and erased thirteen years with a few strokes. Five ten is where it ends. If I top that, I don't want to know. I already tower over half the guys at school, although Rory, thank god, is much taller.

"Why can't we get a table?" I ask, as she propels me through the parking lot.

"Because there's a half-hour drive ahead of us."

"Then why can't we live in Beverly Hills like everyone else? The twisty roads make me queasy."

"The junk food makes you queasy. But if you want to sit awhile tomorrow, try getting ready faster. You should be down to two wardrobe changes by now."

"I already explained. Twice." It astounds me how many times I have to repeat vital information to my parents; they have the mental capacity of four-year-olds. Fortunately, I am a bottomless pit of patience. "I could cut prep time by half if you'd let me take your credit card to the Sherman Oaks mall. You know my clothes are all wrong for L.A. Don't you want me to fit in?"

"What's wrong with your clothes?"

I slouch in the passenger seat. "I'm not sure but everyone else looks cooler."

"Well, when you've figured out exactly where your wardrobe is falling short, we'll discuss strategic additions. There won't be any carte blanche spending."

I stare out the window at the Hollywood Hills flashing by. "If I quit the class, we could spend the tuition on clothes."

She turns so quickly to stare at me that the Beetle swerves into oncoming traffic. "You had better be joking, Vivien. There is no way that you are quitting that class—not after what I sacrificed to get you into it."

Reality Method 101 was booked long in advance and to secure my admission, Mom had to coach a junior class through a production of *The Wizard of Oz*—and star as the Wicked Witch of the West. It was a blow to her pride and it also meant giving up an interesting role in an independent film that would have conflicted.

"I hate it and I'm not learning anything," I say. "All we do is stupid exercises and the teacher never explains the point. I learned more in an hour on *Danny Boy*."

"Duncan Kirk is a brilliant professor and actor."

"Duncan Kirk is already dead, but no one's had the nerve to tell him yet."

"Vivien, that's terrible! The man is a genius. He taught at Berkeley for decades after giving up the stage and the Academy had to coax him out of retirement."

"Maybe it's time he packed it in again. He's asleep half the time."

"I wouldn't be so sure of that. He's probably listening and figuring out how you tick so that he can bring out the best in you."

"Anyway, he hates me."

"He doesn't hate you. Who could hate you?" She smiles. "I mean, you're annoying, but only to people who know you better."

"He singles me out. Yesterday, everyone else got to play cool jungle animals and I had to be 'the first fish to leave the sea.'"

"That's an exercise to help you cast off your inhibitions," she says. "If he gives you harder assignments, maybe he senses that you have stronger inhibitions."

"Or maybe he's a bully. We had a session on it in school and he fits the profile." I prop my feet on the dashboard and ask, "Why are you defending him? It's not like you practice method acting."

"I use some of the principles." She leans over and pushes my feet to the floor, then hands me a tissue to buff a tiny smudge off the dash. "A good actor studies every approach and blends elements of each until she finds what works best for her."

Obviously Annika is still searching for her magic formula.

★ ★ ★

When we arrive at the Academy, Gray, Blake, and Asia are sitting out front. Annika pulls in behind a black Mercedes convertible. Karis climbs out of the car and waves to me.

"That's Diana Russell's car," Mom says, pointing to the vanity plate. "You didn't tell me her daughter is in your class."

"Karis said her mom's an actor, but I assumed she was an unknown like you."

Annika ignores this jab and flings open her door.

"Where are you going?" I call after her, alarmed. "Mom, don't embarrass me."

"Don't be silly, darling. Diana and I worked together six years ago—before she got the Oscar for *Sundown*. It would be rude not to say hello."

Annika clacks toward the Mercedes and crouches beside the driver's open window. "Di, how are you?" she booms. For some reason, Mom always uses her stage voice with fellow actors, although as far as I know, she's never performed on stage.

I jump out of the car, prepared to drag Annika back by force if I have to.

"It's Annika," Mom is telling Diana a little less heartily. "Annika Anderson." She raises her sunglasses to meet Diana's eyes. "We were in *The Missing* together."

I hear Diana say, "Really? What part did you play?"

"I was your sister."

Diana raises her own sunglasses. "I'm so sorry, I don't recognize you. I meet so many bit-part actors that I can't remember everyone."

Karis leans down and says, "Mom, don't embarrass me."

Annika straightens up. "Well, our daughters are in this class together and I just wanted to say hello. Take care, Di. And keep your eyes open for my next film. It's called *Danny Boy*."

She struts back to the car as if she hasn't just been brutally dissed. Leaning over to kiss my cheek, she whispers, "I really just wanted to get a closer look at Diana. We use competing surgeons, you know. Poor girl . . . I hope that eye lift relaxes a little over time. Looks like she's seen the ghost of Duncan Kirk!"

Chuckling, she slides behind the wheel of the Beetle and pulls down the visor to admire her own eyes before gunning it up the street.

★   ★   ★

"Hah, he, hi, ho, huh," the class chants in unison. We do these exercises every morning to warm up our voices.

"Again, from the diaphragm," Professor Kirk commands, patrolling the perimeter of our circle.

"Hah, he, hi, ho, huh."

"Now, let's hear it from your knees," he calls.

"Hah, he, hi, ho, huh."

"Miss Reid, I do not hear your knees."

"My knees are shy, sir."

"Actors do not have the luxury of being shy," he says. "On your own, Miss Reid, and this time from the knees."

I close my eyes and summon the power of my knees. "Hah, he, hi, ho, huh."

"Once more with conviction, please."

"Hah, he, hi, ho, huh!"

And to think I gave up a summer job at the Pita Pit for this.

★   ★   ★

For reasons known only to him, Professor Kirk has announced that we will "become" the four elements: fire, water, earth, and air.

I am to be "whitewater."

"Whitewater *rushes,* Miss Reid," Professor Jerk says after my first pass through the classroom. "It does not flutter like a butterfly in the meadow."

I rush across the room again.

"Arms down, Miss Reid. It's not Swan Lake we're after here but Merced River."

I try to visualize churning, gushing water as I swoop back

across the room.

"Down the gorge again, Miss Reid. More intensity, please."

Panting, I channel the rapids and dash across the class once more.

"Tumbling over the rocks, Miss Reid. Tumbling!"

I throw myself onto the floor and roll. Asia lifts her legs up under her chin, squealing as I crash into her chair.

Lying flat on my back, I look up at Professor Jerk.

"More Roller Derby than river, Miss Reid, but I applaud your enthusiasm."

Walking back to my seat, I channel fire to my face.

"Well done," says Karis, who has already successfully enacted "sand" for the class simply by crouching perfectly still for two minutes. "It was just like being at Yosemite." She plucks a pistachio shell from my hair.

"There's an Oscar category for 'whitewater,' right?"

★ ★ ★

At our first break, I rush outside to check my text messages. Because Asia took two calls during our first class, Professor Kirk now operates on a "catch and release program," locking up twenty cell phones in his desk every morning and releasing them only on breaks and at lunch. People always forget to turn off their ringers so the desk offers musical interludes throughout the day. Gray, with his rotating selection of hip-top ring tones, gets the most calls.

I am anxious for a response from Rory to my two-page e-mail rant about my sorry life. I complained about the snobby students, useless exercises, and mean professor, and finished by saying that I should have stuck with my original plan to become a veterinarian. Acting can't be my true calling.

It was a heartfelt e-mail and probably too much for some guys, but not for my Rory. With him, there is no need to pretend that life is good when it actually sucks. He is so much more evolved than Dad.

```
Leigh,
Went 2 a dedlE concert last nyt.
A frNd wz competing n a battle
of d B&z. hz drummer wz sick
so I sat n & we won! Sounds lIk
acting skul iz intRStN and it's aL
wrkN out 4 U.
R
P.S. Got U a battle of d B&z t-shirt—it's
purple!
```

He may be evolved but he's also got a short attention span. With guys, if you type more than four sentences, they tune out and start thinking about their next game of Halo. Still, he remembered that my favorite color is purple. I can live with that. I'll work on his listening skills later, after we're married.

Leaning back on the bench, I doodle on the back of my notebook:

Vivien Leigh Reid Quinn
Leigh Reid-Quinn
Leigh Quinn
Mrs. L. Quinn
Rory and Leigh Quinn
Mr. & Mrs. Quinn

"Mind if I join you?" Karis is standing in front of me with two Jamba Juice cups in her hands. I slide along the bench to make room for her and she hands me a cup. "Mango-a-Go-Go Smoothie," she says. "It's got a ton of antioxidants for your immune system and it's also high in vitamins B3 and B6. Figured you'd need energy after that tumbling this morning."

"Thanks," I say as she settles in beside me. "How do you know so much about nutrition?"

"My parents are health nuts," she says, "I'm a vegetarian by birthright."

"I tried to become a vegetarian once but my father thought I was anorexic. He's a little uptight."

"Aren't they all?" Karis glances at my notebook. "Who's Rory Quinn?"

"My boyfriend." I love the way that word rolls off my tongue. Pulling out his photo, I tell Karis all about how we met at an Internet café in Dublin and it was love at first sight. Well, more or less. I had to get Sean Finlay out of my system first, which took a few hours.

Karis points to the top signature. "I'd stick with that one: Vivien Leigh was an interesting woman."

"Yeah, right," I say, assuming she's kidding.

"I mean it. My grandfather met her once and he said that she was gutsy and beautiful. And she had a mouth like a trucker." Karis explains that the real Vivien Leigh was so determined to land the role of Scarlett in *Gone with the Wind* that she pestered the director relentlessly until he gave her the part. Then she won an Academy Award for it. "I think it's a compliment to be named after someone who went after what she wanted, full throttle," Karis concludes. "Her footprints might be on the Walk of Fame. Have you looked for them?"

I shake my head. "My mother isn't big on sight-seeing."

She offers to show me around next weekend, and by the time we head back inside, my bad mood has vanished.

★   ★   ★

Asia and Blake are sitting on the patio outside the Urth Café after class. At first, I pretend I don't see them, but then I remember what Dad always says about making peace with your enemies. "Let it go," he says. "Hanging on to anger hurts only yourself." It's a great philosophy but he doesn't live by it. After all, he nick-named our lawnmower "Annie." As well as the blender. In fact, everything in our house that chops or grinds is named after my mother. Still, I know that I should make peace with Asia and Blake. If I am inhibited in class, it's because they're always judging me.

"Hi," I say, in a booming voice not unlike the one my mother used earlier.

Although everyone else on the patio stares, the girls pretend not to hear me.

"Hi," I boom again, my voice now so loud that the coffee cups rattle in their saucers.

They check behind them to see if I might possibly be addressing someone else. Finally, Blake offers a reluctant hi without looking at me.

I wrack my mind for a snappy follow-up and come up empty.

"Nice job in class today," Asia says, smirking. "You make a great lobster."

She's referring to my last performance of the day, in which Karis and I crawled on the ocean floor waving our claws. We'd created a great skit about elephants at a waterhole, but after Blake and Asia eavesdropped on us and stole our idea, Professor Kirk made us play lobsters instead.

Blake adds, "You're quite the comedienne."

I can tell she doesn't mean it as a compliment, but I say, "Thanks! And you make a great pachyderm. Very convincing."

"A what?"

"Don't ask," Asia quickly cautions her.

"A non-ruminant hoofed animal with thick skin," I say, fighting a grin.

"What kind of skin does a smartass have, Doctor Doolittle?" Asia asks.

Unwilling to be surpassed, Blake says, "The great thing about comedy is that you don't even need acting classes for it. Especially with *your* family history. I hear that your mother gets plenty of laughs with her films."

Ouch. It's one thing for me to insult Mom and another for

them to do it. "At least she doesn't have to steal ideas from her colleagues."

Before they can respond, there's a nasal *beep-beep* on the street. Annika's timing is flawless. Rolling down the window, she calls, "Hurry, darling. Roger's in town and he wants to take us for dinner."

"Coming," I call. Turning back to the girls, I say, "Roger was our director on *Danny Boy*. He likes comediennes."

I take a moment to enjoy their scowls before running toward the Beetle.

four

The next morning, Mom is still aglow when she drops me off at the Grove, an eighty-year-old farmers' market with modern shops hidden behind it. "Wasn't it wonderful seeing Roger last night?" she asks.

"Thrilling," I say, making sure that my tone registers no more than three out of a possible ten on the snark-ometer. I'm meeting Karis at Abercrombie & Fitch and I'm not without hope that Mom will offer some spending money.

She darts a quick glance at me. "Oh, come on, it was fun."

"I came to L.A. to expand my horizons, Mom, not tag along on your dates."

"Darling, that wasn't a date. Roger is still married."

That may be but she gussied up in a chic blue dress that matched her eyes and spent half an hour straightening her hair for him. He, in turn, arrived with yellow gladioli (her favorites), drove us to the restaurant in a Jag, picked up the tab, and kissed Mom good night afterward. Apart from the teenage hostage, it fit the classic date profile.

"Admit it, you've still got the hots for him," I say. Last summer, she told me about her long and rocky relationship with Roger, which ended when he married someone half her age. I never saw his appeal, except for the fact that he recognized my raw talent.

Ignoring me, she cranks the volume on the stereo and starts

singing along with Aretha Franklin on *Natural Woman*. I chuckle silently at the irony. It's only silent because of my imminent request for cash.

Eventually, she continues: "It was just a professional meeting in a casual setting. Next week he could find a part I'm perfect for and he'll remember—"

"—how you spoon-fed him chocolate mousse?" My chocolate mousse, incidentally. She'd never order something so decadent, even to advance her career.

"Oh Vivien, it's business. You don't understand how it all works."

If Annika understands how it all works, how come her filmography is so pathetic? "Acting isn't business, Mom, it's art."

"Art alone won't pay for upgrading your wardrobe. And if you hadn't sulked all evening, Roger might have offered to keep you in mind for roles."

"I only sulked when he got my name wrong." Which happened to be all evening. Even Vivien is preferable to Viola or Verna.

"Get over it, Vivien. You have to play the game if you want to catch a break in this business."

I did not come to L.A. to "catch a break," I came to study. My experience on *Danny Boy* intrigued me, and I wanted to learn more about the mysterious process of bringing characters to life. Mom has said herself that acting is not a job but a calling, and I hoped that this class would confirm whether it's *my* calling. That's the only reason I'm sticking with the Reality Method right now.

That and the fact that Annika has threatened to fly Dad down to "talk some sense" into me if I don't stop asking to quit. I could do without another lecture. Before I left, my father delivered the one about how there are no shortcuts in life—that you have to pay your dues and *blah blah blah* (that's when I tuned out). All because I mentioned getting a lucky break on *Danny Boy*.

Anyway, if I decide to pursue acting—and it's a big "if" after week one of Reality Torture—I will do it on my terms, not Annika's. She relies too much on her beauty and her connections, if you ask me. I will rely on my talent alone. Leigh Reid does not suck up to get ahead. Leigh Reid does not compromise her high standards. Leigh Reid does not even need to be paid to act. Art is its own reward.

Annika opens her wallet and pulls out twenty dollars. "Buy yourself something special today."

"Twenty bucks hasn't bought anything special since pterodactyls walked the Earth, Mom. How about giving me an advance on my allowance?"

"You don't get an allowance."

"Every teen gets an allowance. Karis probably has cash falling out of her pockets."

"Only if said teen performs chores. You haven't lifted a finger since you arrived."

"I offered to put ten of them on the steering wheel and chauffeur you around."

"How about offering to cook dinner instead?"

"Cook dinner! I don't know a whisk from a spatula. I take after you."

She grins. "At last, she admits her heritage."

"That was entrapment," I grumble. But she is so pleased with herself that she offers me another twenty dollars.

"Tell Karis to drive carefully. There are a lot of crazies on the highway."

Since I've got all the coin I'm going to get, I say, "Only one of them is wearing maroon driving gloves."

★　★　★

The greeter at Abercrombie & Fitch looks like Benjamin McKenzie, and the guy rearranging the T-shirts is a dead ringer for the model in the Calvin Klein underwear ads. The eye candy in Los Angeles continually amazes me.

"How can we help you today?" a perky voice asks.

I turn to find Karis standing behind me, smiling. There's a staff identification tag hanging from her neck. "You *work* here?"

"Yes, I have to work," she says, understanding what I'm really saying. "My parents are obsessed with teaching my brothers and me 'the value of a buck.'"

"You don't even get an allowance?"

"Only if I do chores. We have a cook, a housecleaner, and a landscaping service, yet they find work for us to do. Last week, I had to mop the floor of a six-car garage."

"Cinderella—with dreads."

"That's how I punish them," she says, pointing to her hair. "I tell Mom that I can't afford regular haircuts and suddenly she's pressing money on me all the time. Of course, I can't take it now: it's a matter of principle."

"I admire your principles," I say, "but I fully intend to spend the forty bucks Annika just gave me."

★　★　★

"So what'll it be?" Karis asks, as we climb into the old jeep she shares with her brothers. "How about joining my friends for Ultimate Frisbee?"

Frisbee? What happened to a leisurely stroll down the Hollywood Walk of Fame? I'm all for making new friends but not if it means breaking a sweat. I should have known that Karis's sporty, ready-for-anything look was more than a style statement. She probably paraglides for kicks.

No one could ever mistake me for an athlete, despite my athletic build. Fortunately, athletics are discouraged at the Nerd Academy where heart rates soar only on report card day. I do swim regularly but only because Dad insists that I be prepared for natural disasters.

"Did I mention my bum knee?" I ask Karis. "I fell off the balance beam in gym class last semester." Actually, I tripped over a soda can while rushing to the school library. "Maybe it would be better to do the tourist thing today."

Karis maneuvers the jeep into heavy traffic with the confidence that comes from having driven daily for fifteen months.

"Listen," I say, "I want to apologize for the way my mother ambushed yours yesterday. She's high-strung."

Karis waves my apology away. "My Mom's a piece of work too, believe me. If it weren't for my Dad, she'd be locked up. You should hear the things she says."

"Let me guess: *There are no good parts for women over forty.*"

She smiles in instant recognition. "Or, *You have no idea how much pressure I am under to look good.*"

I feel like a weight is lifting. Finally, there is someone who can really understand what it's like to live with a diva. "Let's vow not to be like them if we become professional actors."

"*When* we become professional actors," Karis says. "But there's no danger of that. We already know that it's not about being a star, it's about bringing stories and characters to life."

"It's about art. I was just explaining that to Annika."

"We've got our priorities straight," she says. "We'll never become divas."

"We'll never demand the best seats in the restaurant."

"Or a chauffeur."

"Or an upgrade to first class."

"We'll never say, *Do you know who I am?*"

"Or, *Do you think I should get my nose done?*"

Karis pulls into a parking spot and says, "We will not sell out or use our art to promote products—even if that means saying no to free clothes from designers."

We stop laughing and look at each other.

"You can take a point too far," I say.

"Bring on the free clothes," she agrees.

★　★　★

Vivien Leigh's footprints aren't anywhere to be found outside Grauman's Chinese Theater. I'm surprised by how disappointed I am. Maybe unconsciously I hoped to step into her prints and find them a perfect fit. Alarm bells would ring, lights would flash and someone like Stephen Spielberg would shout, "We have our winner." I've been watching too many reality TV shows.

Not that I'm really hoping to be "discovered." Like I said, if I decide to act, I expect to pay my dues. I just thought that standing in Vivien Leigh's footprints might give me a divine sign of whether acting really is my calling. Somehow I doubt the elegant Miss Leigh ever wore size ten sneakers.

"Is your Dad in the business too?" Karis asks.

"My mom is barely in the business, Karis. But my dad is an accountant. They split when I was three and I only got to know Annika last summer."

"That must have been hard."

"In a lot of ways, it was easier before Annika's big comeback in my life." I ponder for a moment and add, "Easier but less interesting."

It feels strange to be telling my family secrets to someone I've only known a few days. In fact, it feels like I'm being disloyal to Abby, who is the only person I fully confide in, especially about Annika. Dad and Grandma still hate my mother, whereas I only hate her part-time now. Still, Karis seems like a normal, decent person—exactly the opposite of what I expected from Hollywood. I think I can trust her.

We stroll along Hollywood Boulevard, calling out the names on the pink stone stars embedded in the sidewalk, until we find Vivien Leigh. Elvis Presley's star is right next door.

"I wonder what she would have thought of her neighbor?" I ask.

"They had something in common," Karis says, explaining that both suffered from depression. "She had to go through shock therapy twice, and that was at a time when it could cause burns or broken bones."

Poor Vivien!

I must remember to check Annika's temples for scorch marks.

★ ★ ★

We're still talking a mile a minute by the time we reach Karis's favorite vegetarian restaurant. I've interviewed her about her parents (still married), her brothers (pains in the butt), her pets (a golden lab and tropical fish), and her love life (no boyfriend, but a big crush on the Benjamin McKenzie clone at Abercrombie).

"I can't believe your parents are still married," I say. "Don't they know it's Hollywood?"

"My father is a patient man," she says. "At least with Mom. With us, he's pretty tough because he wants *us* to be tough. He knows we all want to get into the business and he doesn't want us to crack under the pressure. He's always challenging us to think independently."

"Whereas my father would prefer me to think like a forty-six-year-old accountant."

Karis orders several dishes, rhyming off names like tempeh, tahini, edamame, and wasabi without even looking at the menu. I'm suspicious but determined to try everything. I can always order a pizza when I get home.

While we wait for the food, I cough up the humiliating details of life at the Nerd Academy and share my ambitions to be a veterinarian.

"I thought you wanted to act," she says.

Even if I were one hundred percent certain of that I wouldn't want to say so to someone with Karis's pedigree. "I'm not so sure. Especially after starting this class. I don't have a clue what's going on and I feel like an idiot all the time."

"So do I but everyone else is suffering too."

"Blake and Asia aren't. They never have a hair out of place."

The food arrives and Karis shows me how to pop the soybeans out of their pods. "I go to school with Blake and Asia," she says. "You do not want to be like them."

My chopsticks seesaw wildly as I chase grains of rice around my bowl. "How come they're never mean to you?"

"My mom," she says, simply. "At our high school, that kind of thing counts." Wielding chopsticks with expert skill, she scoops brown rice and vegetables into her mouth and adds, "Plus they know I could kick their skinny asses."

Something tells me she could too. "Well, they're ruining the class for me."

"They're bitches," she agrees, "but you can't let them get you down. They're just jealous."

I almost choke on a soybean. "Of me? Why?"

"Because you've already had a part in a feature."

"I only got it because I happened to be in the right place at the right time—and have the right hair color to replace an actor who came down with mono. It was luck."

"Well, we all want a break like that," she says. "You have connections."

I laugh. "I'm sure everyone in that class has better connections than I do, Karis. Especially you. Look at your parents."

"They're no help," she says, setting an empty pod afloat in her miso soup. "My mother really doesn't want me to act."

"I'm sure she'll come around when she sees how much you want it. Even if she doesn't, it's not all about luck and connections. It's about talent, and with your genes you're going to be great."

"If there's a part for a lobster, I'm so there," she says. But she brightens. "I guess we'll have to make our own breaks."

"A toast to that," I say, raising a glass of herb-infused spring water.

After that, she helps me get the hang of the chopsticks, and soon I am dropping only half of every mouthful. Horizons are expanding all over the place today.

★　★　★

Annika slides a slab of lasagna in front of me. "I slaved all afternoon to cook this with my own two hands."

"That's a fresh manicure, Mom. You wouldn't risk chipping it in the kitchen."

She piles salad onto my plate. "True, but I did push a grocery cart around Gelson's with my own two hands."

I pull a noodle aside with a fork and peek inside. "Is that meat? I'm a vegetarian, Annika."

"Since when?"

"Hello! I've been veg for three years, but I haven't been able to practice because of Dad's totalitarian regime. There's no room for independent thought in that house."

"You're telling me," she mutters.

"Don't use my stand on animal rights as an opportunity to diss Dad."

She shakes her head. "No more playdates with Karis if you're going to come home with a head full of ideas."

"It's time I started taking a position on issues."

"Dare I ask if Karis is a vegetarian?"

"As a matter of fact, she is. Because her parents are both open-minded and health-conscious, they have made it possible for her to live by her principles."

Annika is clearly bemused. "So, you discussed principles all afternoon and now you're boycotting my lasagna?"

"The fight has to start somewhere. After dinner I'm going to hunt for pelts in the hall closet and if I find any, I'm spraying them with the fake blood Karis gave me."

The smile vanishes. "If you get anywhere near my fox coat, you will be in more trouble than you can even imagine, young lady."

"You'd be surprised at what I can imagine, Annika."

She sighs. "I can't believe I volunteered for another summer of this."

I dig into my salad. "Anyway, you were the one complaining about my eating habits. You should be happy I'm taking more of an interest in my health."

"Fine," she says. "I'll let you experiment, but I'm keeping a very close eye on you. If you go home anemic, your grandmother will alert the child-welfare authorities."

I am a practicing vegetarian at last! "Do you have any edamame?"

"Any what?"

"Soybean pods. Karis says soy is good for declining estrogen, so you should load up."

Drumming her shiny nails on the table, she changes the subject. "Roger called today. He wants to send you on an audition."

"Me? I didn't feed him chocolate mousse. You said that was the key to making connections."

Turning her attention to her salad, she says, "When you tire of your own wit, let me know and I'll continue."

I take my time peeling off a noodle and scraping every last bit of dead cow off it. Eventually, my curiosity gets the better of me. "What kind of audition?"

"A friend of Roger's is directing a soap opera. There's a role for a sullen teen and he thought of you right away."

I overlook the insult. "What soap?"

"*Diamond Heights.*"

"*Diamond Heights!* That isn't a soap, it's a—"

"—a drama?" she says. "Or wait, a dramedy. Just like *The OC.*"

"It's hardly a dramedy, Mother. There is nothing funny about *Diamond Heights.*"

At least, not intentionally. The show is about a fictional town inhabited by rock royalty. The characters play loud music, get stoned, spend money, fight, interbreed, and generally stir up trouble. It is quality entertainment. Because it airs at five P.M., it's practically primetime. Dad tapes it and we watch together, although he usually laughs all the way through it and ruins it for me.

Annika says, "They're looking for a teenage girl to play the spoiled daughter of Max Volume, a British heavy-metal star. Are you interested?"

"I'm not sure," I say. "Some people make fun of soaps. Like Dad."

Mom's eyes narrow to blue slits. She's guest-starred in a lot of soaps over the years. Reaching for the phone, she says, "I'll let Roger know you're above it."

"I didn't say that." I grab her wrist but she starts pressing the buttons anyway.

"No, darling, I think you've expanded your horizons enough for one day, what with the vegetarianism and all."

I throw myself on top of the phone, knocking the salad bowl to the floor.

Annika says, "When you've cleaned that up, you can call Roger yourself and thank him, Verna."

★ ★ ★

Ten Actors Who Got Their Start in Soaps:
 1. *Amber Tamblyn*
 2. *Ryan Phillippe*
 3. *Christian Slater*
 4. *Julianne Moore*
 5. *Leonardo DiCaprio*
 6. *Meg Ryan*
 7. *Josh Duhamel*
 8. *Sarah Michelle Gellar*
 9. *Antonio Sabato, Jr.*
10. *Demi Moore*

five

If there is one thing I'm good at, it's homework; the Academy has at least given me that. So when I learned that I had only two days to get ready for my audition, I memorized four different scenes right away. I may have a foot in the door but I can't afford to take any chances. Better overprepared than humiliated, I figure.

I'm trying not to get too excited about it. *Diamond Heights* isn't a feature movie, after all. I also feel sheepish about jumping all over this break after my discussion with Karis. But I figure I can't pass up a chance to work every day when it will help me discover whether acting is my calling. It's not like I'm getting a free ride: Roger may get me in the door but I'll have to prove myself once I'm there. There may be a few others competing for the part.

Annika wanted me to use a scene from a classic, so I've decided to go with something more modern. *Diamond Heights* is very hip, and delivering Titania from *A Midsummer's Night Dream* would send the wrong message—the Nerd Academy message. I need to show the selection panel that I have mass appeal, so I'm doing the scene from *Friends* where Rachel confesses her love to Ross. They'll laugh, they'll cry, and in the end, the director will thank Roger for the ratings boost.

Scene 3: Leigh's Big Audition

INTERIOR STUDIO, DAY

Jane Baxter, director of Diamond Heights, *frowns as she examines the handful of hopefuls. She knows a rising star when she sees one, and no one in this room has what it takes to play Willow Volume, the spoiled seventeen-year-old daughter of English rocker Max Volume.*

                    JANE
            [to the casting agent]
        Where's that kid Roger called about?

The studio door opens and Vivien Leigh Reid enters. Jane notices electricity in the air: this girl has star power.

                    JANE
        Never mind, I think our Willow has ar-
        rived.

                    LEIGH
            [deciding to play the game]
        It's an honor to meet you, Jane. I think
        Diamond Heights is the most intelligent,
        challenging show on television.

                    JANE
        Thanks for taking the time to audition
        for us. I saw an early cut of *Danny Boy*
        and I think you stole the show.

                    LEIGH
            [inclining her head modestly]
        I just hope I do all right today.

                    JANE
        Relax, the part's already yours. We're

just going through the motions of an
audition—studio policy and all that.
I'll let the other girls do a quick read
and get rid of them.

The casting agent calls up the first girl, who deliv-
ers only two lines from Romeo and Juliet *before Jane*
interrupts and dismisses her. It's nearly the same for
the next two. The competition vanquished, Leigh re-
moves her coat to reveal an outfit fit for the daughter
of an English rock god: short skirt, FCUK T-shirt, and
Burberry handbag.

When Leigh finishes her scene, the panel leaps to its
feet and offers a standing ovation.

                    JANE
I have never seen such range in one so
young. And the camera absolutely loves
you. Welcome, Willow!

                    LEIGH
Don't jump the gun, Jane. I'll need to ap-
prove my wardrobe and trailer before I
sign anything.

                    JANE
Of course. *(Snapping her fingers at an un-*
derling.) Take Ms. Reid to wardrobe and to
choose a trailer. Make sure it's the
biggest one. Is there anything else, Leigh?

                    LEIGH
No, I think we're going to get along just
fine.

★ ★ ★

Annika drops me at the main entrance to CBS Studios, lingering at the curb for a few minutes in the hopes that I'll relent and let her come along. I cross my arms and glare at her until she finally drives away. I don't need a chaperone. More importantly, I don't need Annika Anderson stealing the limelight today.

A crowd of young women is milling around outside Building Five, each clutching a large piece of paper with a number on it. Some production is obviously holding one of those "cattle call" auditions Mom told me about. I'm starting to realize how lucky I am to have connections.

Inside, there's an even bigger crowd. I weave through it to a long table at the end of the room, behind which sits a thin man wearing a lime green suit, a burnt orange shirt, and a fat tie that combines both colors. He has a shaggy mop of platinum hair with dark roots and he's wearing full makeup.

"Good morning," I say, giving him my very best smile.

He looks back to his clipboard. "Next!" A Mischa Barton look-alike steps up to the table.

"Excuse me," I say, expanding my smile to include molars. I summon my most professional presence to show this guy he's dealing with a pro—and a pro who now has a screen name. "I am V. Leigh Reid. I have an appointment with Jane Baxter."

Mr. Congeniality smirks and claps his hands to attract the crowd's attention. "Did everyone hear? This one says she has an *appointment* to see Jane Baxter."

A collective giggle swells until it fills the room.

"What's so funny?" I ask.

"All of these girls are waiting to see Jane, Veely. Take a number."

I look around, shocked. There must be a hundred girls here and most of them have patterned themselves after Mischa, Hilary Duff, Jennifer Aniston, or J. Lo. The place is awash in blond highlights. "They're all auditioning?"

He shows me his own molars. "That's right."

"But someone called to make an appointment for me."

"Everyone here has exactly the same appointment."

I lower my voice to a whisper, so as not to seem cocky. "Mine was made by my former director, Roger Knelman."

"Sorry to disappoint but your connections mean nothing here, Veely."

He doesn't sound sorry, but he will be when I've joined the cast and he is back on the drag queen circuit. I say, "It's V-*period*-Leigh Reid. The *V* is an initial—like Samuel L. Jackson or Michael J. Fox."

He pretends to yawn. "End of the line, V-period-Lee."

I can tell that he's spelling Leigh wrong too but rather than correct him, I plead, "Please check your list."

Scanning the list quickly, he says, "Veely, Veely, Veely. Nope. Nada. Nyet."

Another idea occurs to me. "Could you check under Verna?"

He aims his pen at me and flicks it toward the end of the line.

★　　★　　★

It's all Annika's fault. She should have *insisted* on staying with me. Most of these girls are older than I am, yet many are with their mothers. What kind of mother would knowingly sacrifice her underage daughter to the cattle call? The unfit kind, that's what. I've called several times over the past three hours to tell her so, but she must have turned off her cell phone. She's in for a shock when she checks her voicemail.

If I get the part on *Diamond Heights,* my first move will be having Mr. Congeniality run down by one of those golf carts the producers use to zip around the back lot. At the moment, however, he still has the upper hand because that's the hand holding the clipboard. "Numbers eighty through ninety-four," he yells. "Your time has come."

We shuffle after him through the double doors onto the set.

"Here's the last of the plaid warriors," he tells the group of people sitting behind the bank of camera monitors. He's referring,

I suppose, to the fact that many of us have worn Burberry to capture the authentic English look.

A plump woman in a director's chair says, "Thank you, Chaz." Then she calls, "Okay, girls. Hand your pages to Chaz, step up to your mark, give us your name, and deliver your lines."

Number 80 announces her name and on the cameraman's signal, begins:

"Monica, you were supposed to be here hours ago."

"I'm sorry, Rach," Chaz replies, his voice rising a few octaves. "Chandler stopped by and I couldn't get rid of him."

There's a sudden high-pitched whistle in my ears as my ego deflates. Number 80 is Rachel. As are Numbers 83 and 86. Number 88 ups the ante by launching into the exact scene I've chosen. With ten years' worth of episodes, what are the chances? This audition is like a *Friends* retrospective.

No wonder everyone says it's so hard to make it in this business. Even when you have connections and you rehearse until you're hoarse, you're just another face—and never the prettiest one—in a big crowd. There's no way for me to stand out, apart from my mousy brown hair.

Number 89 breaks the pattern by doing a scene from *The OC* where Mischa Barton howls in rage at her mother. I notice the panel leaning forward with more interest than they've shown so far. Full-on drama is clearly the way to go.

By the time Jane calls Number 92, I've switched to Plan B. I hand Chaz several pages of script and take my mark in front of the camera. If Mr. Congeniality thinks I'm a total novice, he's in for a surprise. I know my way around a studio.

"I'm Leigh Reid," I announce, dropping the *V* for simplicity's sake. "Today I'll be doing a scene inspired by *Gone with the Wind.*"

"*Inspired by?*" a voice at the monitors asks.

"The screenplay is kind of dated and *Diamond Heights* is a contemporary show, so I did a little rewrite," I explain, handing Chaz several typed pages. "The scene takes place after the Civil

War, when Scarlett O'Hara is desperate to come up with money to pay the taxes on Tara, the family plantation. The only person she can turn to is Rhett Butler, who is a bit of a player. She knows she needs to wear something hot—I mean nice—to impress him so she uses her mother's velvet curtains to—"

"—Number ninety-two?"

"Yes?"

"It's a long movie. Go ahead."

"Fine, I was just setting the context. Chaz, you'll play Mammy. That's Scarlett's maid."

"I know," he says, "although it's the first time I've had the pleasure."

There's snickering behind the monitors. It's not quite the mood I was hoping to create with my dramatic scene. But I take a deep breath, examine myself in an imaginary mirror, and summon a Southern drawl.

> SCARLETT
> Mammy, I'm so thin after all these months
> of war rations. Not that being thin is a
> bad thing, but I have nothing to wear.
> [Turns to fondle an imaginary set of vel-
> vet curtains, mentally scheming.] Crack
> out the sewing machine. You're going to
> make me a new dress.

> MAMMY
> Not with your mother's drapes, I'm not.

> SCARLETT
> Get over it, girlfriend. They're my drapes
> now, and I need to look like a million
> bucks when I go to Atlanta.

When I stop speaking, there's silence at the monitors. It isn't the standing ovation I imagined, but at least they're not laughing. I decide to continue before anyone says otherwise. I want them to sit up and notice that Leigh Reid is in the house. Fortunately, I learned something on *Danny Boy* that might do the trick.

"Fast forward and we're at the Atlanta jail," I explain. "Scarlett is hitting on Rhett in the hopes that he'll hand over the cash. Chaz, you're Rhett now."

"Got it," he says in a strangled voice.

                    RHETT
        Cut to the chase, babe. You didn't come
        here wrapped up in velvet just to shoot
        the breeze. How much do you want?

                    SCARLETT
        I lied to ye when I said everything was
        brilliant, Rhett. I'm broke and I need a
        C-note for the taxes on Tara.

Chaz falls silent. There's an animated conversation around the monitors. My Irish accent has obviously made quite an impression.

"Chaz?" I say. "It's your line."

"Did Scarlett take a wrong turn somewhere and end up in Dublin?" he asks.

Numbers 81 through 94 start giggling and the group at the monitors joins in. Chaz's grin widens to reveal lipstick on his teeth.

Okay, the Irish thing wasn't such a great idea, but Leigh Reid is no quitter. "If you're not up to playing Rhett," I tell Chaz, "all you have to do is say so."

The giggling continues but I raise my voice and deliver Rhett's line in a Southern accent. For Scarlett's, I switch briefly to an English accent. It's not as good as my Irish, but it works.

Chaz interrupts, "Are you crazy?"

"Willow is English, right?"

He shoves my script pages at me. "Thanks for coming out."

Jane steps out from behind the monitors and raises her hand. "Number 92, I believe you've just covered Atlanta, Dublin, and some part of northern England."

"Liverpool, ma'am," I say. "I'm not sure exactly where Willow is from."

One of the producers whispers something in Jane's ear. She waves him off and says, "Carry on, Number ninety-two," she says. "Chaz, please do the honors."

Chaz reluctantly takes the pages back. "She's giving you a second chance," he whispers. "If I were you, I'd stick to cotton fields and fried chicken. This script is crazy enough without the accents."

But Jane didn't make any restrictions, so I figure I'm free to go with the "green" version of *Gone with the Wind*. Jacking my brogue up another notch, I say,

                    SCARLETT
          Let go of me, eejit! Ye knew ye wouldn't
          lend me the cash before I opened my
          mouth, but ye let me beg fer it.

                    RHETT
          [with an exaggerated Southern drawl]
          Look on the bright side, babe. You can
          come to my hanging and I'll make sure
          you're in my will.

                    SCARLETT
          I'll be there to watch ye swing. I just
          hope it's in time to pay the taxes on Tara.

When we're done, Chaz stalks off with a disgusted shake of the head.

★ . ★ . ★

And then there were three.

Jane, the director, has sent everyone home except Numbers 12, 89, and me. She tells us that we'll be reading a scene from *Diamond Heights* with Sasha Cohen. For the past few weeks, Sasha has been playing Fallon, the teenage daughter of Max Volume's biggest rival in the rock world. There will be a similar rivalry between the girls.

"Take ten minutes and learn the part," Jane says. "Things move quickly on a soap and I need to see how well you can memorize dialogue."

Once again, I am grateful for my near-photographic memory. That's one reason I do so well in school. I'm not smart enough by half for the Nerd Academy, but I can usually take in information quickly and spit it out at the right moment.

The scene we're doing is set at the Diamond Heights Yoga Den. Willow has just arrived in town and it's her first visit to the studio. She arrives early and stakes out the best spot beside the window, not realizing that Fallon has used this spot for years.

Sasha is wearing a white corduroy blazer and ripped jeans rumpled over Uggs. In one hand is a shiny white leash attached to a tiny black dog wearing a white sheepskin coat. It's probably eighty degrees in the studio.

"Cue the fake snow," I whisper to the other girls.

Number 89 holds a finger to her lips. "Careful," she says. "Sasha is the executive producer's daughter and my agent says she's a bitch."

Number 12 offers, "I heard she got a boob job for her sixteenth birthday."

Sasha conveniently removes her blazer to expose her assets in a skimpy white camisole.

"Fake," Number 89 pronounces.

"Totally," Number 12 agrees.

"How do you know?" I ask.

"Too round and too much space between them," says Number 89, sounding matter of fact. "They don't squish."

Sasha is telling Jane, "I don't want to read. Get Chaz to do it."

Jane shakes her head. "I need to know if you have chemistry."

Sasha takes us in with a sweeping glance. "With them? I don't. I can tell you that already." She pulls out her cell phone. "I'm calling Daddy."

Jane takes the phone. "You're getting paid to be here so be professional."

Sasha stares at Jane for a few moments before tying the leash to the monitor stand. "Wait here, sweetie," she tells the dog. "Mummy won't be long."

Chaz pushes me toward the mark. "You're up, Scarlett," he says. He doesn't bother to introduce me, either because he's a rude pig or because he's afraid of Sasha. Or both. Sasha promptly raises her script pages to block me out.

While the technicians finish lighting, I try to figure out how to play the scene. Since Willow is new in town, she probably feels much as I did on my first day at the Academy. Except that Willow has more spirit than Leigh Reid and she'd prevail over the Fallons of her world.

Sasha opens the door of the yoga studio and pauses on the threshold. I reach for the props and unfurl a yoga mat beneath the window.

                        FALLON
            You dropped your mat.

                        WILLOW
            I didn't drop it. I put it there on purpose.

                        FALLON
            That's my spot and it always has been.
            Ask anyone.

                        WILLOW
            Where I come from, it's first come, first

serve. That means I get the good view
today.

By the time we finish the scene, Willow is about ready to pop
Fallon. And on another level, Leigh Reid is wondering if the dis-
appointment she sees in Sasha's eyes is acting or the real thing.

★ ★ ★

And then there were two.

It's hour six and down to Number 12 and me. After a quick
confab with her posse of judges, Jane says, "Okay, ladies, I'd like
to hear you sing."

"Sing?" I say. "Roger never said anything about singing!"

"Roger?" Jane asks. Then it clicks. "Oh, you're the kid Roger
Knelman called about." I nod, hope stirring at the possibility of
escape. "Why didn't you say so earlier?"

I throw Chaz a glare before giving Jane an exaggerated shrug
to convey that I didn't expect preferential treatment just because I
have friends in high places. If I get this gig, at least I will be able
to take full credit myself. "I didn't prepare a song," I say.

"This isn't a deal breaker, ninety-two, but it's a musical show and
the girls could get into the family act. Just sing something you like."

Sasha, standing behind Jane, executes a perfect pirouette in
her Uggs. I know a war dance when I see it and somehow it frees
my frozen brain. Focusing directly on Jane, I belt out *Something
Good,* a song by Herman's Hermits—the sixties band that sang
with an English accent. Dad sings it at home so I know all the
words. I even manage to change all the "she's" into "he's."

"Interesting choice," Jane says, smiling. "You're quirky,
ninety-two."

"Quirky" is just a nicer way of saying "nerd."

★ ★ ★

Abs,
I got d pRt on Diamond Heights!!!

I didn't evN nEd Roger's hlp.
d director sAz Sasha Cohen & I
hav chemistry. Yikes!
I stRt NXT wk. So nw I hav
2 figur out how 2 teL Dad.
L
P.S. Sasha hz fake boobs.

six

Intuition is a mysterious thing. How does Millie, my West Highland terrier, know exactly when to start watching for Dad when he gets home at a different time every night? How does Grandma know to bring over chicken soup when I haven't even told her I'm sick? And how does Abby know to send me a message at the exact moment I have a meltdown?

More mysterious still, how do I know the most direct route to drive my mother insane when we've spent so little time together? I don't have an answer to that, I'm just glad that I do. Unfortunately, it also works in reverse and Mom tends to use her intuitive powers at the worst possible times.

Like this morning. Here I am, trying to put together the perfect outfit for my first day on the set of *Diamond Heights* and the last thing I need is a distraction. I've been pulling items out of the closet one by one, dropping the rejects on the floor, and flinging anything with potential onto the desk. It's a good system. Then along comes Annika to freak out over the mess—the same woman who tried on ten dresses before her date with Roger and left nine of them heaped on the hamper.

Her irrationality has swelled to epic proportions today for the simple reason that I am working and she is not. I know this because I have intuition. Plus, I've watched her tackle her cigarettes like a linebacker every time her agent calls. Mom has turned down a few good opportunities lately because she's taking the summer off to spend time with me. I didn't ask her to, but she has decided that Annika's World will revolve around Leigh's for a change. It's all very touching, but you can't mess with planetary orbits without encountering some turbulence.

To shove her off the warpath, I do an exaggerated doubletake and ask, "Did you change your lipstick? Your teeth look yellow."

She races to the bathroom to investigate, giving me a ten-minute reprieve to decide on white capris and a denim jacket. As much as I'd love to wear my new white blazer, I can't risk having Sasha think I'm copying her look. Because I'm not. The jacket just happened to be on sale at Banana Republic yesterday.

After I dress, I have precisely four minutes to do something I've been avoiding: call Dad. I haven't had the nerve to tell him about *Diamond Heights* and he's going to lose it. At least, I think so. I've never been much good at reading the parent who raised me. I know that if I bring home good grades he'll be happy, that if I whine he'll complain, but beyond that he rarely reacts as I'd expect.

Last year, he wasn't happy about my part in *Danny Boy,* but he let me do it. And when I wanted to take classes this summer, he let me do that too, although he'd hoped acting was a passing phase. Dad and Grandma aren't big fans of the acting profession, thanks to Mom's bad example. In fact, Grandma considers it a vice on par with gambling. That's why Dad hasn't even told her about *Danny Boy.* He says there's no need to upset her when I might end up "on the cutting room floor." I sense she'll be a lot more upset when she finds out we've kept it from her this long, but Dad doesn't believe in intuition. He does believe in avoiding giving bad news until it can be avoided no longer—something I can relate to now as I review the excuses I've prepared.

But again he surprises me. "You beat out ninety-one people?" he asks. "That's amazing!"

Huh? I make him reel off our address and zip code to prove that aliens haven't taken over Seattle since I left.

"Well, Sprout," he continues, "you know I'm not big on the

idea, but if this is what you want to do, I have to support you. Tell me about the character you're playing."

"Her name is Willow and she's a high-strung teenager."

"That's not acting," he says.

"Very funny. I hope she's different from me. I want to stretch myself, you know. I am doing this to expand my horizons."

"Your expansion is putting me in an awkward position with your grandmother. How will I break the news to her?"

"Get her liquored up," I suggest. Dad is quiet so long that I know he's considering it.

Meanwhile, Annika is back in my doorway laughing. She hates Grandma Reid.

"I hear that," Dad says. "Tell your mother her teeth look yellow." Yet the man doesn't believe in intuition!

After I hang up, she says, "The world would be a better place if your grandmother drank more."

★ ★ ★

My dreams of a luxurious trailer haven't quite materialized. Instead, I find myself in a tiny, dim cubbyhole on the "honey wagon," which is also the trailer that holds the washrooms. In fact, the name "Willow" appears on the door next to the one that says "Men." I've been on enough of Mom's sets to know that the honey wagon is the bottom of the barrel, but it's a start. There's a bench that a person of average height (i.e., not me) could stretch out on, a television and VCR, plus my very own restroom. It won't be so bad after I've spruced it up with photos of Rory.

Today, I have only a moment to drop off my things before a production assistant arrives to take me to hair and makeup. Carla, the makeup artist, immediately lets loose with a flurry of brushes, tubes, and cotton swabs. Makeup for film or television has to be exaggerated so that the skin appears smooth and the features "pop" under the bright lights. I know this, yet still I gasp when

Carla turns me around to face the mirror. My face is barely recognizable under the mask of product, and it doesn't help that my hair is still wet and slicked back.

"You didn't cover the mole," I tell Carla, pointing to the black spot.

"Of course not," Carla says. "It's a beauty mark."

Someone is being lazy. "I'd like it covered, if you don't mind."

"I don't mind, but you will when you see it on screen," she says. "If I apply concealer it will look like a pimple—and a large one at that."

"It won't!" I've been covering it for months; it had better not look like a zit.

"It did when you came in today. I was relieved to find a mole under there instead of a carbuncle."

"A carbuncle!" Whatever that is, it can't be good.

There's a snort behind me. It's Sasha Cohen with her little dog under her arm. "You've got your work cut out for you, Carla," she says.

"Well, not everyone has your gorgeous skin." Carla's lip twitches slightly, but Sasha takes her seriously.

"True," she says, admiring herself in the mirror. She takes the seat beside mine and pulls an iPod out of her pocket. "Let's get going, Carla. I have a wardrobe fitting in half an hour."

Tapping me on the shoulder, Carla says, "I'll have to dry your hair later."

"But I have this cowlick," I say. A cowlick is really too nice a word for what happens to my hair when it's left to its own devices. My bangs morph into a thick wedge and migrate to the wrong side. But the new kid in the trailer obviously doesn't stand a chance against the producer's daughter so I sit quietly, watching my hair turn into a fright wig.

Once in a while, Sasha cracks a lid open to eye my hair appreciatively, but mostly she just bobs to unheard music. Finally, she says, "Oh, Carla, I forgot to mention that I had a hive last night and I think it's from your moisturizer."

"I always use that cream," Carla says, "and you've never had a problem before."

Sasha shrugs. "People can develop allergies at any time." She squints at me to convey that the only thing she's really allergic to here is me. "You'll have to start again. Obviously, I can't have hives on screen; Daddy wouldn't like it."

Chaz bangs on the door. "Let's go, Veely. They're ready for you in wardrobe." He turns to help Sasha out of the chair. "You've never looked better," he tells her. "How's your father?"

★　★　★

Chaz's voice crackles across the walkie-talkie. "Where the hell is she?"

The production assistant replies, "I'm bringing her to set now."

"You better be running. The entire company is waiting and Jane is steamed."

The P.A. starts to jog and I struggle to keep up in my mules. The heels are bad enough, but the size is the real problem. Although the wardrobe department had racks and racks of shoes, there was nothing above a size nine. When I joked, "Somebody obviously got to the tens first," the assistant didn't laugh. Then I said that I'm planning to get my feet "done" to take them down to a size seven and she didn't laugh at that either. I am so missing the makeup and wardrobe assistants from *Danny Boy* right now. My shtick is wasted on these people. The Irish, they know humor.

The P.A. leads me through a labyrinth of hallways and surrenders me to a lecture from Jane about punctuality and respect for others. She points to Jessica De Luca, who plays Willow's mother. "She has ten Daytime Emmy awards, yet she never keeps the company waiting," Jane says.

I fight back tears of frustration. Roger taught me last summer that crying and excuses don't cut it on set.

"We gave you plenty of time to get ready," she continues, examining my too-tight jeans and bad hair. "Though clearly not enough."

I shrink on my mules until I am shorter than she is, although that is technically impossible, since she is no more than five foot three.

★　★　★

"*I know my lines, I know my lines, I know my lines.*"

My voice echoes in the empty restroom, mocking me, because I can't actually recall any of my lines right now. I am hiding in a cubicle, trying to remember what I've heard about stage fright. Mom warned me about it, but I didn't think it would happen to me—not after *Danny Boy.*

As a last resort, I am following Professor Kirk's advice and chanting affirmations. It's lame but it's better than anything else I've got. Leaning down to check under the cubicles for feet, I say, "*I can do this, I can do this, I can do this.*" To finish on a strong note, I give a cheer: "*Yes, YES, YES!*"

When I fling open the cubicle door, Sasha is standing in front of me. "Were you alone in there?" she asks.

"I was just saying some affirmations. You know, to psych myself up."

She smoothes her perfectly coiffed hair and saunters toward the door. "Whatever it takes."

★　★　★

INTERIOR POSH BOUTIQUE & CAFÉ, DAY

Fallon is at the coffee bar when Willow Volume and her mother Sumac enter. They cross to a display of cashmere sweaters.

"Cut!" Jane yells. "Willow isn't sneaking into a bar underage, Leigh. Let's see a real entrance, please."

Feeling the eyes of cast and crew upon me, I walk out and try it again.

"Cut," Jane repeats. "Willow Volume doesn't slouch. She

knows people are watching and she loves it. Pull your shoulders
back and give us some attitude."

Anxiety is doing a hip-hop number in my stomach, but I walk
back through the door muttering, *"I can do this."* I enter a third time.

"Cut," Jane says, shaking her head.

Chaz clears his throat loudly. "Jane? May I?"

She nods at him. "By all means, Chaz. Show the girl how to
make an entrance."

Chaz exits the set. When Jane calls action, he kicks open the
door and steps onto the threshold. Posing with one hand on hip,
he shakes out his mop of hair. Then he pulls his shoulder blades
so far back they're practically touching and sashays toward the
cashmere display, chin up, lips slightly pursed. The cast and crew
applaud, and he takes a deeper bow than I would have thought
possible in jeans that tight.

I thank Chaz, even though I didn't actually need the lesson.
The theatrical entrance is common practice for Annika. She pauses
on every threshold to claim the room, even if that room is Starbucks. My mistake was in thinking that that sort of thing is ridiculous.

Throwing open the door, I push my sunglasses up onto my
head and scan the room before walking in. This time Jane continues rolling.

*Willow holds up a sweater and inspects it with obvi-
ous disdain.*

                    WILLOW
        This *cannot* be the coolest shop in town,
        Mummy.

                    SUMAC
        Diamond Heights isn't London, sweetie.

WILLOW
That's obvious. So far, it's naf.

Jane yells cut and I heave a sigh of relief. This time I was flaw-less. My accent sounded just like Renée Zellweger as Bridget Jones. I expect Jane simply wants to congratulate me before we continue.

Instead, she says, "Leigh, you're folding the sweater."

"That's my action," I explain. Mom warned me that soaps aren't like film but I expected more sophistication than this. "The script says Willow inspects a sweater."

"Right. Your action is to *inspect* the sweater—not refold it."

I give the sweater a pat. "I inspected it and put it back the way I found it."

"Here's the thing. As Leigh, you might put things back the way you found them. But Willow doesn't. She's a spoiled rich kid who's shopped in the best boutiques in the world. She doesn't fold clothing. In her world, that's what staff are for."

"Well, that's rude."

Jane turns to Chaz. "I guess I deserve this for going with the novice."

"I am not a novice!" I protest. "I have a credit on a feature film."

She continues as if I haven't spoken. "Roger says she's bright enough."

Chaz says, "Well, intelligence and talent are two different things."

"You got that right," Sasha says.

★　★　★

"Brrrrrrrr . . . Brrrrrrrrrrrrrrrrrrr . . ." I let my lips vibrate loosely as I practice vocalizations. "Hah, he, hi, ho, huh!" Concentrating on my toes, I try to make the sound travel up my body. "Hah, he, hi, ho, huh!"

Sasha materializes without warning. "You mean 'Ha, ha, ha, ha, ha.' And believe me, you're not the only one laughing at your performance."

"Oh, shut up, Sasha," I say. It comes out with the Bridget Jones accent.

"How authentic," she says, making a face to imply it's anything but. She turns on her heels and strides toward the door. "Let's go, Olivier," she calls and exits with a flourish worthy of Chaz.

Olivier? As in Sir Laurence? Could she be more pretentious? But Olivier cannot follow his mistress: the ruff on his sheepskin coat is wedged under the bottom rung of her director's chair.

Before I can rescue him, she slinks back in, snatches him up, and exits again minus the flourish.

★ ★ ★

Willow emerges from the changing room empty-handed, leaving a heap of designer clothing on the floor.

SALESWOMAN
Nothing of interest today?

Willow points to a dress hanging behind the counter.

WILLOW
Maybe that.

SALESWOMAN
[pointing at Fallon]
I'm afraid we're holding that for another customer.

WILLOW
Unless she's paid for it, I'll try it on.

It takes some effort to bite back the please and thank you, but if I'm going to succeed as Willow, I'll have to forget my training in common courtesy. Leigh Reid can be rude and self-centered, especially with a role model like Sasha.

The saleswoman hands the dress to Willow and Fal-
lon rushes over to block Willow's path to the chang-
ing room.

> FALLON
> That's mine.

> WILLOW
> Let's see your sales receipt.

> FALLON
> My boyfriend is on his way over to see it
> before I buy it.

Sasha puts me in an arm lock that is definitely not in the script. I wait for Jane to call cut, but when she doesn't, I shrug Sasha off with enough force that she squeals. My height advantage is starting to come in handy.

★ ★ ★

It takes me awhile to struggle into the low-cut black dress because it's far too small and tighter than a corset. I'm not particularly well-endowed, but what I have is spilling out. I'd never leave my bedroom in this, yet now I'll be flaunting it nationwide. Trying to channel Willow, I step out of the change room and turn to face the mirror. Oh my god, I look like a hooker! Gran will have a breakdown.

> SALESWOMAN
> It looks amazing on you.

> Willow
> Yes, it does.

The door opens and LAKE MATHEWS enters. Fallon
throws her arms around him.

Standing on tiptoe, Sasha kisses the actor playing Lake so en-
thusiastically that the suction can be heard clear across the set.
The guy is at risk of losing his appendix, and when Sasha pulls
away, a thread of saliva catches in the back light. Eew.

"Cut!"

Jane must be disgusted too. It is daytime television after all.

"Leigh, wake up," she says. "It's your action."

I've been so caught up in the porn show, I missed my cue.
"Right, sorry."

Willow nudges Fallon aside to shake hands with Lake.

                    LAKE
        What a beautiful dress.

                   WILLOW
        Do you really think so?

                    LAKE
        Oh, yes.

His eyes blatantly drop to my cleavage and I clap my hand to
my chest.

"Cut!" Jane walks onto the set. "Leigh, lighten up. Willow is
flirting with Lake."

"The script doesn't say she's flirting."

"Read between the lines. The girls are competitors and that's
what Willow would do to annoy Fallon."

"But the guy is a pig," I say. Turning to the actor, I add, "No of-
fense." He's even better looking in person than he is on TV, but
also far older than the college-age guy he plays. He should not be

checking out my cleavage. Especially when he almost has to stand on tiptoe to do it. "That leer wasn't in the script," I point out.

"Maybe not but it fits with his character. So we'll go with it."

"Well, could I get a scarf or something?"

Jane laughs. "Leigh might be a prude but Willow certainly isn't."

Everyone in the general vicinity joins in the laughter. It's hard to say who's loudest, Sasha or Chaz.

"I'm not a prude. I just need to understand what Willow is thinking, that's all."

"She's thinking about doing Lake," Chaz says.

"Chaz, stop," Jane says. "In the future, Willow is going to steal Lake from Fallon so you have to start the flirting here, Leigh. Make eye contact. Lean in a little. Giggle."

We repeat the scene again and again but I sound wooden and I know it. No matter how hard I try, each time "Lake" looks at my chest, my hand twitches and my shoulders collapse.

Sighing, Jane says, "Show a little chemistry."

Chemistry is the only thing I'm *not* showing right now. I wish I'd thought to inquire whether Willow is a tramp before I accepted the part. I don't have much experience to draw on in that department. In fact, my most significant acting experience so far is playing a Catholic schoolgirl. But now that I'm here, I'm going to have to master the art of seduction or Jane will cut back my storyline.

Fortunately, I know just the person to study. She's hurtling toward me right now in her vintage rocket.

seven

Scene 4: Acting Class Field Trip

EXTERIOR DAY, GRIFFITH PARK GAZEBO

The ancient relic stops his lecture when he notices one of his students has her nose in a script.

            PROFESSOR KIRK
    Miss Reid. Would you like to share your
    script with the rest of the class?

            LEIGH
    Sorry, Professor. I'm trying to learn my
    lines.

            KARIS
            [proudly]
    Leigh has a recurring role on *Diamond
    Heights*.

            GRAY
            [high-fiving Leigh]
    Cool.

                    PROFESSOR KIRK
Congratulations, Miss Reid. Why didn't
you say so earlier?

                    LEIGH
I didn't want to brag, sir.

                    ASIA
Diamond Heights is the best!

                    BLAKE
I love analyzing the storylines. They're
so intense.

                    LEIGH
The writing is pretty good but it's just
a soap.

                    KARIS
Just a soap? I don't think so: it's a drama.

                    BLAKE
The best drama on television. When Fallon kissed Lake Mathews for the first
time at the Halitosis Relief Ball, I
cried my eyes out.

                    ASIA
Me too. It was so selfless of her to orga-
nize that ball. How many people suffer
from bad breath and don't know it?

                    PROFESSOR KIRK
That is one of the merits of soap operas.

They bring attention to important so-
cial issues.

                    BLAKE
          Yeah, remember when Lake tried to get
          butt implants and practically died on
          the table?

                PROFESSOR KIRK
          Exactly. Soaps are good training and
          they help actors stretch themselves emo-
          tionally. I predict great things for you
          now, Miss Reid.

*The Ancient Relic asks for Sumac's autograph and pro-
poses a class trip to CBS Studios to watch Leigh in
action.*

                    ★   ★   ★

Karis and I are flat on our backs on the dusty floor of the Griffith
Park Gazebo. Professor Kirk has brought us here to teach us how
to focus in public places so that we'll be able to perform easily in
front of strangers. He's been walking us through various medita-
tion techniques, but each time he turns around, Karis and I stop
relaxing and start talking.

"I could have used these techniques on set yesterday," I say,
trying to prompt her to ask about my first day on *Diamond
Heights*. We've been together a full hour, yet she hasn't mentioned it.

"Oh right," she says. "You started yesterday. Were you nervous?"

"Freaking out," I confess. "Sasha Cohen deliberately made me
late to set. She's a bitch, you know."

"She's a crap actor too," Karis says. "She's probably jealous
of you."

Karis seems to think everyone is jealous of me. It's ridiculous.

I tell her about my problem with getting into character. "I only got the script the day before shooting and they didn't give me much to go on. It turns out Willow's a rude, arrogant diva—and a slut to boot. Anyway, I didn't make a very good first impression. The director was disappointed."

"It was only your first day," Karis says. "I'm sure you were fine."

I thank her for the vote of confidence. "By the way, Karis, have you mentioned this to anyone?" I'm kind of hoping she has.

"God, no," she says. "Your soapy little secret is safe with me."

I raise my head to get a better look at her. "*Diamond Heights* isn't really a soap. It's more of a drama."

She closes her eyes without answering and takes deep, even breaths.

"Before you go into a trance, I wanted to tell you that the director is looking for three daily actors for a party scene. Why don't you audition? It would only be a couple of lines, but we could hang out in my trailer and make fun of Sasha."

Karis opens her eyes. "I don't think so. My parents wouldn't like it. They don't think much of soaps."

Before I can defend myself against the blatant soap-snobbery, Professor Relic interrupts. "What's this about a soap opera, ladies?"

"A friend of mine is on one, sir," Karis says. "No one you know."

"Glad to hear it," he says. "Soaps are the junk food of the acting world and my role is to educate you about good nutrition."

★ ★ ★

Karis has fallen silent to search for what Professor Kirk calls our "still center." I am trying to stop my mind from racing around like a trapped bird when I hear Asia's voice. Opening my eyes, I see her leaning over the guy lying next to me.

"Excuse me. Jesse, isn't it?"

"Jonah," he says, instantly turning bright red.

She smiles at him. "Jonah. Of course. I'm Asia."

"I know," he says, growing redder still. At this rate, his head is going to pop right off and float above the gazebo like a helium balloon.

Giving Jonah's forearm a gentle squeeze, Asia says, "That's such a great shirt. Egyptian cotton?"

"Uh, just regular, I think," Jonah stammers.

"Well, you know, it would get less dusty over here. Why don't you take my place and I'll take yours?"

"Oh no, you keep it," he says, his voice cracking.

Asia's hand glides up his forearm to rest lightly on his scrawny biceps. She meets his eyes for a moment. "Jesse, I insist."

And before Jonah realizes he's just embraced a new name, he's surrendered his spot. Twice. Because no sooner does he move than Blake gives him a sweet smile and eases him even further away so that she can slide in next to Asia.

Jonah/Jesse stares at the ceiling of the gazebo for a few moments, stoned on his newfound popularity, before raising his head to say, "Uh, thanks Asia."

Asia doesn't answer him. She already has what she wants, which for some strange reason, is a place beside me. Whatever she's up to, it can't be good.

"Hey, Blake," she says, "look who's next door: Vivien Leigh."

"So it is," Blake says. "Maybe she'll share some more animal trivia."

"What could be better than that?"

They giggle and look over to make sure I'm taking it all in. Karis shakes her head to signal that I should ignore them, but I can't. Propping myself on one elbow, I say, "Hey Karis, do you think one of them has a crush on me?"

Ignoring this, Asia says, "Blake, I think our Leigh has landed a part."

"No kidding. Tell me more, Asia," Blake says.

"That's all I could pick up with Jesse's butt in the way, but I'm sure she's dying to tell us all about it."

"Not really," I say, no longer eager to share my news.

Professor Kirk has started talking and he interrupts. "Ladies, am I boring you?"

"No, sir," I say. "I'm really interested in anything you have to say about . . ."

". . . about the importance of character history and motivation, Miss Reid. Now pay attention, please. You must be familiar with every detail of your characters' lives, right down to their favorite color," he continues. "Then you'll understand why they behave the way they do."

That's exactly what I need to work on for Willow, and soon. As a brand-new character, her storyline is evolving every day. I suppose, in a way, I'll be helping to create Willow's character myself. Jane seems open to that approach. Yesterday, when the actor playing Lake decided that his character is a pervert, Jane encouraged him.

Interrupting my musing, Professor Kirk assigns an exercise designed to foster trust. "That's what acting is all about," he says. "You must be open and supportive of one another at all times. The absolute worst thing an actor can do is reject what another actor gives."

Like anyone in her right mind would trust Asia and Blake.

★ ★ ★

Gray and I stand five feet apart, facing each other. If there is one person in the class I didn't want to be matched with, it's Gray, the undisputed class leader.

The Relic deliberately broke up the usual pairs, saying it wouldn't be a real exercise in trust if we already trusted each other. Judging by the bickering in Team Karis/Asia, there's more going on under his gray thatch than I gave him credit for.

There's no bickering in Team Leigh/Gray because I'm too intimidated even to look at him. In the natural order of things,

Gray's world and mine would never collide. He has a golden aura about him and not just because of his streaked hair. It's because he was brought up in the Hollywood royal court. I feel like a commoner around him. Although Karis comes from as distinguished a lineage, it doesn't show outwardly. Gray carries himself as if there's an invisible crown on his head.

Not that I have any great desire to run in Gray's circle. It's too much work. There are always trends to follow, or trends to set. There's the upkeep on clothes, hair, and everything else. Besides, I like my life—at least most of the time. My friends are cool enough for me. And Rory, well, he's actually cooler than me, but in an arty-cool sort of way that defies the usual laws. You can't rank Rory on the American scale. Things are different in Ireland where they seem to value quirkiness and individuality. Maybe I should emigrate.

In my opinion, Gray isn't as attractive as everyone else seems to think. Sure, he has great features, great hair, and a great body, but he's artificially blond and his tan is too even. In short, he's trying too hard. Rory's casual look is so much sexier. In fact, compared to Rory, Gray seems plastic. Still, I am intrigued. Mixing with Hollywood royalty is valuable character research for my work on *Diamond Heights*. Willow Volume is rock royalty and I could learn a lot about her world by studying Gray's.

At the Relic's command, I stretch my arms out in front of me. Gray sets his hands on top of mine. In this "seeing eye" exercise, we will take turns at guiding our partner around the gazebo. Both of us automatically assume that Gray will take first lead, so without word, I close my eyes and allow his hands to urge me backward. After a few nervous steps, I stop dead.

"Would you relax?" he says.

"I am relaxed," I say, taking another tentative step.

"You're stiffer than a corpse."

"How would you know?"

He pauses for a moment. "You got me there." I can hear that he is grinning. "Anyway, you have to trust me."

"I do trust you," I say, although I don't, not one bit.

He pushes me sharply to the right and someone grazes my shoulder. "Close call," he says. "The drivers are crazy here on Highway Gazebo. So what were you saying?"

"I was saying that I trust you."

"Most girls don't, especially when their eyes are closed."

His voice sounds almost flirtatious, which is odd. Can't he see he's paired with a commoner? Maybe he's like Annika, who flirts with all members of the opposite sex.

Propelling me forward again, he says, "You're doing great." Then he gives my hand a squeeze.

Professor Kirk says we have to accept what fellow actors give and offer something in return. So I wrack my brain for a moment and spit out, "If I'm doing great, it's because you're such a great leader."

"Why thank you," he says, his voice warming to liquid honey. "We're a good team. I thought that might happen."

It worked! I, Leigh Reid, am flirting with a Hollywood prince. He's lying, of course, but that's okay. It's part of the game. Maybe the same thing will work on the *Diamond Heights* set if I try to be a little more trusting of the guy who plays Lake. He is a professional actor, after all.

I try another serve with Gray. "You did?" I allow my voice to swoop up at the end as Annika's does when she's really turning it on. "What made you think so?"

"I can just tell. You're so—" He gropes for the word. "—*dynamic* in class."

I laugh. I'm striving for a giggle, but it comes out more like a cackle. Well, never mind, I doubt "dynamic" is exactly what he was striving for either. I'll have to work on the giggle though. Willow cannot cackle. She must have more finesse if she is going to snatch Lake from Fallon's arms.

Professor Kirk tells us to change leaders and when I open my eyes, Gray is smiling. I smile back and glance quickly away, just as

I've seen Annika do. Then I start leading him around the gazebo and he follows without resistance. Since his eyes are closed, I take the opportunity to stare at him. At close range, I can see razor stubble and it's quite fair. What's more, he has real tan lines at his collar. Obviously I was too hasty in judging him earlier. He isn't plastic at all.

So intent am I on searching for the real Gray that I don't even notice Team Asia/Karis looming until Asia deliberately rams Karis into us.

Gray's eyes open. "Hey! What happened, partner? I trusted you."

"I'm sorry," I say, blushing as if he could see right through me.

And maybe he can because we continue to hold hands until the Relic says, "You can let go now, Miss Reid. This isn't a square dance."

★ ★ ★

I sit at a picnic table with my cell phone, trying to think of something to say to Rory. Although it was character research that led me to flirt with Gray, I still feel as though I cheated on Rory. After all, if there wasn't an ocean between us, I'd be practicing on him. Not that Rory and I have to flirt. We are fated to be together.

Anyway, flirting seems to work better face to face. It's like improvisation, where each person reacts to the other spontaneously and then it's gone. In fact, if you decide the whole thing was a bad idea, you can always give the other person the cold shoulder later and pretend that he read too much into it. That's what I intend to do to Gray, in case he gets any big ideas.

The magic disappears when you try to flirt in writing. I've already drafted and deleted a couple of flirtatious messages because they sounded so lame. I worry that Rory will laugh. Or read them ten times over looking for hidden meanings, as I would. So I stick with the safe route.

```
Rory,
I'm not LuvN Diamond Heights yt.
It's harder thN I thawt. Isn't evrtng?
hOp it's goin gr8 w d B&. ms U,
Leigh
```

There's no magic in it but it will have to do. By the time he arrives, I'll have my giggle in working order.

★ ★ ★

"Sorry, I'm late, darling," Annika says, as I climb into the Beetle. "Your grandmother called just as I was leaving."

"Uh-oh." Gran always calls my cell phone so that she doesn't have to speak to Annika. If she called Mom directly, there can be only one reason. "Dad told her about *Diamond Heights*."

"I'm afraid so. She thinks you've been brainwashed by your evil actor mother and wants to fly out here for an intervention."

"I hope you talked her out of it."

"Barely. It took a lot of patience and repetition, but I think I convinced her that you're okay."

I tell her about Professor Kirk's comments on soap operas. "Karis thinks they're garbage too."

"That's absurd," she says. "You came down here to learn how to act and you're acting. Any project is worthwhile if you're learning. Which reminds me, Roger got a tape of your first episode and sent it over."

"I don't want to see it." Watching the *Danny Boy* footage last year didn't put me off acting, but it did put me off seeing myself act.

"It's part of the learning experience, darling," Mom says. "I'm warning you though, your hair was a fright. And who in god's name is the costume designer? That dress was far too small."

"Tell me about it. I looked like a hooker."

"You're exaggerating. But your grandmother will probably have a heart attack." She chuckles at this. "Anyway, you did fine— and much better than that Sasha."

I explain how I came by my cowlick.

"I don't understand why Sasha gets more priority than you do," Mom says. "Next time you're on set, I'm coming along to get it straightened out."

"Oh no you're not!"

"I won't have you playing second fiddle to a hack."

"That hack is the executive producer's daughter," I say.

"And you are Annika Anderson's daughter."

Like that's ever done anything to win friends or influence people.

eight

Sasha beat me into the makeup chair again and it's all Annika's fault. Although I was up and dressed in record time, I wasted nearly an hour convincing her that spending the day on set would be a huge mistake. How can I impress Jane if my mother is hovering in the background?

Chaz steps into the trailer just as Carla pronounces Sasha done.

Sasha shakes her head. "I don't think so. My hair is curly and I specifically told your assistant that I want to wear it straight."

"First I've heard of it," Carla says, looking at Chaz. "A blow out will take twenty minutes and I've got to start on Leigh in five."

"YP, not MP," Chaz says, meaning *your problem, not my problem.* "Just let me know when Sasha's ready." He stops beside me on the way out. "What's with the pink script pages, Veely?"

"I'm reviewing my lines." Duh.

"How about reviewing the right ones? We're on blue pages now. You do know that each version is printed on a new color?"

"Of course I know that," I say. "This isn't my first job. When did blue come out?"

"Someone dropped a copy in the honey wagon an hour ago."

"Are you kidding?" I ask. The number of revisions on this show is ridiculous. Still, it's my fault for avoiding the honey wagon this morning. I took one look at the sewage truck parked out front and bolted.

"Do I look like I'm kidding?" Chaz pulls several blue pages out of the envelope he's carrying and hands them to me. "You've got a few minutes before rehearsal, so get going. And try to be on time today, will you?"

I stick my tongue out at his back as he leaves and it's still protruding when I notice Sasha staring at me. I flip through the new script pages, trying to stay calm. If I can recite the names of the state capitals and all the presidents, I can memorize a few new lines. It's not like the writers are going to radically change the script at the last second.

Except that they have. Almost every one of my lines in the Fourth of July party scene has been altered.

"I can do this . . . I can do this," I chant to quell the rising panic.

Seeing my lips move, Sasha pulls out her headphones and says, "What?"

"Just trying to memorize my new dialogue. Almost everything has changed."

"Yeah, mine too," she says. "Hey, I know just how to put you in the mood for the party scene." Jumping out of her seat, she connects her iPod to Carla's stereo and cranks the volume on Ashlee Simpson.

Carla reaches over and turns it down. "Leigh needs peace right now."

Sasha turns it up it again. "Jane says it's important that we build the tension between our characters. Right, Leigh?"

"Right, Sasha," I say. "But I figured we'd just act."

★　★　★

When Chaz enters the wardrobe trailer, I am sitting with my arms folded over my chest in defiance.

"What's going on?" he asks.

"I called for Jane," I say.

"She sent me. Jane doesn't have time to consult on wardrobe."

"This is a personal issue and I'd be more comfortable discussing it with a woman."

"Consider me one of the girls," he says. "We can swap makeup tips later."

The designer says, "Leigh doesn't like her costume."

"A bikini is not a costume," I say.

"It is when the scene is a pool party," Chaz says. "What did you expect, a parka?"

"I expected something G-rated," I say. "This is daytime TV. We're not even shooting at a real pool: it's a fake sunroom opening onto a fake terrace."

"In the fake town of Diamond Heights. This is a fantasy and your job as an actor is to sell that fantasy to our audience."

"I know, but—"

"No buts. Except yours. In a bikini. Now." Chaz grabs the bikini off the rack and drops it in my lap.

"I refuse. It's gratuitous."

"This isn't some rinky-dink school play, young lady. You're getting paid to be here, so get changed, get on set, and start acting like you smell chlorine."

★ ★ ★

I hold the bathrobe closed around my throat as I walk onto the set in flip-flops. I suppose there's nothing gratuitous about a bikini at a pool party, but why am I the only actor wearing one? Jessica De Luca is in a one-piece bathing suit with a cover up, Sasha is wearing a gorgeous sundress, and Lake is in swim trunks.

I, meanwhile, am wearing a tiny white bikini with a push-up bra top. The designer said it suits me, and I took her word for it without so much as looking at the mirror. I do not need to see myself through Grandma's eyes. I can't worry about things like that anymore. I am an artist, and an artist keeps it real.

"Bathrobes off," Jane tells me and the extras.

"Could I have one of those?" I ask, pointing to Jessica's sarong. There's no harm in keeping it real under a skirt.

Jane shakes her head and I decide not to push it. I've been down the "prude" road before and I didn't like the scenery. Doffing the robe, I try to cover as much of myself as possible with fanned script pages.

Sasha points at me. "Hey, if she's wearing a bikini, I'm wearing one."

"You're wearing the sundress Drew Barrymore wore on last month's cover of *In Style*," Jane says. "I wouldn't complain."

Sasha flounces over to her director's chair and pouts. "I want a white bikini."

"I'm all for trading," I say.

She rolls her eyes. "*I don't need a push-up.*"

"Enough, Sasha," Jane says. "Where did you girls get the impression that this is a democracy? There is only one boss here and it's me. Fallon is in a dress for a reason. Willow is in a swimsuit for a reason. End of discussion."

I walk backward to my mark on the "terrace," still holding my script pages in front of me. Chaz swoops in with outstretched hand to collect the script. He beckons a special effects guy who is carrying a small tank with a hose attached.

"Hose her down and let's roll," Jane says.

Why does expanding one's horizons have to be so excruciating?

★ ★ ★

INTERIOR TERRACE, DAY

Lake is sitting on a sofa beside Fallon when Willow enters. Dripping water on the floor, Willow crosses the terrace and sits on the arm of the sofa.

"Cut it, Jane," Sasha says. She jumps off the sofa and turns to face me. "You're all slimy and disgusting. If you'd read the script, you'd know you're supposed to sit on the *arm* of the sofa, not right beside me, you moron."

"You said you wanted to build tension between the characters," I say. "I'm just doing my part."

"Good idea," Jane says. "We'll take it again the same way."

A waitress enters and offers lemonade. Willow takes a glass and sips it.

> WILLOW
> [grimacing as she sets the
> lemonade back on the tray]
> It's too sour. Tell the caterer to get it
> right or she's history.

> WAITRESS
> Yes, miss.

> WILLOW
> British servants have much higher
> standards.

"Cut!" Jane steps onto the set. "Tighten up your cues, Leigh. There's too much lag time after the waitress enters. And don't speak until after you put the lemonade back on the tray because the noise interferes with your dialogue. I want you to pump up the attitude a little more. And watch the accent: you sounded Irish by the end of your second line. The line was wrong too."

"Other than that, the Emmy nomination is in the bag," Sasha says.

I take comfort in seeing that her damp dress is now sticking to her leg.

Jane says, "Hose Leigh down and let's go again."

> WILLOW
> British standards are so much higher.

Willow rises from the couch and stands in front of Lake.

                    WILLOW
       And where are your standards? An En-
       glishman would have offered me his
       towel by now.

Lake jumps to his feet and holds out his towel.

Improvising, I take the towel and toss it onto the sofa, clipping Sasha in the head.

                    WILLOW
       On second thought, I'm ready for another
       dip. Why don't you join me?

"Cut," Jane says. "Leigh, jack up the flirting and get the line right." She snaps her fingers and Chaz instantly produces a copy of the script.

He reads, "On second thought, I'm going for another dip. The water's warm, care to join me?" Although he sounds like Hugh Grant on helium, he manages to inject a lot of campy flirtatiousness into the line.

"I'm sorry," I tell Jane. "I was focusing on the character."

Sasha heaves a dramatic sigh. "This isn't rocket science. It's only a few lines. And watch what you do with the props, by the way." She whips the towel back at me, but Jane snatches it out of the air before it makes contact.

"It was a good ad-lib," Jane says. "It's something Willow would do. You've got a better handle on her character today, Leigh, but you've got to get the lines down."

"I only got the new ones this morning," I say.

"I warned you that last-minute script changes are part of life on a soap," Jane says. "Everyone got new pages this morning."

"But you're the only one screwing up," Sasha adds.

Jane shakes a finger at her. "When I need your help to motivate my actors, I'll ask for it."

★ ★ ★

Jessica De Luca offers me a steaming Styrofoam cup. "It's chamomile tea with honey," she says.

It tastes like brewed garden compost. "Delicious," I say.

Jessica smiles at my expression. "The chamomile is soothing and the honey is good for your voice."

"I need all the help I can get."

"You're doing fine," she assures me. "Your accent is quite good, but learning to sustain it takes time."

I'm thrilled that she's speaking to me as if I'm a real colleague rather than the show's mascot. "I'm so embarrassed about flubbing my lines," I say. "Normally, I have a good memory."

"Memorizing under pressure gets easier with practice. If it's any consolation, you had more line changes than the rest of us."

"I did?" I ask, brightening.

"Sure. I just had a couple of minor revisions."

"What about Sasha?"

She scans the room before answering. "Sasha's lines rarely change. Daddy makes sure of that."

Jessica obviously sees through Sasha too, which makes her my new idol. "I expected this to be easier," I confess.

"A soap is actually a tough gig, and not just because of the memory work," she says. "The characters go through such a wide range of emotions in a short time. Personally, I think it's a great opportunity to stretch."

"Willow is definitely a stretch for me," I say. "She's totally obnoxious."

She laughs. "Count your blessings. The divas are the most fun to play."

"I'm not having fun yet," I say.

"That might have something to do with getting hosed down before every take."

"It might," I agree.

"I remember my first bikini scene like it was yesterday," she says, with mock nostalgia. "It ranks right up there with my first sex scene for embarrassment. But it will help you get over your inhibitions, which is one of the toughest things about acting."

"What's tougher?" I ask.

She sips her tea for a moment and ponders. "The day the wardrobe department assigns you a sarong, I suppose. It's hard to accept that your bikini days are over."

"My mother says the same thing. She's an actor too."

"I've met her. She's a delight to work with—always professional and very funny."

I glance at her quickly but she doesn't appear to be joking. "You must be thinking of someone else. My mother is Annika Anderson."

"I know that," she says, slapping my arm. "I worked with her on *Terror in the Teahouse*. I hope she'll visit you on set one day."

Not if I can help it.

★   ★   ★

"My baby is naked!" A familiar voice echoes through the studio, followed by the rapid clip-clopping of spiked heels. Annika appears on the terrace set just as special effects starts to hose me down.

"Don't worry, Shamrock," the guy says, "the water's still warm."

"Shamrock?" Annika asks. "What does he mean? Oh my god, your tattoo is showing." Grabbing my bathrobe from a nearby chair, she tries to wrap it around me.

"Mom, it's no use. It's what Jane wants. I'm trying to see it as an opportunity to expand my horizons."

"Do your horizons have to include a full moon?" she asks.

"I'm not mooning anyone," I say, craning over my shoulder to be sure. "What are you doing here, anyway? You promised not to come."

"It's a good thing I did," she says, swatting at the water hose. "Stop that," she tells the special effects guy. "You're ruining her hair."

"Director's orders," he says.

"Mother's orders trump director's orders." When he continues to spray, she starts slapping him with both hands. He fends her off briefly before turning the hose on her instead. She lets out a piercing shriek.

"Mom, stop," I say, trying to break them up. "You're going to get me in trouble."

As if on cue, Jane comes over to see what the fuss is about. I yank up the strap of my bikini top before something pops out and introduce my mother reluctantly.

"It's a pleasure to meet you, Annika," Jane says. "Roger tells me you were wonderful in *Danny Boy.*"

Annika releases the special effects guy and offers Jane a dripping hand. He massages his arm where her nails gouged him. Chaz materializes with a towel and hands it to Annika with a look of veiled contempt. He has some nerve; I'm the only one entitled to give her that look.

Pulling Mom aside, Jane says, "Your daughter has obviously inherited your professionalism. She hasn't complained and that wet bathing suit must be very uncomfortable."

"It's going to make her father a lot more uncomfortable," Annika says.

"But it's really going to sell the scene," Jane assures her.

"A fifteen-year-old girl shouldn't be selling anything."

"Sixteen," I say.

"And Willow is seventeen," Jane adds.

"Just the same, I want to see *my* teenager in a bathing suit with more coverage—something that isn't transparent when it's wet. And I want that tattoo covered with waterproof makeup."

"Mom!" I grab her purse to cover transparent spots.

"Hush, darling. You can thank me when your father doesn't arrive with the authorities."

Jane sizes Annika up. "All right," she says. "We'll cover the tattoo but the bikini stays because I don't have time to reshoot. A couple of well-placed Band-Aids will help with the transparency.

While we get Leigh fixed up, come sit with me by the monitor. Let me get Carla to give you a touch-up."

Annika trails after Jane like a rat on the heels of the Pied Piper.

★　★　★

In the next scene, Lake has to pat Willow's shoulders with a towel. I feel more self-conscious than ever. How am I supposed to flirt with my mother watching and a wet bathing suit riding up my butt?

"Cut," Jane calls. "Leigh, you need to—"

"Loosen up, darling!" Annika voice cuts her off. "And take more time with your lines. You're rushing them."

I try to relax but Jane cuts the next take early too. "Your mother is right, Leigh. You've got to loosen up. The hottest guy in town is drying you off so let's see a smile."

On take four, another voice yells "cut." Jane looks startled as Annika rushes onto set and bats at Lake's hand. "Easy with the hair," she says. "It's bunching."

"Sorry," he says, backing quickly away.

Annika studies him for a moment. "Jane, can we put this boy on a box? He's not tall enough for Leigh."

"Mom," I repeat, "this is not helping me loosen up." I mouth a silent apology at the guy who plays Lake.

Jane says, "They're the same height, Annika. It's fine."

"It is not fine. The prince is taller than the princess in any fairytale."

Sasha, who is dying to join the fray, says, "But the princess is never a giant."

Annika turns on her. "Excuse me? Do you really want to go there?"

Sasha retreats speedily and Carla steps in to retouch her makeup.

Jane puts Lake on a box and announces that she's ready to roll again.

"Wait a second, Jane," Annika says. "Leigh needs a touch-up.

Her hair is matted." She tows Carla over to me. "Give her a little more gloss. And a touch of bronzing powder. Use the Bobbi Brown shimmer brick."

★　★　★

Annika sits on the sofa in Carla's trailer, sulking. "I can't believe Jane barred me from set," she says.

I study her reflection in the mirror as Carla blows out my hair for the last scene of the day. "And I can't believe she lasted as long as she did."

"I was just looking out for your interests, darling," she says. "Carla, not an up-do, please. It makes her face look too long." Annika met Carla and several other crew members long ago on the *Passionate Hearts* series. "And use the violet liner. It brings out the green in her eyes."

Carla, who hasn't smiled before in my presence, smiles now. Hair and makeup people always like Annika, probably because she values their work so highly.

"I'll give you the eyeliner, Annika," Carla says, "but the hair goes up. Sasha's is down for the next scene, and word from the top is that Fallon and Willow must have distinct looks."

"You mean word from the top is that Fallon must look better than Willow."

Carla shrugs but doesn't deny it.

"Well," Annika says, "we'll just see about that."

★　★　★

The costume designer greets my mother like a long-lost sister. "Why didn't you tell me you're Annika's daughter?" she asks me when we're alone in the back room.

"Because it's not a name that opens doors," I say. "I'm sure you heard that Jane kicked her off set earlier."

She nods. "I was surprised. Annika is usually so professional."

Where are people getting that idea? Her behavior today is consistent with the meltdowns I witnessed on *Danny Boy*.

"I give you about two minutes to cling to that notion," I say, slipping into the frilly dress she's set out for me. "She's about to tell you how to do your job."

Annika pushes open the door and announces, "No, no, no. That color makes her look sallow and with her height and build, she's better in simpler designs."

"Mom, I like it."

"Darling, that little man you're paired with will get lost in those ruffles."

"I am not a giant."

"Of course not. He's stunted." She selects a pink dress with spaghetti straps and a hint of lace from the rack behind her and hands it to me. "This is the one."

"It's too plain," I tell her.

"It's also reserved for Sasha," the designer says, taking it from me.

I turn to Annika. "It's growing on me."

Annika pries the designer's fingers off the hanger and hands it back to me. "That's because it's perfect for you. Try it on."

Off the hanger, the dress is anything but plain. It's sleek and stylish and it flatters my figure.

"Perfect," Annika says, "just as I thought."

I allow her to bask in her victory because even I can see that I haven't looked this good since *Danny Boy*.

"That's my dress," Sasha says, joining us. "Take it off right now." It's just like the scene we did a few days ago, only unlike Willow, I have Annika to fight my battles.

And fight she does. "Who are you?" she asks, as if she's never seen Sasha before.

"I'm Sasha Cohen, the star of this show."

Annika laughs. "Jessica De Luca will be surprised to hear that. I'll tell her about her demotion when we have coffee later."

Sasha isn't fazed. "Take my dress off," she repeats.

I stand a little taller and say, "No. I'm wearing it."

Annika chimes in, "It doesn't suit you Slusha."

"That's Sasha," she says. "My father is the executive producer of this show and I'm calling him now." She takes her phone out of her purse and hits speed dial.

Annika grabs the phone. "Jacob? Hello, it's Annika." Her voice takes on the musical quality she reserves for the highest profile flirtations. "I'm on the *Diamond Heights* set with my daughter, Leigh. I know, sweetie, it's been years. It's so nice to hear your voice too. How's Linda?"

Sasha's jaw drops right onto her plastic boobs as she hears her mother's name.

"Oh dear, I didn't realize you two had split. What a shame." Annika eyes gleam as the stakes change. "I've been there and I know how rough it is. Yes, yes. I'm afraid we've broken up too." She glances at me and I know she's referring to Roger.

The designer selects a pair of shoes in size ten to match the dress and hands them to me. Sasha is going down and we all know it but she's not quite out yet.

"Tell him about the dress," she shouts.

"Yes, that's your daughter," Mom says. "Lovely girl. Wardrobe was putting her in something that doesn't do her justice and I stepped in."

Sasha grabs for the cell but Annika moves out of reach and continues. "You're right, I do know what flatters a figure on screen. Why thank you, Jake." She turns sideways to the mirror and runs a hand over her flat stomach. "I work at it. Anyway, you know how girls are, with their opinions. You wouldn't want her to look dumpy."

Sasha grunts in frustration as Annika holds her off with one hand.

"I couldn't agree more, Jake," Annika says. "They do need guidance at this age. If you like, I'll weigh in on Sasha's wardrobe whenever I can. It's no bother, really. I've put my career on hold to spend time with my daughter this summer, so I expect to be here often. You'll drop by? I can't wait, sweetie. All right, yes . . . uh-huh. 'Bye then."

Annika hangs up and passes the phone back. "A word of advice, Slusha: never play princess until you've checked out the size of your opponent's tiara."

Sasha stomps to the door, turns and hurls the cell phone at Annika, who steps nimbly aside to let the phone crash against the wall.

nine

"Come on, darling, let's have a look at your body of work,"
Annika says, popping a disc into the DVD player. Jane gave Mom
a copy of my first three episodes of *Diamond Heights* as a consolation prize for kicking her off set.

"No thanks," I say. "I'm going to my room to learn my lines."

As if I'm not self-conscious enough on set without actually
knowing what the audience will see. When Roger showed me the
rushes on *Danny Boy*, my face looked as if it had been stretched by
a fun house mirror. Meanwhile, my so-called beauty mark looked
like it was about to sprout legs and take shelter in a nostril. That
thing is so big it should have its own trailer.

Annika pats the seat beside her. "Now, Vivien, I know what
you're thinking and you're being too hard on yourself."

"So says the woman who is known for her good looks." And
not, regrettably, for her talent.

She fluffs her hair and smiles. "True. And you will be too, I
suspect. Jane says the camera loves you."

"Jane was just trying to get rid of you," I say, trying to change
the subject.

"She was not trying to get rid of me. I don't know where you
got that impression. She thanked me for my advice and invited
me to come back any time."

It's amazing what the human mind can rationalize. Jane flattered Mom right out the studio door and locked it behind her.

"What she actually said was, 'Give Chaz a call if you want to visit again next month.' My role is only supposed to last a few weeks, so you do the math."

She gives me the "whatever" eye roll and reverts to her previous subject. "Jane says you're a natural beauty."

"Emphasis on the word 'natural.' It's a nice way of saying I'm average." I hover in the living room doorway for a moment. "Did she say anything about my acting? That's what really matters, right?"

"Actually, she thinks you have potential."

"She does?" It's the first positive feedback I've had from Jane.

"Why so surprised? Roger obviously saw something in you, or he wouldn't have suggested the audition."

"But Jane is constantly harping at me. I never seem to get anything right."

"It's a director's job to push actors to do their best work. You'll appreciate it when you see the results." She pats the couch again and hits PLAY.

"I'll wait for the boxed set," I say, heading into the kitchen to fortify myself with ice cream.

"Darling," she calls after me, "did I mention that Jake Cohen said you were doing a great job?"

I pop my head back around the corner. "Sasha's father?"

"That's right. He said you have a 'believable presence.' When an executive producer makes comments like that about you, it can only mean—"

"—that he wants to date my mother?"

"Don't be silly," she says, hitting FAST FORWARD until my face appears on the screen. "Jake is just a colleague. You see romance blooming everywhere."

I'd take issue with that comment if I weren't distracted by the close-up of my face on the television screen. It's not quite as hideous as I remember. Thanks to the heavy-handed makeup, it barely looks like me. My face still looks ridiculously long, but it is more balanced than it was last year. I guess my cheeks have filled out a little.

Annika hits PAUSE and stares at the screen for a long moment before turning to me. "Darling," she says, sounding surprised, "you look just like me. I don't see your father in you at all."

"What about the brown hair and muddy eyes?" I ask. "Those don't come from the Scandinavian side of the family."

She studies me as if seeing me for the first time and her brow furrows—at least as much as it can five weeks into a Botox treatment. "I guess it's your smile."

"That's what Colleen said last summer," I tell her, noticing that her own smile has disappeared. "What's wrong?"

She reaches abruptly for her cigarettes. "Nothing."

It doesn't take an expert on nonverbal communication to read the signs. "Mom, you've got plenty of good years left in you."

"Of course, darling, I know that."

She doesn't, though, and the tremor in her hand proves it. Why is it that anything that goes well for me seems to come at a cost to her? It means that I have to feel guilty.

"At least you don't have a nose like a brussels sprout," I say. "You know where I got that, don't you?"

"Your Grandmother Reid," she supplies, with a hint of a smile.

"And the cowlick?"

"Definitely your father."

The scene she has frozen on TV is the one at the boutique, in which I am wearing the low-cut dress. "And what about those?" I ask, pointing to my assets on display.

"I take credit there," she says, sounding almost cheerful again. "For slim women, we have nothing to complain about in that department."

She hits PLAY and turns up the volume. I wince at the sound of my squeaky voice, although the British accent does distract the ear somewhat. Willow is flirting with Lake and it's so over the top that it is hard to watch. But then it's Fallon's turn to flirt and I realize I haven't even neared the top, let alone gone over it. In real life, that sort of behavior would be ridiculous, but on a soap, it's entertainment. In fact, Sasha's exaggerated acting somehow makes her character more appealing. Well, maybe "appealing" is the wrong word, since she comes across as a nasty piece of work, but definitely fun to watch. Willow is pale and wishy-washy by comparison. If I were Lake, I'd choose Fallon.

More importantly, if I were an audience, I'd choose Fallon. Jane is always after to me to pump up the attitude and I can finally see why. I must find a way to unleash Willow's potential. I'll need to use what I'm learning in acting class. Better yet, maybe if I start thinking more like Willow off set, I'll be better able to get into character on it.

There's no time like the present to get started. "Mom," I say, "pass me your cigarettes. I just realized that Willow smokes."

She is so shocked that she drops the TV remote. "Oh no she doesn't."

"It's not like I haven't smoked before. Sean Finlay taught me to enjoy a fine cigar last summer."

"Well, if Jane decides that Willow enjoys fine cigars, tell her I'll be on set to witness it."

"I'm sure Jane will be open to the idea: we're co-creators of Willow and she values my input."

Mom's response to this is lost in the sofa cushions as she gropes for the remote.

★　★　★

When we meet in front of the Academy of Dramatic Arts, Karis looks me over from head to foot. "What happened to your clothes?" she asks.

I'm wearing Annika's Lululemon yoga pants paired with her Juicy Couture cashmere hoodie. I sold my soul to extract them from her closet. More specifically, I promised to clean both bathrooms tonight. "What do you mean?" I ask.

"I mean that you have a totally new look. For you, that is. It's standard for Asia and Blake."

"What's your point? It's not like you wear the same clothes every day."

"True, but my basic style doesn't change."

I glance around the classroom as we enter as an excuse not to meet her eyes. "It's good to shake things up sometimes." To prove it, I deliberately choose a different seat from my usual one. Willow wants a new view.

Karis sits beside me and whispers, "That's Blake's chair. She always sits beside Gray."

"Not today."

"She's going to flip when she gets here. What's wrong with you?"

"Nothing's wrong, why?" She bugs her green eyes at me until I crack. "Okay, I'm just doing some research for my role on the show."

"Does 'Willow' have a death wish?"

I smile. "She does like a challenge."

When Blake sees me, it's like a thundercloud passes over the sun: I get a little chill. Fortunately, I don't have to *be* tough, I only have to *act* tough. So, I lean back in the seat and cross my legs with deliberate nonchalance.

"You're in my chair," Blake says, glowering.

I turn to examine the back of the chair. "Really? I don't see a sign. Are you sure?"

"Yes, I'm sure," she says. "Get out."

"I don't think so. I feel like mixing it up today." I turn to Gray and ask, "Do you mind?"

"Free country," he says.

Karis slides a little lower in her seat, embarrassed. But I'm starting to enjoy myself. It's so much easier to hold my ground when I can tell myself it's Willow doing the holding. I only wish I'd discovered this skill years ago. Not that I've had to face down many bullies. There is no fighting at the Nerd Academy, only spirited debate.

"Get out of my chair," Blake repeats. "Now."

"Nope," I say, opening my purse and pulling out lip gloss. I twist the cap off the gloss and apply it without a mirror, praying I don't ruin the moment by slicking my chin as well.

Gray laughs. "She could take you, Blake. I'd give it up if I were you."

Wow, guys really do prefer bitches. Which explains why Gray likes Blake and Asia in the first place.

Well, they've got competition now: there's a new bitch in town and she's twice their size.

★   ★   ★

Today's lesson is on "emotional memory," a technique for making characters believable. It involves calling up a personal emotion and applying it to our acting. If a scene requires a character to show joy, for example, we would recall an event in our lives that was particularly joyful, such as a childhood birthday, or a special vacation. Meaningful objects can help to evoke this emotion.

"Close your eyes and think of something that makes you happy," Professor Kirk says.

Naturally, I think about Rory.

"Put yourself into a specific setting," he says.

I mentally place myself in Terminal Burger in Dublin, where we met. The setting is very clear in my mind. We are sitting across from each other in a booth. I see the burgers and fries on the wooden table, but somehow I can't see Rory's face. I try to focus on his green eyes, his dark hair, and the gold stud in his left eyebrow. It's nothing but a blur.

"Miss Reid," Professor Kirk says, "you look more puzzled than happy. You do have happy memories, I hope?"

"Yes, sir," I say. Ignoring the class's laughter, I return to Terminal Burger. I can remember being happy, but I can't actually *feel* it. Maybe it's a result of pretending to be Willow. It could be distancing me from my own emotions.

"Now, I want everyone to imagine holding an object related to your memory," he instructs.

My memory of Dublin is a year old, so I focus instead on Rory's visit to Seattle and how we walked in the park near my house. *He reaches over to take my hand.*

"How does it look?" Professor Kirk asks.

His hand is large, square and tanned. There's a silver ring on it.

"How does it feel?"

It feels warm and strong and smooth.

"And how does it smell?"

It smells like Calvin Klein cologne.

Except that Rory doesn't wear cologne. I open my eyes. I smell Calvin Klein all right but it isn't a mental whiff of Rory, it's Gray beside me. His tanned hand is resting on his thigh and there's a silver ring on it.

I don't get it. I am usually pretty good at this sort of exercise but today everything is all jumbled up in my mind.

"Sense memory is a powerful way of getting in touch with your emotions," Professor Kirk concludes.

Not for me. My receptors have gone haywire.

★ ★ ★

Professor Kirk tells us to remember feeling sad.

Instantly, I think about the time when I was nearly twelve and Dad and I went to the hospital to visit Grandpa Reid. I sat in the waiting room for what felt like hours and finally Dad came out to get me. Once I was standing beside his bed, Grandpa opened his eyes. His fingers twitched a little on the white cover so I held his hand.

"Hi, Sprout," he whispered. That's why Dad calls me Sprout; Grandpa started it. "I have something for you," he said. His voice was dry and raspy, and there were gaps between the words.

Grandma unclasped his watch from his wrist and handed it to me.

"No," I said, "I can't take it Grandpa."

He squeezed my hand. "Keep your eye on the time," he said. "And keep your head."

So I smiled instead of crying because that was our private joke.

Grandpa Reid wasn't just my grandfather, he was my pal. Every Thursday, he'd pick me up from school and drive me to swimming lessons. Afterward, we'd go to a café around the corner called the Long Shot and drink mochas topped with whipped cream.

"Don't tell your Grandmother," he'd say. She wouldn't let him eat whipped cream because of his cholesterol level.

"As if," I'd say. She wouldn't let me drink coffee in case it stunted my growth.

Grandpa would hand me his wristwatch and tell me to keep my eye on the time. "If we're not home by six, your Grandmother will have my head."

The watch was worn and smooth as a river stone, and the gold was thin in a couple of places around the rim. Sometime after six o'clock, when we were good and late, I'd give it back to him. Then Grandpa would drive home really fast on the back roads, pretending to be scared of Grandma.

The next time I saw him, I'd say, "I see you still have your head, Grandpa."

"Just got it back," he'd say. "You should have seen me yesterday."

It was our shtick and when he gave me his watch in the hospital, I knew we'd never get to use it again. I was heartbroken.

"Miss Reid," a voice says. I open my eyes, startled to find myself in a classroom with tears streaming down my face. "Stand please," Professor Kirk says.

I wipe my eyes on my sleeve and say, "Sorry, sir."

"Don't apologize. I think you've mastered the technique. Let's see you channel it into your acting."

He hands me a sheet of paper and invites me to read a scene with him.

★ ★ ★

"Who died and made you scream queen?" Blake asks. "Kirk chooses you for one exercise and suddenly you're an expert on accessing emotions?"

The class has broken into groups of four to study the emotion of fear and rehearse scenes from classic scary movies. Blake, Gray, Karis, and I are preparing a scene from *Dawn of the Dead.*

"I don't need to be an expert to see you're not trying," I tell her. "A zombie is about to rip your arm off and I've seen you look more worried over a bad manicure."

Karis laughs. "And Willow makes five," she whispers.

"No, that's Leigh talking," I tell Karis. "I just think we could do a better job with this scene. Your reaction seemed a bit weak too, if you don't mind my saying."

"Uh, yeah, I do mind."

"Come on, Karis. You've just seen a zombie remove someone's arm. You'd be terrified."

"So now you're directing too, are you?"

"I'm just trying to help. I know you want to be the best actor you can be."

"Thanks for the input, Willow. For your information, I was acting stunned."

"Who's Willow?" Blake asks.

Karis raises her eyebrows at me. I've been keeping quiet about *Diamond Heights,* but the first episode airs in a few days and I might as well face the music now. After all, Willow Volume wouldn't give a rat's ass what people think of her.

"Willow is my character on *Diamond Heights,*" I say.

Blake wrinkles her nose in disdain. "*Diamond Heights*? It's crap."

"I don't know about that," Gray says. "I like it."

Karis looks stunned by Gray's reaction and she's not acting this time. I'm stunned myself.

"It's a soap," I tell him, in case that fact has eluded him.

"I know," he says. "Some soaps are cool."

"But they're so . . . *not* art." Karis says.

"Sure they are," Gray says. "They're pop art. Right, Blake?"

Blake is visibly torn. She doesn't want to support anything I'm involved with, but at the same time, she can't go against Gray.

"You're out of your mind," says Karis, the only person who routinely challenges Gray's opinion.

"Miss Reid," Professor Kirk interrupts, "I hope your group is rehearsing over there."

"Yes, sir," I say. "We're just discussing motivation."

"Why does he think this is *your* group?" Blake asks.

"Maybe because I'm the only one taking the exercise seriously," I say. "We'll pick it up from Blake's line. But first, let's take a moment to get into our emotional space."

"Hope there's room in there for two, Willow," Karis says.

★　★　★

"What's with you?" Karis asks later, at Urth Café. "You were sucking up to Kirk all day."

"I was not," I say. "I just wanted us to do well, and we did. Kirk thought we rocked."

"That's great, Leigh, but this isn't a competition, it's a class. We're here to learn."

"I know but I want to get the most out of it that I can. I don't always want to be doing soaps, you know. You keep reminding me of that."

She dodges this issue. "Well, you were more fun last week."

I probably was. That was before Jane got on my case over in *Diamond Heights*. All of a sudden Reality Method class isn't just something standing between me and the beach. "The class is more demanding now. We should probably get started on our final project soon."

"Maybe you need a new partner—someone who won't disappoint you."

"Karis, don't be like that. You know I want to work with you. We're a team."

She studies me for few moments. "Leigh and I are a team. Willow and I, not so much. She reminds me of my mother."

I laugh. "Then I'm doing something right with her, I guess. How about I promise to leave her at the studio when we're rehearsing?"

She gives me a high five and we're back on track again.

★ ★ ★

I check my messages while waiting for Annika to pick me up.

```
Leigh,
Haven't hErd frm U n a few
dAz. hOp evrtng iz kewl.
plAD 1st gig w B& last nyt.
It wz brilliant, bt wud hav
Bin BetA f U c%d hav Bin ther.
Rory
```

That's the closest Rory has ever come to saying he misses me. A month ago, I would have been so thrilled I'd have danced around the block, but today I am so drained it barely makes an impression. Maybe Willow is taking over again. Let's face it, Rory wouldn't be her type at all. With her expensive tastes, she'd definitely be looking for a guy with cash.

"Hey," a voice behind me says. It's Gray and he's gliding along the sidewalk as if that invisible crown is still resting on his head. "Nice work today."

He punches my arm and my stomach does a weird flip. "Thanks," I say.

"If you have some time, I'd love to hear more about that soap you're doing," he says, continuing past me to a black SUV parked on the street.

"Oh. Sure. I guess. Whatever." It comes out as a series of verbal burps.

"Okay, great. I think." He smiles and his teeth are so bright that I have to raise a hand to shield my eyes.

If I were interested in Gray, I'd be pretty embarrassed. Fortunately, I am not interested. Maybe he's Willow's type but he sure isn't mine.

```
Rory,
Thx 4 d msg. Everything's
kewl, I've jst Bin BzY 18ly
w skul & wrk.
```

I look up from my phone as Gray reaches for his surf board to make sure it's secured to the roof of the car. The movement causes his T-shirt to ride up and I catch a glimpse of a perfect six pack. Willow would rate that view an eleven out of ten. Even I can appreciate it, although I care more about other things, like artistic integrity.

```
Glad d concert went weL.
Bet U wer amazn.
Leigh
```

I glance at Gray again and see that he is bent over his backpack, searching for something. I try to look away but it's impossible. I am mesmerized. When he turns, my eyes are still at butt level. I drag them back to my cell phone and glue them there.

```
P.S. I wsh U wer her.
```

Finally, after I've stalled so long that Gray should be safely behind the wheel, I look up. He is leaning against the driver's door. Watching me. Grinning.

If Willow were here she might grin back, but she's left for Diamond Heights.

★ ★ ★

Ten Things You Need to Make It in Hollywood
1. *A surfboard or boogie board (regardless of whether you can actually surf)*
2. *Yoga wear (regardless of whether you take classes)*
3. *Designer purse (must cost more than a year's earnings from the Pita Pit)*
4. *Teacup dog (half the work of a normal-sized dog, and cheaper than a designer purse)*
5. *Designer bag to carry dog (likely costs more than the dog but less than the designer purse)*
6. *An attitude (easier to carry than dog, purse, or surfboard and totally free)*
7. *Ripped, faded, or wrinkled jeans (brand-new but distressed to look like they're about to disintegrate)*
8. *Real bling (cubic zircons are for amateurs)*
9. *Designer shoes (see note for designer purse)*
10. *Designer sunglasses (see note for designer shoes)*

★   ★   ★

Annika makes good time on the cobblestone streets of the Grove, especially for a woman in heels. She's trying to stay ahead of me, but I pick up the pace and continue my sales pitch. "Please? Pretty please? Just a standard surfboard—nothing fancy."

"Vivien, you do not need a surfboard. Unless there's something you've been keeping from me, you do not surf."

"I'm thinking of taking it up."

"Then you can borrow one."

"A borrowed board is the mark of a beginner."

"I'm not buying you a surfboard."

I give her a few minutes to let her guard down before moving to Plan B. "How about a purse?" I ask. "Just a small Louis Vuitton bag."

"I thought you loved your Puma bag," she says.

A slight hesitation suggests she'll crack on the bag if I keep up the pressure. "I do like it, but I've matured since I've been here and I need something more sophisticated. You're a woman of style, Mom. You know how important these things are." I'm shoveling for all I'm worth now. "We have time to buy one before hitting the spa."

"I don't know," she says. She's holding out for sport now. I know the bag is in the bag, but there's still some dancing to do.

"You said you'd get me something special for landing the part on *Diamond Heights*."

Annika stops so abruptly that I crash into her. "You've cashed in that promise already. Or have you forgotten all about your white blazer?"

"I love my white blazer and I want to do it justice with the right accessories. Please, Mom? Just one small purse."

She checks her watch. "We have six minutes."

"I can do it in four," I say, hauling her into the closest handbag store.

"I'm warning you, Vivien, do not make me late for the spa. I'm having lunch with Roger tomorrow and I need to look my best."

"How old is his wife, again?" I ask, feeling bold.

"You can't afford that comment, darling, you don't have the purse yet."

She's got a point.

★   ★   ★

Wrapped in a white robe, I follow Annika into the treatment room. "I can't believe you made me settle for a fake."

"You could have settled for nothing at all," she says, taking one of the seats. "Surely you didn't think I was going to buy you a two-thousand-dollar purse?" Mom looks at the esthetician, who shakes her head in sympathetic agreement.

"They weren't all two grand."

"Six hundred dollars is still far too much for a handbag. No one will know yours is a knockoff."

"If that's true, why do you have a real one?"

"I got it at an auction for a fraction of the original cost." She leans over to take a closer look at me. "Excuse me, are those my diamond earrings?"

Oops. I meant to take those off earlier. "I didn't think you'd mind," I say.

"I most certainly do mind." She holds out her hand and I deposit the studs in it. "I mind your borrowing my clothes too."

"I wouldn't have to if you'd buy me something decent to wear."

The esthetician starts smearing cream over Mom's face, mercifully cutting short the lecture. Meanwhile, an assistant starts my facial. "What is that smell?" I ask.

"It's the cleanser," the assistant replies. "We use a lot of botanicals."

"It smells like rotting vegetables. Could you use something else, please?" The woman reaches for a new product, which tingles on application. "Is this for sensitive skin? I don't want to be blotchy. And no extractions, please. I've read that manhandling delicate facial tissue leads to premature wrinkling."

Annika's head snaps toward me. Even with eye pads and an inch of goop on her prematurely wrinkled face, she manages to convey soundlessly that I'd better shut up.

★   ★   ★

"What's gotten into you?" Annika asks, as she leads me through the spa's parking lot. "I was so embarrassed by your behavior that I had to tip everyone double."

"Embarrassed? What do you mean?"

"You rejected thirty shades of nail polish."

"Mother, I just know what I want. And I wanted purple."

"There were half a dozen purples."

"But not the right shade." I wave indigo-tipped fingers in front of her. "This is so wrong. Surely you can see that it clashes with my knockoff bag?"

She grabs one of my flailing wrists and tows me along. "Seriously, what's going on? Why the sudden interest in designer handbags and expensive jewelry?" Then the light dawns. "Ah ha! This is some sort of method acting, isn't it? Willow Volume is a demanding diva, so now Vivien Reid is a demanding diva."

"That's Leigh Reid," I say. "And you're the one who chose this program. I'm just putting the Reality Method into practice. I don't think there's anything wrong in expanding my horizons or communing with my character."

"Commune faster please. We're going to be late for our dinner reservation."

"Where are we going?" I ask, suddenly suspicious.

"The Wasabi Bistro."

"Forget it. I hate sushi."

"You haven't tried it yet. Besides, I hear Willow loves it."

Like I'm stupid enough to fall for that. "Willow does not like raw fish. I should know, I wrote her back story."

"Then Willow is not as interested in expanding her horizons as you are."

I suppose if it's really disgusting, I can survive on edamame until we get home.

ten

I stand on the desk chair inspecting my outfit, as per my usual morning routine: Navy blue yoga pants (my own, acquired during negotiations for the release of Annika's black ones); powder blue Adidas zip-up jacket (a new hostage); Gap T-shirt (two years old but mostly covered up by jacket); and Louis Vuitton purse (fake, fake, fake).

Annika pops her head into my room. "What's that noise? I heard an odd sort of . . . yodeling."

"It was the TV."

"There's no TV in this room. Otherwise, I'd never see you."

Precisely why I keep asking for one. "I was rehearsing, if you must know. Jane says my giggling isn't very convincing and obviously she's right."

"I could help you with that, darling," she says, looking concerned. "Why don't we work on your giggle tonight?"

"It's probably something I should master alone, Mom." I stare my reflection, seeing only the cheap bag. "Where's your Louis Vuitton?" I ask. "I want to compare this to the real thing, in case there's some obvious difference that screams 'fake.'"

"Don't be ridiculous, Vivien. That is a high-quality reproduction and it looks *exactly* like mine. No one will suspect it isn't the genuine article."

★ ★ ★

"Can't afford a real one?" Sasha asks, pointing to my purse.

I grope for a comeback and come up empty-handed. There must be a joke about her fake boobs in there somewhere, but I can't see it. So I do the only thing I can do, which is to stomp away. When I get back to Seattle, I'm selling it on eBay.

I'm still sulking on the juice bar set when Jane stops to say hello. "You're early today. Got your lines down?"

"Yes, ma'am," I say.

"Glad to hear it. And you look good too." She points at the bag, which is sitting on the counter. "Nice bag."

I'm not reassured. Jane has such a sensible, no-nonsense style that she probably wouldn't recognize a fake bag if she saw one. But I am happy that she noticed my appearance. Thanks to Annika's threat of daily visits to the wardrobe trailer, the designer has updated my look with Rock and Republic jeans and a purple wraparound top that chases the mud color out of my eyes.

After Jane moves on, Chaz swoops down on me and grabs my purse. "Hey, where did you get this?" he asks, letting out a whistle of admiration. "It's a beaut."

"I got it at the Grove," I say, feeling better instantly. If this bag can fool a style maven like Chaz, maybe I won't have to hawk it after all. Sasha must have been guessing it was a fake earlier. I'm glad I didn't give the game away.

"Don't leave it sitting around, Veely. Someone might steal it." He runs a finger over the Louis Vuitton label on the front of the bag. "It's the best replica I've ever seen."

★ ★ ★

The first scene takes place in the Buddha Juice & Raw Bar. Fallon and Willow will be at the counter with Lake Mathews when a beautiful young woman enters and shocks the girls with the news that she is Lake's fiancée.

I take a moment to summon an emotional memory to anchor

the scene. Closing my eyes, I think about the day I got the biggest shock of my life—my ninth birthday.

Dad greeted me at the door after school, which was shocking to begin with, as he is rarely home before seven. "There's a surprise for you in the family room," he said. He didn't look too happy about it, so I knew he'd relented and bought me a guinea pig. Dad had this idea that one pet is enough for any family, but I'd enlisted Grandpa's support. When Grandpa went to bat for me, I usually got what I wanted.

I skipped through the house and jumped down the three steps into the family room at one go, feeling the world fall away for a moment. Mid-flight, I saw her: Annika. She was sitting in the old armchair by the window. By the time my feet hit the sisal rug, my smile was gone. Although I hadn't been in the same room with her for a couple of years, I could hardly forget what she looked like due to the constant stream of photos and movie clips she sent.

"Hello, darling," she said. "Happy birthday."

I deliberately wiped my face clean of expression and glanced around. "Where's the guinea pig?" I asked.

She looked taken aback. "What do you mean?"

"Dad said there was a surprise in here."

"I think he meant me, darling. You do know who I am, don't you?" Her voice was pretty shrill by the end of the sentence, so I could tell she was freaking out too.

"One of his girlfriends?" Dad dated now and then, but if he had any girlfriends, he'd never introduced them.

"No, I'm your mother," she said, still smiling. Her lipstick was so bright it made the rest of the room look dull and shabby by comparison. "I was filming in Vancouver and drove down."

"Okay," I said, noticing Dad in the doorway behind me. "When are you leaving?"

"Leigh," he said, "Don't be rude. Your mother has driven a long way to see you."

"I was just wondering when we could go and buy the guinea pig."

His frown told me that he hadn't broken down on the guinea pig front, so I turned to Annika. "Or maybe she'll buy it for me." I may not have had the benefit of pitting my parents against each other for a long time, but I was always a quick study.

"Of course I will," she said, getting to her feet. "I'm sure you don't mind, Dennis."

Dad clenched his teeth. "I'm not big on vermin in the house, Ann."

But Annika was already leading me out to her rental car, a sporty black convertible. At the pet store, she bought the biggest cage they had and approved my choice of a dainty, honey-colored female guinea pig. "Call her Estelle," she said. "It's the character I play in my new movie, *Risen from the Ashes.*"

Two hours later, she was gone and I renamed the guinea pig Annika. Dad pretended to disapprove, but after all, he'd named our cocker spaniel Deedee, after Grandma Anderson. The next afternoon, I came home from school to find the guinea pig had disappeared. Dad and Deedee looked equally innocent and that was the end of the story. Fortunately, I hadn't had time to get too attached to her.

Mom should try this emotional memory stuff. She'd save a bundle on psychiatry bills—money that could be used to finance real Louis Vuitton bags.

★ ★ ★

INTERIOR BUDDHA JUICE & RAW BAR, DAY

Willow enters the restaurant and several teens beckon. Max Volume's daughter has already established herself as one of the hip elite. She could have her pick of any guy in the room, but Willow has set

her sights on Lake Mathews, who is sitting at the
counter beside Fallon. Fallon wraps a possessive arm
around Lake as Willow stands beside them, waiting
for another customer to order.

>   CUSTOMER
>   I'd like an Energizer, please. No ginger.

>   SERVER
>   [pointing to a sign]
>   No omissions, no substitutes, no excep-
>   tions. Next!

>   WILLOW
>   One Beta Booster. Hold the blueberries,
>   double the carrot and wheatgrass, and
>   throw in a shot of bee pollen.

Willow stares at the server, daring him to protest.
Much to the other customer's dismay, he begins making
the drink. Willow smiles at Lake, and Fallon tightens
her grip on him.

The door to the shop opens and a beautiful young
woman crosses over to the counter. She spins Fallon
around on the stool.

>   BEAUTIFUL YOUNG WOMAN
>   Take your hands off my fiancé.

CLOSE UP ON: Fallon and Willow as they gape in
shock.

"Cut!" Jane says. "Sasha, I need a bigger reaction," she says.
"And Leigh—"

"Yes?"

"Well done. Same again, please."

I think of my ninth birthday again on take two. And take three. And takes four through ten. Who knew I'd get so much mileage out of my dysfunctional past?

Jane approaches Sasha. "You *are* aware that the cameras are rolling?"

"Yeah," Sasha says, cautiously. "Why?"

"Why?" Jane turns to the cameraman and signals him to cut. "Because it's customary to act when the cameras are rolling."

"I was acting."

"No. Leigh was acting. You were just standing there."

At the end of the next take, Jane is back on set. "This is a close-up of your shocked reaction," Jane explains to Sasha. "Try using your eyes and your posture to show bewilderment and dismay."

Sasha won't even look at me, and as much as I'd like to taunt her, I don't. It could very well be me in the next scene.

After a few more takes, Sasha gives a credible reaction and Jane moves on. Patting my shoulder, Jane says, "Good work, Leigh. I was impressed by your consistency. It's not easy to look genuinely shocked fifteen times in a row." She raises her voice at the end to ensure Sasha hears her.

Sasha hears her alright. She glares at me over Jane's shoulder before heading over to the craft table to drown her sorrows in chips and cookies.

★ ★ ★

INTERIOR BUDDHA JUICE & RAW BAR, DAY

Fallon and the Beautiful Woman storm out of the shop and Willow sits at the counter beside Lake.

LAKE
You're not running away too?

> WILLOW
> [shrugging as she reaches for her drink]
> Why would I?

I take a sip of the Beta Booster and my eyes immediately start to water. It's so spicy that my lips and tongue feel like they're blistering. I hold it in my mouth for a moment, afraid to swallow.

> LAKE
> It doesn't bother you that I'm engaged?

I don't want to blow the scene now that I'm finally on a roll with Jane, so I swallow the noxious brew, gagging audibly, and say my line.

> WILLOW
> Engagements...are broken...all the time.

"Cut! The gagging didn't do much to sell the scene, Leigh."

I let out a cough that threatens to drag my lungs with it. The spasm continues until I am light-headed.

Jane rushes over. "Chaz!" He hands me a bottle of water. "What's going on?"

I fan my mouth and point to the juice. "Hot," is all I can manage before the next wave of coughing hits.

Jane takes a tiny sip of the juice and yells for the props department. "There's Tabasco sauce in here," she says. "Is this someone's idea of a practical joke? I don't have the budget to burn on pranks, people."

She races off the set, passing the real culprit on the way: Sasha is sitting in her director's chair, calmly stroking Olivier. A tiny smile plays on her pretty face.

★   ★   ★

It's a clear, balmy evening and the Third Street promenade in Santa Monica sparkles with hundreds of tiny twinkly lights. Karis and I leave Fred Segal and find an empty bench on the crowded promenade to listen to a Peruvian flute band.

"You promised to leave your alter-ego at the studio," Karis says.

"I did," I protest. "Willow is missing in action."

"You made the sales guy take every pair of sunglasses off the rack so that you could examine the hinges."

I retrieve my new Dolce and Gabbana shades from a shopping bag and polish the lenses on my T-shirt. "So? I didn't want to pay for damaged goods."

"Newsflash: they were on the 'damaged' rack."

"At least I got the best of the bunch." Removing the sales tag, I prop the glasses on my nose. There's a tangle of scratches on the left lens, but I can see around it no problem.

"Only poseurs wear shades at night," Karis says.

"Even at seventy percent off, I paid good bucks to get the real thing and I intend to wear them. And Sasha can bite me if she tries to say they're knockoffs."

Karis laughs. "I still can't believe she put Tabasco in your juice. She must hate Willow even more than I do."

My hackles rise at this. Willow has many good qualities that Karis doesn't even know about yet. Still, if I argue, it will look like I've lost perspective on my character. "So glad you can laugh at my suffering."

"Oh, come on, Leigh, it was funny," Karis says. "You'd laugh if it were me."

Not in front of her, I wouldn't. I guess I'm just a nicer person, which explains why I try suggesting another *Diamond Heights* audition even though she dissed the idea the first time. "There's a big scene at the yoga studio and they're looking for a couple of girls. How about it?"

"I don't think so."

I let the shades slide down my nose and look at her. "Why not?"

She mutters something about her mother and fumbles with her shopping bags.

"Just ask her, Karis, she might surprise you."

"She won't surprise me."

I notice that she still isn't meeting my eyes and wonder if there's more to the story than soap-snobbery. Why wouldn't Karis just stand up to her mother? We've spent a lot of time together lately and, while she always seems confident and independent, maybe she just puts on a good act.

"Then just audition without telling," I say. "When she sees how well you've done, she'll be proud of you."

"My mother is tough, Leigh."

"And Annika isn't?"

Karis looks away. "Well, she got you the job, didn't she?"

This is insulting, and for a second I think Karis may be jealous of my luck too. But then I realize that she is probably just upset about her own situation, so I decide not to make a big deal out of it. "I told you what happened. Hank recommended me and Jane didn't even know it until right at the end."

"But your mother encouraged you. Mine has high standards and she puts a lot of pressure on me."

Okay, now I'm getting it. Karis thinks she's under more pressure than I am because her mother is an A-lister. Well, she should try living in Annika's B-list shadow for awhile and see which is harder.

Before I can say so, she steers the conversation into a safer channel. "Anyway, we're not the only people struggling with difficult mothers. Sasha's got problems too."

"What do you mean?"

Karis explains that Sasha's mother is a Broadway star who really wanted one of her daughters to follow in her footsteps. She initially focused on Sasha's older sister who won a part in *The Lion King*. Then the girl got trampled by a giraffe during the show and she'll never dance again. "Now Sasha's mom is turning all her attention to Sasha's career," Karis says. "That's why Jake Cohen had to cast her in the soap."

"Is that story true?" I ask, suspiciously.

"Sure. It was in *The Inquisitor*."

"You don't read *The Inquisitor*."

"No, but my brothers do."

Even if it's only partly true, I can understand why Sasha is so difficult. If it's her first real acting gig, she probably feels overwhelmed. Maybe I should share some Reality Method techniques with her. It would be the nice thing to do. More Leigh than Willow but that's okay.

"Let's decide on a scene for our class project," I say.

"How about some Tennessee Williams?" Karis asks. "He's Kirk's favorite playwright so we might get bonus points. *The Glass Menagerie* has a couple of strong female roles."

"I don't know. That's pretty advanced and we're not going to score bonus points if we're in over our heads."

"Have some guts, Reid," a male voice says. I turn to see Gray Cowley and another guy standing behind us, grinning. Before I can answer, he points to my new Dolce and Gabbanas. "Incognito already? Your first episode hasn't even aired yet."

"I was just trying them on," I say, removing the glasses as Karis smirks. "What brings you down here?"

"Just hanging with Skippy," he says, nodding toward his friend. Skippy, who's wearing boarding shorts and flip-flops, gives us a peace sign. Gray picks up our shopping bags. "Let me carry your stuff."

Karis tries to take the bags back. "This is supposed to be a girl's night."

"But it's not like we had anything specific planned," I say. "It'll be fun."

"Don't leave me alone with Skippy," she whispers. "He's obviously crazy. Look at those pigtails."

"Why would I leave you alone?"

"I can see what's going on between you and Gray."

"There's nothing going on. I've barely spoken to him."

She rolls her eyes. "Tell it to Rory."

★ ★ ★

It was an impulse buy and it's Karis's fault. Despite her complaints about Skippy, she joined him in a surf shop and left me alone with Gray. Just to have something to talk about, I led him into a nearby pet store where a fluffy white puppy barked at us from the window display. Gray lifted him out of his pen and handed him to me. The puppy snuggled under my chin, while Gray leaned against the counter to watch us, all golden perfection. That's when I lost it. I whipped out the charge card Annika gave me for emergencies, and when we left the store a few minutes later, the dog was mine.

Gray was totally supportive but Karis is another story.

"Are you out of your mind?" she asks when she sees the puppy. "Your mother is going to kill you."

"She'll be fine with it Karis, trust me." I'm embarrassed that she's making such a fuss in front of Gray.

"I doubt that. In fact, I'm coming in to watch the fireworks."

"I'm not afraid of *my* mother, Karis," I say, striding ahead of her.

Gray follows and eventually I stop and set the puppy on the ground. Karis is now far behind us on the promenade, watching, hands on hips, as Skippy demonstrates surfing moves on a bench.

"You should call the little guy Brando," Gray suggests. "Brando was so brilliant in *A Streetcar Named Desire*." Gray bellows, "STELLA!" and Skippy echoes the cry from his bench.

"Stop that," I say. "You're scaring the dog."

He pulls me toward an Italian restaurant. "Come on, let's get a pizza. There's a patio, which works for Brando." He scoops the dog into his arms and I catch a whiff of Calvin Klein cologne.

"The jury is still out on the name," I say, following him onto the patio. I notice that some girls at the next table are checking him out and I can't blame them. He looks incredible in his rumpled shirt and khaki shorts. They're probably wondering what he's doing with me. There's no Hollywood crown on my head.

As soon as we're seated, Gray tells me he's auditioning for a part on a soap opera.

"Ah-ha," I say. "So that's why you think soaps are cool."

"Guilty." He gives me one of his dazzling smiles. "I thought you might share some pointers."

He leans toward me and rests a tanned hand on my arm. I don't want to offend him by leaning away, but my entire landscape now consists of his huge, perfect teeth. Coupled with the cologne, it's sensory overload. I can't remember which one of us is holding the dog. Or if I only imagined the dog.

After a minute, I push my chair back and look over my shoulder, only to find Karis standing on the other side of the patio railing watching us. Skippy casually slings an arm around her and gives her a squeeze.

★　★　★

The jeep squeals to a stop in front of my mother's house and Karis pops the lock on the back door in silence.

"Come on, Karis," I say. "You haven't spoken to me the whole way home."

"You promised you wouldn't abandon me," she says.

"You abandoned me first." I'm sure this has more to do with my crack about her mother than it does with a pig-tailed surfer dude, but I am not going to apologize. Her superior attitude is starting to get on my nerves.

With Brando still tucked securely into my hoodie, I hop out of the car and unload my things.

Karis points to my hoodie and says, "You've sprung a leak."

I look down to see that Brando has had a little accident. A big accident, really, for such a small dog.

When I look up again, Karis is pulling out of the driveway. She really must be mad if she's willing to give up seeing Annika's reaction to the dog.

★　★　★

Annika is standing in the front hallway tapping her watch. "You were supposed to be home two hours ago."

"I know. I'm sorry. We ran into some friends," I say.

"I called your cell phone five times."

"I forgot to take it with me. Sorry." Two "sorrys" in such quick succession ought to disarm her. She hasn't heard that many in my whole life.

Her sharp eyes scan me for signs of further misconduct, lighting on the wet lump in my hoodie. "What the hell is that?"

I unzip to reveal the puppy, hoping his adorable face will melt her heart. I may have bought him on a whim, but I've already fallen for the dog. It happens with every animal I touch. "This is Brando."

Annika's groomed brows gather ominously and she snatches her car keys off the hall table. "We're taking him back right now."

"We can't. He's nonrefundable."

"Don't tell me you *paid* for that thing?"

"He's a purebred Maltese."

"I'm no expert on dogs, young lady, but that's no purebred anything."

I take a closer look at Brando and see that his snout and ears are awfully pointy for a Maltese. His pedigree certainly looked more respectable when I was blinded by Gray's beauty. "Well, the clerk said he was." Come to think of it, she didn't offer any details—or paperwork.

Annika rattles her keys menacingly and Brando scrambles back into my hoodie, away from the big bad witch. Reaching for her cigarettes, she says, "We're taking him back right now."

"Come on, Mom, we need this puppy. It will make us more of a family. Families have pets."

She sniffs. "This family will manage without. Tomorrow he goes."

I still have one card to play and I play it shamelessly. "Do you remember Estelle?"

Stalling for time, she runs a finger along the cigarettes before selecting one. "No, I do not remember any Estelle."

"Estelle was the guinea pig you bought me on my ninth birthday. Remember, when you came to Seattle to surprise me?"

She watches me warily as she lights the cigarette and I wonder if she is going to tell me she doesn't. But finally she says, "What about it?"

"I was so thrilled that you got her for me, especially after Dad said no."

Exhaling smoke in my direction, she says, "I didn't have to live with it."

"You named her Estelle after the character you were playing."

"*Risen from the Ashes,*" she says, momentarily distracted. Then she snaps out of it. "I know exactly what you're doing, Vivien. I will not be manipulated into keeping this dog."

"Of course not. I was just thinking about it on set today. It's the only time you ever visited on my birthday."

Annika drops the cigarette on the floor and curses. "We'll discuss the dog further in the morning."

On cue, the puppy pokes his head out. I make a show of kissing him to conceal my smile of victory. "Hi, little guy. That lady's your Grandma."

"Don't you dare!"

"Would you mind not smoking in front of Brando, Mom? I know you don't care about *my* lungs, but he's only a baby."

She grinds the cigarette out in an ashtray and turns on her heel. "You're impossible," she says.

That's the first "impossible" I've won all summer and I didn't even need Willow's help to earn it.

eleven

Brando sits patiently on the bench of my honey wagon hideaway while I groom him with a custom-made natural bristle brush that has a silver handle encrusted with crystals in the shape of an *A*. He's mostly Maltese, I'm sure of it. I researched teacup breeds online and my best guess is that he also has a healthy dose of Papillon. That would explain the pointy ears and snout. Not that I care much about his bloodlines. He's a sweetheart and worth fighting for, although I took a cab to avoid Annika this morning. I think she'll cave eventually, but the less she sees of him today, the better.

Following the dog's gaze, I notice the calendar on my wall. Rory's visit is flagged in bright purple highlighter, and I'm surprised to see that it's only thirteen days away. When I arrived in L.A., I knew exactly how many hours remained before he landed on American soil. I've been so distracted with the show that I lost track.

I'm sure that's all it is. Karis may think I'm interested in Gray but she's wrong. I've come to appreciate some of his good qualities, such as his acting ability, but that's where it ends. I'm still crazy about Rory, even if I've been too busy to count the hours until we're together. But I think he might be worried. Lately, his e-mails and text messages have become both longer and more frequent. I used to be the one writing all the time and asking tons of questions, only to receive a reply like the following:

Leigh,
Halo 2 is brilliant. Have already mastered the covenant's deadly
energy sword, even with warthogs in turbo boost! Gotta go, the
guys are here to play Slayer death match.
R

What's really sad is that I printed that e-mail and brought it in
here to re-read, just in case I'd missed something on the screen.
The only hidden meaning is that a long distance relationship
sucks.

Last night, however, I received this:

Leigh,
I've hardly heard from you all week. Hope everything's going
okay. How's the show? Is Sasha still being a bitch? I can't wait to
see your first episodes. I'm going to watch them all when I get
there. Looking forward to seeing you. I miss you,
Rory XO

XO? Those letters have never appeared together in anything
Rory has sent me. His turnaround totally supports my theory that a
guy's interest in you increases or decreases in direct correlation to
your interest in him. Abby and I call it the "Myers Phenomenon,"
after Glen Myers, my first boyfriend. Glen and I were only together
a few weeks when he dumped me for another girl. I went to Ireland
heartbroken and returned fully recovered, thanks to Rory. By that
time, Glen had dumped the other girl and started hanging around
me again. Even though I told him about Rory, he asked me out six
times during the school year. I guess all guys are freaks. But Rory is
my freak and he'll see that with his own eyes when he gets here.

In the meantime, I'll keep the notes short and let him wonder
a little. Willow prefers her nails long, so it's hard to do much typ-
ing anyway.

★　★　★

Carla is so startled when I step into the hair and makeup trailer she almost takes flight. "What are you doing here so early?"

I point to the little face peeking out of my jacket. "Brando is anxious to meet my favorite crew member."

She's onto me immediately and shakes her head. "I'm not a pet sitter. Take him to set like Sasha does."

"But Brando is only a baby."

"Meaning he isn't trained and you want him peeing on my floor instead."

"That won't happen. At least, not as long as you take him outside every two hours."

"How convenient. I'm sure the talent will understand if I have to put my dryer down and walk your dog."

Who knew she could be so sarcastic? "Come on, Carla. Do it for Annika. I got him for her. She's lonely when I'm on set all day and I worry about her nerves."

Carla becomes more sympathetic. "Okay, I'll keep him for the day. For your mother's sake."

Before she can change her mind, I haul in Brando's crate, bowl, leash, and chew toy. "Thank you so much. And don't worry, you won't even notice he's here."

★   ★   ★

"Carla must be waxing Lake's back today," Chaz says, stepping onto the craft truck where I'm making myself a peanut butter and banana sandwich. "You should hear the wail coming out of that trailer."

I drop the sandwich and race back to the hair and makeup trailer, terrified that something has happened to Brando. Maybe he got burned by a curling iron, or blown to bits by a dryer. Maybe Annika put a hit on him.

I fling open the door to find Carla standing over Sasha, who is lying on her belly in front of the sofa. Brando is standing beside her, his tiny fringed tail wagging. The howl is emanating from under the sofa.

"For god's sake, Carla, get rid of that rat!" Sasha shouts, slapping at Brando.

"Don't you dare hit him," I say, snatching up the puppy.

The wailing sound immediately stops and Sasha rolls onto her back to glare at me. Her white camisole is covered in hair clippings from the floor. "That beast terrorized Olivier," she says, pointing a finger at Brando. "He's a menace and he should be put down immediately. I am calling Animal Control."

"Olivier is a drama queen," I say. "Brando is less than half his size."

Sasha's eyes narrow. "Is that thing yours?" She's on her feet before I manage a nod. "And you named it after an actor? How original." She pauses to examine Brando for a second. "What is it?"

"He's a Maltillon." I announce it with pride.

"A what?"

"A cross between a Maltese and a Papillon."

"You mean he's a fake, just like your handbag."

"Actually, he's a brand-new breed, practically one of a kind."

Olivier, having lost his audience, starts wailing again. As Sasha tries to coax him out, Carla explains that Olivier cornered Brando in his crate and stole his chew toy. When Brando tried to reclaim it, Olivier ran under the sofa and turned on the siren.

I help Carla lift the sofa and Sasha grabs Olivier. Then she retrieves her cell phone from her real Louis Vuitton bag and asks Information to connect her with Animal Control.

"Hey, when you're finished, could you call your Dad?" I ask. "I want to tell him that I figured out who put the Tabasco sauce in my juice."

Sasha eyes me for a moment, assessing whether I'm bluffing, but finally she hangs up. "The line is busy," she says. "I'll try again later. In the meantime, keep your mutt away from my baby." She heads for the door.

"My Mom sends her love," I say. "She's up for a wardrobe consult anytime."

She mutters something nearly unintelligible.

"Excuse me," I call after her, "I don't like that language used in front of Brando."

★　★　★

"It's like watching a train go off the rails," Jessica De Luca whispers to me as we sit in our director's chairs. "Horrible yet utterly riveting."

"I don't get it," I say, as Sasha flubs her line for the tenth time. "Why is she so much worse than usual?"

"One of the daily actors is sick and the scene had to be rewritten at the last minute—including all of Sasha's lines."

At the monitors, Jane's anger has reached boiling point. We are now a full hour behind schedule. Instead of taking responsibility for her mistakes and striving to do better, however, Sasha is looking for a scapegoat.

"Jane," she says, calmly, "In case you haven't noticed, this dialogue isn't working. I'm going to ask Daddy to fire the writer."

"Duck," Jessica says, as Jane springs from her chair.

If this were a cartoon, Sasha's hair would be blown back from her face by the force of Jane's yelling, and eventually she starts to look chastened. I should be enjoying the moment, but Karis ruined it by mentioning Sasha's family situation. Now I have to feel sorry for her. Her parents have split, her mother is overbearing, and she's trying to make everyone happy. That sounds a lot like my life. Except that I get knockoffs and she gets the real thing.

At any rate, I can identify with the pressure she's under.

Being too nice is such a curse.

★　★　★

Clambering aboard my white charger, I gallop toward the damsel in distress, who is now sulking in her director's chair.

"What do you want?" she demands.

I smile. It's going to take a lot more than misdirected anger to deter this Good Samaritan. "I notice you're having some trouble with your lines."

"I notice you're having some trouble keeping your big fat nose out of other people's business." She taps her own shapely nose to make her point.

Nobody ever said being a savior was easy. "I'm not being nosy, I'm just trying to share a tip I learned in my acting class about memorizing lines."

"How about memorizing this line: *Leave me alone.*"

A hero persists even when the going gets tough. "Are you sure? This memory technique could really help."

"I don't need help from a loser like you." She jumps out of her chair and stomps off the set.

I wonder if Mother Theresa ever had it this hard?

★   ★   ★

Broccoli salad, Caesar salad, bean salad, spinach salad. As the lunch line inches forward, I help myself to some of each until my plate is piled perilously high. One scoop of peas, one stuffed pepper and, draped over the top of the heap, three grilled zucchini slices. A feast fit for a vegetarian hero.

Carla calls, "Leigh, come join us."

I grab a couple of cookies and head in her direction, only to find that Sasha and several other girls have beaten me to the free seats.

Sasha eyes my plate. "With your mother's career, I guess she can't afford to feed you at home." Everyone except Carla laughs. Before each girl is a plate holding nothing but greens.

Pulling up another chair, I say, "Variety is crucial for good nutrition." At least, according to Gran.

"And a good figure is crucial to ratings," says Chaz, pressing down on my shoulders with both hands. "We wouldn't want phone calls from the studio recommending diets, would we Veely?"

"No, Chaz, we wouldn't," I say, trying to unhook his talons. Here I thought Annika was just paranoid about her weight. I never believed her that studios would actually complain if she gained a few ounces.

He reaches for my cookies. "I'll take those."

"Not the oatmeal," I say, slamming a hand down over the last one and breaking it. "It's my favorite."

Chaz grimly collects the bits, down to the last raisin.

"Oh, give her a break," Jessica De Luca says, coming up behind Chaz and whacking him with a rolled up magazine. "This is a big day for Leigh: her first good review. Listen up everyone." She unfurls the magazine and I see it's *Soap Opera Digest*. "Allow me to do the honors:

> The *Diamond Heights* Fourth of July episode airs tomorrow. As always, Jessica De Luca sparkles in her role as Sumac.

Jessica pauses and smiles. "Well you don't need to hear that. Let's see, skipping . . . skipping . . . more about me . . . oh, here it is. . . .

> Newcomer Leigh Reid delivers a delightful portrayal of Max Volume's spoiled daughter, just arrived from across the pond. Miss Reid's British accent is spot on, and her portrayal of Willow Volume is enchantingly wicked. This charming, fresh-faced young actor is a name to watch for and a new reason for audiences to tune in every day."

"Our Willow has done well for herself," Jane says, joining us. "Congratulations, Leigh. How does it feel?"

It feels amazing but I don't want to overdo it so I settle for, "Cool."

Sasha and Chaz roll their eyes at each other before leaving together.

Jane says, "I overheard you offering to help Sasha today. She wasn't very gracious about it, but I thought it was a nice thing to do. This show needs more team players like you, kiddo."

After she goes, I collect the last oatmeal cookie from the dessert table. I'm a hero and a star and no one is going to stop me from eating a cookie. Just to be sure, I hide it in my knockoff purse to eat later, in the privacy of my own cubbyhole.

★ ★ ★

At the end of the day, I practically skip over to the security booth to ask the guard to call me a cab.

"No need, Miss Reid," he says. "Your chariot awaits." He points toward a domed roof peeking over a line of parked cars.

My good mood evaporates as Annika springs out of the Beetle. Her lips have been freshly injected with collagen.

"You are in so much trouble young lady," she says. "I woke up this morning and you'd just disappeared. No note, no message. It was just like last summer when you ran off to Dublin. You promised your father and me that you would never do such a thing again."

Wow, someone's cranky. That's what happens when you let people jam needles into your lips. "Mom, I did call when you were in the shower."

"At eight o'clock when I'd been up for over an hour."

"And when did you call security to see if I'd made it, five after seven?"

"That's not the point. The point is that you skulked out with that little fleabag." She points at Brando. "And how much did the cab cost?"

It's a shame those injections don't have a paralyzing effect. "You don't have to pay for it. I make my own money now."

"Your money is for your university education."

"It's my money and I can spend it any way I want to."

"Not until you're eighteen, I'm afraid. In the meantime, you're going to live by the rules your father and I set. And speaking of your father, we're calling him when we get home."

Before I can protest, a black convertible pulls up alongside us. "Well, well," the driver says, looking at Annika. "You're even more beautiful than I remember." His hair is thick and silver and his eyes are as blue as hers. For an old guy, he's pretty hot.

Mom obviously thinks so too because she turns her frown upside down in a 0.2-second world record. "Jay-Jay," she squeals, throwing herself into his arms before he's quite out of the car.

"I've been looking for you here, Nika, but you're hard to find."

"That's because Jane barred her from set," I offer. "Nika" squeezes my arm hard enough to snap my humerus.

"Impossible," he says. "I'll have a word with her."

Ah. Jay-Jay is Jake Cohen, Sasha's dad.

"Jane was joking," Annika says, still pinching my arm. "But I admit I was a little overprotective." She shoves me forward a few paces. "Have you met my daughter?"

"We haven't officially met," he says, extending a hand. "I'm Jake Cohen."

"Pleased to meet you, sir," I say, reluctantly offering my hand. The man spawned the devil: he'll probably leave the charred outline of a pitchfork in my palm.

"You're a real asset to the show, young lady," he says, smiling.

Maybe Sasha was adopted. "Thank you, sir."

"You and my daughter have terrific chemistry."

On the other hand, I do smell brimstone. "The conflict comes pretty naturally."

"Congratulations on the good review."

"What review?" Annika asks.

"I'm sure Leigh wants to tell you all about it herself, Nika. But I will say she's inherited your talent."

Nika giggles until I wonder if she's skipping like a scratched CD.

"I trust you've set your VCR," Jake says. "Your first episode aired today."

"Are you kidding?" Annika laughs. "She notified everyone we know—and many we don't."

"I did not!"

Jake leans over to pat Brando, who has been watching the show from his front-row seat in my jacket. "And who's this cutie?" he asks. The puppy wisely licks the hand that feeds him.

I tell Jake about how I rescued Brando while Annika looks on disapprovingly.

"Brando, eh? I like it," he says. "He's a friendly little guy. Dogs bring so much joy into our lives, don't they, Nika?"

"I . . . Yes, they certainly do," she says, refusing to meet my eyes.

"Nika isn't a fan of dogs," I offer helpfully.

"Darling, I have allergies, you know that."

"Fortunately, Brando is hypoallergenic," I say. "He's a Maltillon." I use my best French accent.

"Well, that's a mouthful," Jake says. "I can't keep up with the new breeds these days." I notice that Mom is covering her mouth, although her delicate hand is barely up to the task. "Sasha's dog has been a constant comfort to her since the divorce. I don't mind telling you, before that little mutt came into our lives, Sasha was a real handful."

"Really?" I say. I must get Olivier a chew toy to thank him. "That's so hard to believe." I sound insincere even to me.

"It was great seeing you, Nika," Jake says, giving my mother a peck on the cheek. "May I call you sometime?"

My mother nods so hard her curls polish the Porsche.

★ ★ ★

I reach for the remote control. "Just one more time."

"We've watched your scene five times. I think you've learned all you can."

"But do you think I was annoying enough? That was my first day and Jane was really riding me."

"Trust me, you've mastered annoying." She's smiling, though, because she's still riding the wave of Jake Cohen's pheromones.

I'm hoping it carries her right past the urge to call Dad and tell on me.

I pick up my copy of *Soap Opera Digest* and turn to page sixteen. "Was I 'fresh-faced and charming'? 'Enchantingly wicked'?"

"Remember, that's a review of tomorrow's episode. Let's leave room for improvement."

I look at the television and freeze the frame on a close-up of Sasha and me. With her dark hair, blue eyes, and white skin, Sasha is striking on camera. But I don't look bad at all. Now that I know a reviewer thinks I'm fresh-faced, I can see my own appeal. Somehow, even the mole is working. It makes me look older and a little mysterious. It sets me apart.

Actors with Flattering Beauty Marks:
Kate Winslet
Julia Roberts
Cindy Crawford (not really an actor but definitely a babe)
Kim Cattral
Matt Damon

Mind you, none of them has a bulbous nose overshadowing their beauty marks.

"Can you book me an appointment with Dr. Gerrardi?" I ask. "I want a nose job." I don't really but I want to see what she'll say.

"Not a chance. There's nothing wrong with your nose."

"You said it's Grandma Reid's nose and you didn't mean it as a compliment."

Cornered, she says, "On you, it looks fine. Your grandmother's problem is the simian brow."

"Mom!"

"I'm kidding," she says. "Which reminds me, we were going to call your father."

"Let's not. I promise to wait for you to drive me to set in the mornings as long as you promise Brando can stay."

"He's on probation," she says. "If he so much as nibbles a

shoe, he's gone. And for the record, Dr. Gerrardi is my dermatol-
ogist. I deny having a cosmetic surgeon."

"Your lips are telling a different story, Mom."

"If you're not careful, my lips will be telling the story of a girl
who's grounded."

twelve

Annika screeches to a stop in front of the Academy of Dramatic Arts. "Show me your ears," she says.

"They're where they always are," I say. "And I'm not wearing your diamond studs, if that's what you're thinking."

"You're wearing just about everything else I own," she says, taking inventory. "Pull your hair back."

I roll my eyes behind my designer shades and display my naked lobes. As if I'd be stupid enough to get caught wearing her earrings twice. "Satisfied?"

"No. Empty your pockets."

She's definitely getting sharper in her old age. I pull a small velvet bag out of my pocket and surrender it. "I hope you're happy I look like the poorest kid in the class."

"Karis definitely looks poorer than you."

"But she *isn't* and everyone knows that."

"Little Miss Soap Star has it rough, all right."

"I don't like your attitude," I say, getting out of the car and leaning into the back to say good-bye to Brando. I've stowed him in his crate and belted it so that he'll survive Annika's driving. "Maybe I should take him with me."

She flips down her visor to freshen her lipstick. "I said the little rat can stay for now and I meant it. Annika Anderson does not go back on her promises."

"What about the one where you said you'd love, honor, and cherish Dad till death do you part?"

She smacks her lips together and blots before looking at me. "Who's doing you a favor? Right, that would be me."

She guns the engine and I leap to safety before she runs over my toes.

★   ★   ★

Karis isn't in class when I take my regular seat. She hasn't answered my calls since she dropped me off the other night so she must still be mad. I suppose I am too but I'd still like to smooth it over. Between fights, Karis and I have a lot of fun.

"If it isn't my favorite soap star," Gray says, slumping into the chair beside mine.

"That's Karis's seat," I say. Today isn't the day to play musical chairs. And Willow is going to have to make herself scarce if Karis and I are to recover lost ground.

He flashes a copy of *Soap Opera Digest*. "And how is the 'delightfully wicked' Willow Volume today?"

"That's 'enchantingly wicked,'" I correct him.

"I'll let you know whether you're 'enchanting' or 'delightful' after I've seen the episode. I've got you TiVo'd."

"Really?" Well, that's flattering. I've never been TiVo'd before. It's the kind of thing a girl remembers forever.

"Sure. I watched your first episode too." He describes his favorite parts in such detail that I mentally roll over and purr, stoned on praise. "That was some dress," he concludes.

My face ignites but Karis's arrival saves me from responding. "Hi," I say, sounding slightly hysterical. "Sit down."

"My seat's taken," she says.

"No, it's not," I say. "Gray is just leaving."

"Right," he says, making no attempt to shift his butt.

Karis crosses the classroom to take another seat. She doesn't look back.

★ ★ ★

Professor Kirk sets his briefcase down with a sigh. Each morning, he shuffles into class looking so frail that I am grateful I learned CPR in swim class. But once he starts talking about acting, a strange thing happens: his voice gets stronger, he stands a little taller, and his movements become more fluid. This must explain his decision to teach this class after retiring from Berkeley's theater school. He could be chilling in a rocking chair somewhere, but this is his passion.

Today he divides us into two groups of ten, directing us to form tight circles, with the shoulders of one person touching those of the next. One by one we will step blindfolded into the center, fall backward into the waiting hands of the others, and allow ourselves to be passed around the circle.

"This exercise requires more trust than any of our previous exercises," Professor Kirk says. "Now that you all know each other, you can put your trust to the test."

I'd prefer not to put my safety into the hands of my classmates. The only people I like are Karis and Gray, and Gray is in the other group today. That leaves eight people who would as soon drop me as otherwise, especially Blake and Asia.

I focus on keeping my body rigid as I fall backward, blindfolded, into someone's hands. That person shoves me up and I fall forward, until someone catches me gently. Rocking forward and back, I move slowly around the circle. The steady motion is hypnotic and my fear soon dissipates. It's like riding an air mattress on a sea of gentle waves. But then a particularly vigorous push sends me shooting backward. The fall seems to go on forever and a voice in my head shouts, *"Warning! Warning! Abort this mission! Abort!"* I fight the urge to flail. Then my scalp scrapes against something that feels like a belt buckle and—OOF!—I'm flat on my back, the wind knocked out of me.

I push back the blindfold to see nine pairs of eyes staring at me. The professor breaks into the circle and leans down. "Are you all right, Miss Reid?" he asks.

"I think so," I say. "What happened?"

"Karis dropped you," Asia says.

"I didn't *drop* her, my wrist gave out," Karis says, rubbing her hand. "Old surfing injury."

"We did the best we could, professor," Blake says. "But look at her: she weighs five thousand pounds."

★ ★ ★

"Do you have a partner for the final project?" Gray asks during a break.

I look across the classroom at Karis. I had a partner and a friend, but I don't seem to anymore. A real friend wouldn't drop me; she'd throw herself under me to break the fall. Karis may have good reason to be angry about the other night, but it doesn't warrant this. I could have cracked my head open and she didn't even apologize. I don't see why I should have to honor a commitment to work with someone I never should have trusted in the first place.

"I'm available," I say.

"Great," he says. "I've got the perfect thing to showcase our skills."

Like Karis, Gray is convinced that Tennessee Williams is the ticket to a good grade, but he's going with *A Streetcar Named Desire.* I've seen the movie version with Annika. She agrees that it's dark and disturbing and says it's a challenge even for seasoned actors. Still, Gray is one of the best actors in the class, and if anyone can pull it off, he can. It's a compliment that he wants me in the scene with him.

Blake and Asia are eavesdropping again. "You said you'd be my partner," Blake whines.

"And mine," Asia echoes. "What gives?"

"Nothing personal," he says. "But I had to cast the right girl for the role."

"You mean you cast the girl who can help you get that soap job," Blake says.

That's an odd thing to say, since I've already shared any information I can with Gray, but I suppose she's jealous.

Professor Kirk joins our group. "You're sure you're all right, Miss Reid?"

"Yes, sir," I say. "Although my head aches a little." I glance over at Karis and notice that she isn't wearing a belt. I wonder what my head hit on the way down?

Blake says, "I hope it won't keep you away from *Diamond Heights*."

"Don't tell me you watch that soap opera, Miss Reid?" Professor Kirk asks.

"Watch it? She stars in it," Blake offers gleefully.

"Hardly," I say, "but thanks for the promotion."

Professor Kirk silences us by assigning our foursome an improv exercise. We are to play strangers who meet on a park bench. Asia is a homeless woman, Gray a street musician, and Blake an executive.

"And you, Miss Reid, are a lost child," he says.

★ ★ ★

I tug on Asia's sleeve. "Have you seen my mommy?"

"I already told you," Asia snaps. "Mothers always leave. They bring you into this world and then they dump you."

My eyes fill as my character reacts to her words. Gray puts a comforting arm around me. "Don't worry, your mother's looking for you right now." He turns to Asia, "Ease up on the kid. Just because you've had a hard life doesn't mean you have to take it out on her."

Asia gets off our imaginary bench. "A hard life?" she asks. "You have no idea what I've been through."

Professor Kirk interrupts. "Miss Pearl, unless you want to dance in MTV videos for the rest of your life, it's time you started working." He sounds annoyed. "Don't *tell* us you've had a hard life, *show* us. Right now, I'm quite aware that I'm watching Asia

Pearl play a homeless woman. I can't get lost in the character be-cause you aren't."

"I am, sir," Asia protests. "I can feel what she feels."

"I'm not buying it. Get inside your character's head and stay there. How does she see the world? How does she think? Feel? React?"

Asia begins to pace back and forth in front of the "bench."

"If you've lived your life on the streets, why are you moving like a dancer?" Kirk asks. "This isn't *Park Bench: The Musical.*"

Asia changes her gait. "I was only twelve when I ran away from the foster home," she begins, looking nervously toward Kirk.

"Don't tell me, tell them." He points at Blake, Gray, and me. "They're sharing this moment with you."

Asia then tells a devastating story of poverty, mental illness, and isolation, becoming so caught up that, at the end, she is on the floor sobbing gustily.

Blake pulls her Uggs out of harm's way.

★   ★   ★

"Miss Reid, how would you rate your performance in that scene?" Professor Kirk asks.

"Okay, I guess," I say.

" 'Okay' isn't what we're striving for," he says. He walks to the door and opens it. "If you're willing to settle for that, you can leave now."

This attack must have something to do with *Diamond Heights* and it isn't fair. "I was trying to be modest, sir. I actually think my performance today was pretty good."

"Pretty good?" he presses me, still holding the door. "I hardly heard your voice."

If he thinks I'm going to crack like Asia did, he can forget about it. "Just because you didn't hear my voice doesn't mean it wasn't a strong performance, sir. I stayed in character and reacted as a child would to a crazy woman. I think I did well."

"Glad to hear it." He closes the door and turns to the class. "In the future, you will have hundreds of auditions and you must have confidence in your abilities. If you doubt yourself, it will show in your performance. Miss Reid's portrayal of a lost child *was* convincing. Even when she didn't speak, the character's emotions were obvious from her expression and gestures."

I look over at Karis to see if she's starting to appreciate what she lost, but she's rubbing her bum wrist as if she doesn't hear.

The Relic peers at me over the top of his spectacles. "I see talent in you, Miss Reid. It's a shame you've chosen to waste it on a tawdry medium. Perhaps, one day, you'll put it to better use."

★　★　★

At the end of the day, Gray approaches, flanked by Asia and Blake. "We're hitting the surf in Malibu on Saturday," he says. "Want to come?"

I wait for the girls to shout "psych" but they don't. Maybe our group bonded over Asia's breakthrough. Or maybe they've plotted to drown me.

"I left my board in Seattle," I say, "but I'd love to hang out and watch."

"No worries, I have a spare," he says.

How lucky for me. "Oh, great, thanks."

Gray glances over at Karis. "Invite Karis if you want."

"I think she's working," I say.

He offers to pick me up and leaves with his harem.

Karis crosses the classroom to join me. "So, now you're hanging with Archie, Betty, and Veronica," she says. "I guess that makes you Midge."

"A girl's got to hang with someone when her real friends let her down."

"I didn't drop you," she says.

"You said so yourself."

"I didn't drop you, I just couldn't catch you."

I notice again that she isn't wearing a belt and wonder if she might be telling the truth. "Well then, what happened?"

"Why don't you ask your new friends, Midge?"

"I don't understand why you're acting like this, Karis. We were supposed to be a team."

"If we're such a team, how come Tennessee Williams sounded so much better when Gray suggested it? I heard you."

She actually has the nerve to look hurt—after what she did to me. "It was obvious that you didn't want to work with me anymore."

"No, it was obvious that I was mad you offloaded me onto Skippy."

It is even more obvious that she's jealous of my success on the acting front. But I don't say this because I am a nice person. "You could have given me a concussion."

"Oh, there was plenty of hot air in there to cushion the fall."

She takes a step toward the door but I dart ahead of her to leave first. If I've learned anything on a soap opera, it's that making a big exit is even better than having the last word.

★   ★   ★

It's a good thing I like a challenge because I've never had so many marks to hit or props to juggle in the course of one scene as I had today. I sat down, stood up, crisscrossed the set half a dozen times, boiled water, made a pot of tea, and served cookies—all the while injecting my lines at the right moment.

"Cut! Print! Moving on!" Jane says. "Great job on the continuity, Leigh. You hit every mark and nailed every line. You're going to make my job in the editing room very easy."

"We all hit our marks," Sasha says.

"You had one mark to hit and one line to say," Jane says.

"Yeah, but I did it perfectly. Didn't I?"

I shake my head. It's sad that she's so needy. Even if Jane hadn't showered me with praise, I already knew I nailed it. The confidence has to come from within. Still, it wouldn't kill me to toss the poor wretch a bone. "You did great, Sasha," I say, when Jane is out of earshot. "Keep up the good work."

"Don't patronize me," she says. "And don't think that sucking up to Jane is going to get you the permanent gig."

"What permanent gig?"

"Jane plans to keep one teenage storyline going and it's going to be Fallon's. My father has way more influence at CBS than Jane. He's the executive producer on three separate soaps, you know. So even if the network lets Jane make the choice, it's in her best interests to keep Daddy happy. Besides, I have way more seniority than you."

"If you're so sure the job's yours, why are you trying to convince me?"

Sasha forfeits the last word and goes for the big exit instead, slamming the door of the "spa" until the whole set rattles.

★ ★ ★

Annika is stretched out on a yoga mat in front of the television, but she isn't exercising: Brando is asleep in her lap. I think it's safe to assume there'll be no more talk of returning him.

"How was your day, darling?" she asks, handing over the dog as I sit down on the couch.

"Pretty good." I reach for the remote control and she gets to her feet. "Hey, aren't we going to watch the show together? I thought you enjoyed this."

"Not as much as you seem to these days."

"Oh, come on Mom. You said yourself that I can learn from watching my own performance. Look, here's the part where I wedge myself onto the sofa beside Fallon and get her all wet. That was my idea and Jane loved it."

I replay my scenes several times and to my relief, I actually look fine in the bikini. "Do you think I could get a new bathing suit?" I ask. "I'm going surfing on Saturday."

Annika laughs. "Surfing? Not seriously."

"What's so funny about that?" I ask, bristling. "I told you, I'm expanding my horizons."

"Well, if you're willing to get up on a surf board, the least I can do is finance a new bathing suit," she says, still chuckling.

"Then let's go over to Sherman Oaks Mall. It's open till nine."

"Now? You still need to review your lines."

Jeez, she's as bad as Dad with the homework lecture. "I know my lines and Jane says I'm doing great. Even Quirky Kirky loves me."

She tosses me my script. "In the world of acting, only the paranoid survive."

"No, only the talented survive. That's why Jane is going to extend my role."

"When did she say that?"

"Well, it's not official yet, but she's going to extend one of the teenage storylines."

"And you're assuming it will be yours."

"Well, yeah. Sasha sucks."

"Sasha is the daughter of the executive producer, and I've told you how important connections are in this business."

"The network is letting Jane choose and I'm the better actor."

"That may be so but there's much more at play than that."

"Talent rules, Mom."

"Talent is only the beginning, Vivien. I've told you, it's a tough business. All you can do is work hard, be professional, and hope for the best."

I hit REPLAY and crank up the volume to block her out. What does she know? Just because her career has been blighted by bad karma doesn't mean mine will be.

She takes the remote out of my hand and turns off the television. "Who's going to hire you when your head is too fat for the screen?"

"I'm not conceited. Professor Kirk says actors have to be confident in their abilities, so I'm just calling it the way it is."

"There's a fine line between confidence and arrogance, darling."

The poor woman is wracked by jealousy. It's a good thing I am so indulgent of her insecurities. "I'm just trying to take advantage of my bikini days while I can."

Annika gets off the couch and replaces *Diamond Heights* with her yoga tape in the VCR. Then, with Brando hanging onto her pant cuff, she gets down to work.

```
Abs,
L%kz lIk Ill b stAyN n LA.
Jane plans 2 Xtend my role.
c%d b d stRt of somTIN big!
L


Leigh,
I knew you'd blo evry1 awA!
saw d 1st two episodes & U wer
amazn. alredi pasted d review
n my scrapbook. kEp it up!
A
```

thirteen

I throw a pair of Roxy board shorts onto the sales counter beside my new bathing suit and hurry over to help Annika, who is standing, dazed, in the tennis section. Jake Cohen called an hour ago to book her for a game at his club. Mom hasn't played tennis since the eighties, but that didn't stop her from yelping "I'd love to." Reality set in after she hung up and she froze. I folded her into the Beetle's passenger seat and drove to the mall before she could snap out of it. She has since approved several wardrobe upgrades so readily that I see the potential for a coup. Leigh Reid never lets opportunity pass her by. When the good times roll, she grabs a shopping cart.

It is almost worth the pain of knowing that my mother is dating Sasha's father.

"Try this," I say, selecting a skirt and a halter.

"Are you sure?" she asks. "They're very short."

"That's the point. You won't be able to hit the ball so you might as well give him something else to look at."

She puts her hand to her forehead. "I should have faked an injury. What was I thinking?"

"You were thinking of Jay-Jay's blue eyes," I say, putting a fleece hoodie into my cart. "Please tell me this isn't going to be a true-life Brady Bunch adventure."

"Don't be silly, darling, it's just a tennis game," she says.

I drop a denim mini skirt on top of the hoodie. "Because if Sasha becomes my stepsister, I may do something desperate."

"That won't happen," she assures me.

I select a Paul Frank beach towel. "I hope not. You can imagine how uncomfortable this is going to make it for me on set."

"You're overreacting, Vivien. We're two former colleagues batting a ball around, that's all." But her eyes get a faraway look and I know, as surely as if I were watching it on the big screen, that she is seeing the wedding.

"I know what you're doing," I say, grabbing a Lulu Guinness beach tote. "And I'd better not be a bridesmaid in that scenario."

Annika flushes. "Oh, stop it."

"Seaside or backyard?"

She takes the Paul Frank towel out of the cart and puts it back on the shelf. "I will not play this game."

"Sasha mentioned a house in Santa Monica, so I'm guessing beach." I replace the towel and add a rainbow of T-shirts for good measure.

"It's a lovely house," she says, dreamily.

"Really? You've already been there?"

"Yes, years ago."

"Does that mean you had an affair with Jake before he got divorced?"

"No," she says, indignantly. "You think my love life is more sensational than it is." Now she is taking things out of the cart faster than I can put them in.

"Sorry. I'm just traumatized by the whole thing. Can you blame me?"

She stops unloading and looks at me. "Would you rather I not see Jay-Jay? Just say the word."

I think she really means it. Of course I would rather she not date my boss, but it doesn't seem fair to ruin it for her. He's a better bet than Roger. And chances are she'll scare him off soon enough. Beauty only goes so far.

"It's okay," I say, leading her to the surfboard department. "Go ahead and play tennis."

She looks around as if she's just awoken from a coma. "What are we doing here?"

"Choosing a surfboard."

"Absolutely not!" She turns and heads back toward the cash register. "Darling, how are you doing for sunglasses?" she asks, as I busily refill the cart right under her nose.

"I've got my D & Gs, so I'm covered. What I'd really like is a nice dog carrier."

"Forget it. That plastic crate is fine."

"Mom, there are going to be times when I'm busy on set and you'll need to take Brando with you. Do you want Jay-Jay to see you carrying that crate?"

Tossing tennis outfits into the cart, Annika turns to me. "Where did you learn so much about extortion, darling? That must be your grandmother's training."

She hands the cashier her credit card and braces herself for impact.

★ ★ ★

If I had half Willow Volume's nerve, I'd have a real bikini instead of this "tankini." It may be bolder than my usual one-piece, but it's still the safe choice. The thing is, Willow frolics beside a fake pool, whereas Leigh could end up saving someone from a treacherous undertow. Reality comes with a dress code.

Brando hops willingly into his new Juicy Couture bag. Well, new to us, anyway. When Annika held out on the carrier, I resorted to eBay and got an amazing deal. The vendor couriered it right away, and I was able to sell four Madame Alexander dolls with equal speed. It was meant to be.

Annika calls, "Vivien, your grandmother's on the phone."

"Hi, Gran," I say, walking into the kitchen. "I can't talk long, I'm going surfing."

"Surfing! That sounds dangerous," Gran says. "Do you have a helmet?"

"You know I'm a good swimmer."

"That's not going to help with sharks. They're attracted by thrashing. And blood. You don't have your—"

"Don't say it, Gran. I might just stay on the beach."

"That's probably best, dear. But I really called to talk about *Diamond Heights*."

"Yeah, I figured. What do you think so far?"

"Well, I'm no judge of acting but I think you're the best person on it."

She's taking this better than I feared. "Thanks, Gran."

"My issue is with your wardrobe, dear. Is the show on a tight budget?"

"Those are designer clothes—better than I can afford in real life."

Annika, still reeling from the bill at the mall, rolls her eyes over her coffee cup.

"There's so little *of* them," Gran continues. "You're walking around practically naked in every episode."

"It's not me, it's Willow, remember? The clothes are an extension of her."

"But what will Rory think? You know the old expression: why buy the cow, when you can—"

"Gran, I gotta go. Say hi to Dad and tell him I'll call as soon as he's over the bikini episode."

I didn't expect Gran to get the whole acting thing. The Reids are not arty. In fact, I had a culture-deprived youth, although I didn't know it then. Gran prefers Wal-Mart to the Seattle Art Museum, and Dad's idea of live theater is watching a bunch of guys chase a basketball around Key Arena. I learned more about art, literature, theater, and film in the six weeks I spent in Dublin than I did in my previous fifteen years. But then Annika, with her languishing career, has time to indulge in that sort of thing.

At first, I resisted liking anything Annika liked, but now I admit art is an interest we share. Over the past year, she has sent me books and DVDs, and taken me to exhibits and the theater. Studying acting has done even more to open my eyes to this world. Professor Kirk is always referring to writers, painters, composers, choreographers, and philosophers that I never knew existed. He believes that a well-rounded knowledge of these subjects will make us stronger actors.

Fortunately, I am all about acquiring knowledge. It's almost as much fun as shopping.

★ ★ ★

The ocean is a cobalt blur as Gray tears up the Pacific Coast Highway. "Tell me about Sasha Cohen," he says.

"She's not very nice," I say. That's a huge understatement, but I don't want to sound too harsh. "She isn't much of an actor either."

"She's hot though," Gray says.

I stare out my window without responding.

"Oh, come on," he says. "She is and you know it."

Sasha is hot and I do know it, but Gray is my friend and he should be on my side. It's not like we're on a date, but if it weren't for Rory, we might be. Would it kill him to be civilized? I wouldn't comment on hot actors in front of him.

Gray laughs. "What I should have said is that she is probably behaving like a bitch because you are so much hotter and more talented than she is. Is that what you want to hear?"

That is exactly what I want to hear. "Of course not. This is business. All I care about is whether Sasha behaves like a professional."

"Okay," he says, still laughing. "But you are."

I hold out for ten full seconds. "I am what?"

"Hotter than she is."

"It doesn't matter," I say, shaking my head in disgust. "And if it did, it wouldn't be true. She's gorgeous."

I can tell that he is staring at me and I can't look at him. He isn't serious. If he were, I'd have to tell him about Rory immediately. But he's still grinning, which means it's just flirtatious banter and I should take it as such. So without turning, I say, "We'd stand a better chance of making it to the beach alive if you kept your eyes on the road."

Although he does face forward and I continue to stare straight ahead, I can still see a hint of big white teeth in my peripheral vision.

He ought to give those babies a rest.

★   ★   ★

When we pull into the parking lot at Malibu, Skippy, Asia, and Blake are waiting beside a beat-up old Land Rover stacked with surfboards. Each of the girls is clutching a designer dog carrier and I breathe a sigh of relief about my Juicy Couture bag. I don't want poor Brando to feel as much of an outsider around these rich dogs as I do around their owners.

Skippy dances over to us as we climb out of Gray's SUV. "Dudes, I am stoked!" He sucks in a lungful of sea air and the breeze lifts his pigtails. "Offshore wind," he says. "Those waves are going to be sweet!"

I squint out over the water and see dozens of people on surfboards, darting in and out of the waves like skiers gliding down a slope covered in fresh powder.

Skippy points to a surfer who is cutting in and out of the waves with a girl on his shoulders. "Check it out. That guy is like totally ripping."

Thanks to my research, I know that "ripping" is actually a good thing. I spent a few hours online preparing for today's role. Then I mapped out a surfboard on my bedroom floor and practiced the "pop up," in which you go from prone to a standing position. It was so easy that I've decided to give surfing a try. I was born and bred by the sea after all; it's in my blood.

Scene 12: Leigh Rips the Wave

EXTERIOR SUMMER'S DAY,
MALIBU BEACH, CALIFORNIA

The sun beats down from a clear blue sky as novice Leigh Reid strides into the pounding surf, a board tucked under one arm and her little dog Brando under the other. She places the board in the water, sets Brando on the front of it and climbs on herself.

She paddles out to join the other surfers and when a wave starts to carry her board, she pops up into a crouched position. Pivoting her shoulders toward the water, she turns into the bottom of the wave. It lifts the board and when the wave flattens out, she cuts back across the flat part to the breaking crest. Brando barks into the wind, his tail wagging ecstatically.

On the shore, people have begun to notice this unknown surfer ripping with her dog.

Leigh locks into the curl of the wave as it gathers momentum. The water holds down the tail of her board as she glides toward the bottom of the wave a second time. Then she leans over and grabs the dog as she attacks the lip vertically. The crowd cheers as she reenters at the top and sets the dog on the front of the board again.

A sports reporter covering beach volleyball directs his cameraman to turn his lens on this incredible talent.

SKIPPY
Look at her go! She's shooting the curl!

When the next swell carries them into shore, Leigh raises Brando high before bowing to the roaring crowd.

★ ★ ★

This is what it would feel like to be trapped inside a washing machine with an ironing board strapped to your ankle. I tumble around in the frothy water, my "leash" tightening until the surfboard tugs me back to the surface. When the churning finally stops, I pop my head above the surface and sputter. Brain damage sets in after four minutes of oxygen deprivation and I think I got pretty close that time. If the damage is cumulative, I'm in big trouble, because I've spent the better part of an hour under water.

Gray is perched comfortably on his board, watching me. Tiny beads of water glisten on his broad, tanned shoulders. "You're a little rusty," he says.

"No kidding." I spit out a mouthful of brine. Each time I heave myself onto the board, I slither off the other side. Finally, I manage to stick for a moment and Gray throws himself down and plows toward the other surfers. I try to paddle after him but small waves keep pushing me back into the shallows.

"Move back on your board," someone shouts, as he paddles by me.

I push myself back and the front of the board shoots up.

"Too far!" he calls when I surface.

I struggle onto the board again and start paddling but I'm already exhausted. The surfer who just spoke to me is already far ahead and Gray is nowhere to be seen. Looking back, I see I'm still pretty close to the shore.

"Leigh, look out!"

Gray's voice reaches me as I am lifted by an enormous wave. It sucks me up its face and tosses me out in front of it. I tumble through the air and hit the water hard. The wave breaks on top of me and pushes me under. The washing machine becomes a cement mixer and for a few terrifying seconds, I can't tell which way is up. Finally, the wave spits me out like a cannonball and I scrape across the sand on my back.

Asia is standing over me pointing at a slimy blob to my right. "You missed a jellyfish by inches," she says, sounding disappointed.

★ ★ ★

"Surf's up," Blake tells me. "Grease your board."

Land sharks. No one ever warns you about those. "You guys have fun. It's my turn to look after the dogs. Besides, I've got some reading to do."

Asia examines my book. *"Get the Agent You Need for the Career You Want,"* she reads. "Getting an agent will probably be tough for you, now that you've been labeled a soap sud."

"I won't be labeled after a month-long stint," I say. At least I hope not. "A lot of stars started out in soaps," I remind her. "It's a great training ground."

"Prancing around in a bikini is good training for . . . what, exactly?"

"Oh, you tuned in," I say. "I'm flattered."

"I happened to be flipping past," she says. Without even trying to be discreet she checks out my body. "You know, in person you don't look fat at all. I guess the camera really does add ten pounds."

"Maybe you'll get a chance to find out for yourself one day," I say. "Especially after your breakthrough as a bag lady this week."

★ ★ ★

I am roasting comfortably when Skippy wrings out his pigtails over me.

"In case you haven't noticed, it's like a thousand degrees, he says."

"There's a breeze," I say, to explain why I'm hiding in a towel cocoon.

"Primo wipe out," he says. "At least your board didn't hit you in the head. That happens to me a lot."

I laugh and Skippy stares at me intently. "Hey, you look just like Kate Hudson."

"I don't think so, Skip." Not even an oversized, brunette Kate Hudson.

"If you dyed your hair blond, you'd be twins," he insists. "By the way, I know your friend Karis was really into me and I feel bad. I'm just not in a place to be tied down right now. Can you let her down easy for me?"

Someone has taken one too many surfboards to the head.

★ ★ ★

The sun is kissing the horizon when Gray pulls the SUV into the parking lot at Venice Beach. Since the others haven't arrived yet, Gray and I stroll along the promenade alone. He doesn't even seem aware that everyone is admiring him.

I pause to look into a shop displaying rows of beautiful hand-blown glass vases in every color of the rainbow.

"Do you mind if I slip in here for a second?" I ask. "My friend Abby would love one of these for her birthday. Do you think they're typically California?"

He gives me a dubious look. "Well, typically Venice Beach, anyway. If it's the kind of thing your friend likes . . ."

"Oh yeah," I say, taking a beautiful aqua vase off the shelf and examining it closely. "This is totally Abby." I point to a little spout sticking out at the bottom.

"What do you suppose that's for?"

"That's where the water goes," he says, as if the answer is obvious.

"Oh, right," I say, taking the vase to the cash register. "Of course."

Skippy is waiting outside the shop as we leave and he peeks into the paper bag.

"Cool, a bong," he says. "My kind of girl!"

★ ★ ★

When Skippy stops laughing at my mistake, he volunteers to carry my new cannabis pipe. He already has one himself in mauve, he says. Unless New York has changed her Abby would probably prefer a T-shirt.

We stop outside Skippy's favorite restaurant, a fake bamboo and grass shack at the end of the strip. The sign reads: *Fresh Air Nut Hut: Home of the Best Raw Hemp Burger.*

"Raw food?" I ask, following him inside. "What's on the menu? Carrot sticks sliced five different ways?"

"Not into raw?" Skippy asks. "No wonder you can't stay on a board."

"Skippy's a diehard," Gray says. "I gave up eating raw a year ago, although I felt better while I was doing it."

"That's because you're killing the life force in your food, man," Skippy says. "Heating food over 118 degrees destroys the enzymes. It changes the molecular structure and makes food toxic."

I don't bother pointing out that what he puts in his bong might be toxic too. I am nothing if not open-minded.

Gray smiles at my skeptical expression. "I'm telling you, it works. Eating raw boosts your energy and your immune system. And it lowered my body fat too."

Asia, who has just joined us, says, "Yeah, you were really cut last year."

I can't imagine anyone being more cut than Gray is now.

"What do you mean 'were'?" he jokes.

She shrugs. "You still look good, sweetie, just a little bloated."

It's good to see I'm not the only one she abuses.

Two girls around our age come over to the table. One touches my arm and asks, "Excuse me, aren't you on TV?"

I look around to make sure this isn't a set-up by Asia and Blake before answering. "Uh, yeah."

"I knew it. You're Willow Volume!" She slugs her friend in the arm. "Told you so! We love *Diamond Heights*. Could we have your autograph?"

"Sure. Asia do you have a pen?" She grudgingly digs through her purse and produces one.

"Dude, you're like famous," Skippy says, after the girls leave. And once the waitress tells us that dinner is on the house because of my newfound celebrity, Skippy's enthusiasm can barely be contained by the thatched roof.

★   ★   ★

Blake and Asia warm up considerably over their free dinner and walk me though the array of mystery dishes: yam pie, sea veggie pizza, a wheat milk shake, and cinnamon date bread. All uncooked. The date bread consists of sprouted wheat mixed with dried fruit and cinnamon and put into a dehydrator for twelve hours. It sounds horribly unappetizing, but to my surprise, all of the dishes are tasty and filling.

As she clears the plates, the waitress offers us a complimentary visit to the O_2 bar on the patio. Gray hesitates. "We should be heading back," he says. "It's late and Leigh has to shoot tomorrow."

I'm happy that he's being so attentive, but I don't get a lot of offers for free drinks and I intend to take advantage of it. "Come on, let's stay," I urge him.

"Don't you need to run your lines tonight?"

"Nah, I'm good."

Disappointingly, the "bar" is serving not alcohol but scented oxygen. The staff offer us plastic prongs and our choice of peppermint, cranberry, or plain O_2.

I was hoping for a real Cosmopolitan, but I settle for a small tank of cranberry oxygen. I don't feel the slightest effect from it, and as far as this daughter of an accountant is concerned, anyone who shells out for canned air is a sucker.

★ ★ ★

On the ride home, Gray seems to feel that he can confide in me and I'm happy about that. After hanging around with Blake and Asia, it must be a relief for him to have a sympathetic ear. I would never in a million years tell him he's bloated. The guy could be an underwear model!

The thought makes me feel disloyal to Rory. Despite all his good qualities, Rory is unlikely to make it onto a billboard in his briefs. I think he's gorgeous, but the broader public would probably see a pasty Irish lad who looks like he could use a few extra potatoes. Rory spends all his time inside, either playing music or computer games, and it shows. What's more, he comes from a long line of pub regulars, and the only crown he stands to inherit is the head on a Guinness.

Still, I have nothing to feel guilty about. I am simply hanging out with Gray as a friend and enjoying a pleasant chat. If Rory were doing the same thing with the female equivalent to Gray—say Asia, Blake, or Sasha—I would be fine with that.

Okay, I wouldn't be fine with that. I'd be insanely jealous. I would probably steal Annika's car and run them off the freeway. Better yet, I'd let her drive. Even if I knew they were only talking about family problems, I would throw a tantrum and threaten to dump him just to make my position clear. Rory is free to talk to any girl he wants, just as long as she is unattractive, untalented, and unintelligent—all the "un's."

Not that I am in any position to set laws today. But I had fun and I'm in no hurry for it to end. I really enjoyed hanging with Gray and Skippy because I don't have a lot of male friends.

"I got a callback for a second audition for the soap opera," Gray says.

"That's so great!" I say. "Why didn't you say so earlier?"

"It's just a callback," he says, modestly. "I don't want to make a big deal out of it."

"I'm sure you'll get the part. You're such a good actor."

"Do you really think so?"

"Absolutely. I think you're the best in our class." Certainly the best looking, and as Annika always says, that counts for a lot in Hollywood.

"Thanks, Leigh," he says. "If you really think so, there's something you could do to help me."

"Me? How could I help?"

"I think you might know the person I'm auditioning for: Jake Cohen."

"Yeah, I just met him last week."

"Do you think you could put in a good word for me?"

"With Jake? Gee, I don't know." Jay-Jay may have a thing for my mother, but I'd feel weird asking for favors. "That's Sasha's dad and she hates me."

"Hey, no problem," he says, reaching over and patting my leg. "I completely understand. I just thought you'd have a little pull because of your good reviews."

"I might have some pull but Jake doesn't hang around the set much." I'm very much aware that Gray's hand is still on my leg, but I don't want to look like it fazes me.

"I shouldn't have asked," he says, withdrawing his hand. "I'm embarrassed."

"Don't be," I say. I feel a bit light-headed, either from sunshine, health food, or cranberry oxygen. Strangely, I can still feel the imprint of Gray's hand on my leg. "Jake does seem to like me. I guess it wouldn't hurt to chat to him about it."

"Really?" He reaches over again and this time he takes my hand.

"Sure. We're in the same acting class. That ought to mean something to him."

He squeezes my hand and when I open my mouth to tell him to put his hand back on the wheel where it belongs, all that comes out is a gust of cranberry air.

"Did you say something?" he asks.

I shake my head and so he continues to hold my hand. Every time he changes gears, he lets go of it for a moment. Every time, I hope he'll remember to take it back again. And when we pull up in front of Annika's, he's still holding it.

fourteen

Annika pounds on my bedroom door. "Vivien, get up!"

I squint at the two alarm clocks on my bedside table. The one without a shamrock sticker says it's four-thirty in the morning, which means that Annika's screeching is just a bad dream. Unless there's a fire.

"What do you want?" I croak.

"Get up!" She hammers on the door again. "You're going to be late."

"I don't have to be on set for hours."

She throws the door back and flicks on the overhead light. "Chaz called last night to pull your start time forward."

I roll over on my stomach. "Why didn't you say so before I went to bed?"

"I would have if you hadn't flounced off in a snit."

Sometimes a snit is your only recourse. What else are you going to do when your theatrical mother works herself into a fury because you're a little late coming home and forgot to call to let her know? I have a lot on my mind these days; I can't remember everything. Anyway, it's her job as a parent to make sure I hear important information pertaining to my career.

"I'm not going," I say, my voice muffled in the pillow. "I can't work on two hours' sleep."

"Two hours? You went to bed at midnight. Why didn't you sleep?"

"Leave me alone."

She crosses the room and pulls the blanket off me. I hold onto it, groaning.

"What's wrong with you?" she asks. "Are you ill?"

"No. Just stiff from surfing."

"I warned you," she says, snickering. "Now get a move on. There's just enough time for a shower and breakfast. You'll have to review your lines in the car."

When I sit up, she turns and walks out, leaving my door wide open. I throw myself back on the pillow, averting my eyes from the clock with the shamrock sticker.

I missed Rory's call last night. We scheduled it in advance to accommodate the time difference, but in the excitement of my day at the beach, I simply forgot. I felt awful when Annika told me. And told me. And told me again. She couldn't shut up about "Poor Rory," who got up at five in the morning, Irish time, for nothing. By the time I had some peace to call him, there was no answer.

Rory arrives in L.A. tomorrow and now he'll be wondering what's going on in our relationship. At least, that's what I did from midnight to two in the morning. Not that he'll be wracked with guilt, as I was. What was I thinking allowing—no, encouraging—Gray to hold my hand? I doubt he's really interested in me. He's probably a player.

I groan again and curl up on my side. Annika soon reappears and walks over to my dresser. She opens my top drawer and starts pawing at my T-shirts.

"What do you think you're doing?" I ask, leaping out of bed and pushing her toward the door.

"Just checking. I'm worried about you, Vivien."

Meaning she's worried that I've descended into a life of drugs, sex, and mayhem. Annika has a very active imagination and she's missing the experience most mothers have to judge the seriousness of a situation. If I sniff, she wants to take me to the doctor. If I'm too quiet, she wants to book a psych consult. She is so unsure about her own judgment that she looks for support from "experts." I'll bet she was up half the night too, reading reference books on troubled teens.

"I'm fine."

"If *Diamond Heights* is more than you can handle, I'll pull the plug. Don't think I won't."

"Does everything have to be a big drama with you?"

"I could ask you the same thing."

"I just didn't sleep well. When did that become a crime?"

Peering over my shoulder, she notices the paper bag on my desk. "What's that?"

"A present for Abby," I say, pressing the door closed on her fingers.

I grab the bong and stuff it into my Puma bag to dump on set. Otherwise, she'll have me in rehab by nightfall.

★ ★ ★

I shake my head over Annika's offer of cereal. "I'm giving up processed food. Do you have any raw almonds?"

She reaches into the pantry and tosses me a container of nuts. "We're going to have to meet with a nutritionist if this keeps up."

"These are roasted." I toss the can back and wince at the pain in my arm.

"You'd better not move like that when you're shooting."

"Duh." Would Jane be extending my role if I were that stupid?

She squints at me warningly. "In case you were wondering, I told Poor Rory that we'd meet him at the airport tomorrow. Or have you forgotten about that?"

"No."

"You don't sound very excited."

"I'm just worried that Rory and I are growing in different directions." Before she can say more, I add, "I'm sure you know all about that."

★ ★ ★

"What are you doing?" Carla asks, as I let the dog out of his bag and set up his water bowl.

"Getting Brando settled. Annika had an appointment and couldn't take him."

"Well, I can't take him either. The entire cast is in today and I'll be under too much pressure."

How much pressure can there be in hair and makeup? It's not cardiac surgery.

I climb into a chair and Carla starts brushing out my hair. "I don't like being taken for granted, Leigh."

What is it with everyone today? It's one lecture after another. A girl could get a complex. "Carla, how do you think I'd look as a blonde?"

She examines my reflection in the mirror. "In a word? Ridiculous."

It's amazing how someone can be so oblivious to another person's feelings.

★　★　★

Jane signals the cameraman to stop taping and walks onto the set to speak to Sasha. "Lake is telling Fallon that he wants a time-out," she says. "But she knows that what he *really* wants is to hook up with Willow. She's hurt. Got it?"

"I get it," Sasha says, "but I think Fallon would be more pissed off than hurt."

"At first she is angry," Jane says, "but after he leaves, she's devastated. That much is spelled out in the script. Chaz!"

Chaz materializes with script in hand and reads: *"Lake exits and Fallon breaks down."* He curtsies and disappears as quickly as he came.

Sasha manages to work up a concerned expression, but she still can't access the waterworks. If she'd been willing to take my advice, I'd have told her how to access her emotional memory.

After six more fruitless takes, Carla has to rush to set with fake tears.

Poor Jane. At least she has one actor she can count on.

★ ★ ★

INTERIOR DIAMOND HEIGHTS
RECORDING STUDIO, DAY

Sumac sits with her husband, Max, just back from his tour of the United Kingdom. Willow enters carrying a magazine.

MAX
Well, if it isn't my long-lost daughter.

Willow crosses the room to give her father a hug.

WILLOW
Welcome home, Dad.

I wrap my arms around the actor and wait for him to deliver his line. He holds on to me so long I start to wonder if he's a creep. Then I realize I didn't finish my line.

WILLOW
Did you say hello to London for me?

MAX
London wants you back: the stores are going out of business.

WILLOW
You're a funny man, Dad. Maybe you
should give up music and get into comedy.

Max looks thrown. Maybe I bungled a line, but it was pretty close.

                    MAX
          I may have to if my CD sales continue to
          tank.

                    SUMAC
          You're exaggerating, Max.

Jessica pauses for what seems like an eternity.

                    SUMAC
          Willow has something to show you.

Jessica stares at the magazine in my hands until I realize I dropped a line. I pass the magazine hastily to Max.

                    WILLOW
          Yeah, lighten up, Dad. *Billboard* says
          your album's still number one in Ger-
          many, France, and the U.S.

Or something like that. I may have gotten a country wrong. Fortunately, I've trained in improv and Jessica is such a pro that she's already delivering her next line. I guess that's what comes of being on the same show for so long. In fact, I bet she has a ton of pull with Jake Cohen. Maybe she could tell me the best way to pitch Gray to him. She might even offer to do it herself.

Jessica gives me a strange look, almost as if she's reading my mind. Oh crap, it's my line again!

That is the last time I stay up worrying about Rory's feelings on a work night.

                    ★   ★   ★

"Sorry I stumbled a little there," I say, joining Jane at the director's chairs. It wasn't a big deal, but it never hurts to look humble before one's director.

"It was more than a stumble," Jane says. "You got nearly every line wrong. Fortunately the ad-libbing gave it a realistic quality that I actually liked."

She doesn't thank me for the spectacular recovery, but I suppose hiring me permanently will be reward enough.

Jane peers at me closely. "Are you feeling okay?"

"Yeah, why?"

"You were moving so stiffly. And there are dark circles under your eyes. I didn't know if it was the lighting or if you didn't get enough sleep."

I had a rough night, but it's not up to me to erase the evidence. Frankly, someone in the hair and makeup trailer has gotten careless. If I did my job as sloppily as Carla, I don't think Jane would be extending my role. Still, I am too professional to rat her out to Jane, so I offer a vague excuse about allergies.

Later, I have second thoughts. If Carla's skills are slipping, she'd probably want to hear about it from me before Jane gets to her. I hate being the bearer of bad news, but Leigh Reid does not take the easy way out. Carla is an old friend of Annika's. I owe it to her to give her a heads-up.

★   ★   ★

Carla is flipping through *Vogue* when I open the door to her trailer. Slacking off isn't going to help her cause one bit.

"I thought you were swamped today," I say, as Brando runs over to greet me.

"I was. This is the first break I've had since five A.M."

"Brando's water bowl is empty."

"Is it? I didn't notice. He's been asleep all day."

"All day? But what about his walks? He needed to go out at eleven and two."

Carla doesn't even look up. "I told you, I don't have time to look after dogs."

Not with all those magazines to read. To think I was planning to give her some career guidance. She can forget about that. If her ship's sinking, I'm not bailing her out.

⋆ ⋆ ⋆

I've decided to dispose of the bong near the technical trucks, where drug paraphernalia probably isn't that newsworthy. No sooner have I dropped it in the trash than Chaz appears.

"Hi, Veely," he says. "What are you doing over here?"

"Just getting some fresh air. How about you?"

"Delivering next week's scripts." He hands me one. "Big news for Willow."

While he takes a call on his cell phone, I flip though the script eagerly until I find it: concerned about the decline in Max's record sales, Sumac has decided to create a whole new generation of fans by producing a reality television show starring her daughter, Willow Volume. *Between a Rock and a Hard Place* will document Willow's adventures as she gives up the high life to stay with a working-class family in London.

That's it! If Willow is getting her own show, the permanent gig is definitely mine!

Scene 15: Leigh Hits the Big Time

INTERIOR NIGHT, HOVEL IN THE VALLEY

Annika dabs at her eyes after hearing that her precious daughter Leigh is getting her own place.

LEIGH
Relax, Annika, I'm moving to a better neighborhood.

ANNIKA

Darling, I can't let you go. I've as-
sembled a panel of youth experts to
convince you that you're better off
here.

LEIGH

You should have thought things through
before you started dating my boss. It's
just too weird seeing Jake in your
bathrobe at breakfast. I'm losing all respect for him.

ANNIKA

Let's get a mediator on board to help us
set some new ground rules. I could stay
at Jay-Jay's place more often. And we
could hire a raw food chef to prepare
your meals.

LEIGH

Nah. I'm too embarrassed about your
house to invite my friends over anyway.
Gray lives in a mansion, we live in
squalor. Even my trailer on set is nicer—
especially now that I've taken over
Sasha's.

ANNIKA

It's a great trailer and you deserve it.

LEIGH

I know, but since she got fired, she's been
leaving threatening voicemails. She's
gone off the deep end.

ANNIKA
Why didn't you say so, darling? I'll hire
a security guard. Better yet, I'll call in
the FBI.

LEIGH
I can handle myself. And I don't want to
make trouble for you and Jake. My moving
out is the best thing for everyone. I need
privacy to focus on the show and my studies. I'm still going to college one day.

ANNIKA
[wiping away another tear]
You're becoming everything I wanted to
be myself.

LEIGH
There's a point in every mother's life
where she has to take a back seat to her
daughter. It's my turn to drive.

ANNIKA
[offering her car keys]
Take the Beetle.

LEIGH
I meant that metaphorically. I'm actually buying an SUV.

ANNIKA
You've become so sensible and mature.

LEIGH
I always was. By the way, Dad is giving

up his job to manage my career. If you
think there's a role for you in my company, why don't you send him your re-
sume?

ANNIKA
I can't really do anything but act, I'm
afraid.

LEIGH
How about dog-sitting? I'll be away
shooting in London sometimes.

ANNIKA
Anything to help. I'm so proud of your
success, Leigh.

LEIGH
Me too, darling.

Chaz snaps his fingers in front of my face. "Earth to
Leigh. . . . Be a doll and drop this script off with Sasha on the way
to set, will you?"

I take the script. I don't want to get in the habit of running er-
rands for Chaz, but this will give me a chance to break the bad
news to Sasha in private. Once I'm officially headlining *Diamond
Heights*, I'll have to stop being so nice, though. Jessica De Luca
certainly isn't doing favors for Chaz. If I want people to treat me
like a star, I am going to have to start behaving like one. No one
respects a pushover.

How to Act Like a Star by Vivien Leigh Reid:
1. *Inconvenience yourself only for people who can afford to thank
    you properly.*
2. *Stay on top of your beauty team.*

3. *Hire an assistant. You can't afford to be seen picking up your dry cleaning.*

4. *Hire a dog walker. You can't afford to be seen picking up after your dog either.*

5. *Never walk when someone can drive you.*

6. *Order off the menu. When your custom-made dish arrives, send it back and order something else.*

7. *Travel first class. It's all about image.*

8. *Expect upgrades and freebies and you will get them.*

9. *Never settle for knockoffs.*

10. *Demand the biggest trailer on the lot.*

★   ★   ★

There's no answer when I knock on the door of Sasha's fifty-foot Winnebago. I open the door, planning to drop the script and leave, but once I'm inside, I can't resist looking around. After all, this trailer will be mine before long.

It's exactly as I imagined it: all-white, sleek modern furniture and a huge plasma screen TV. Compared to my cubbyhole, it's a palace. There's a white bowl holding white jelly beans on the coffee table and I help myself, even though they're not exactly healthy. A girl can't transform all her bad habits overnight.

"What are you doing here?" Sasha is standing at the bedroom door.

"Dropping off a script," I mumble around a sticky mouthful of jelly beans. "You didn't answer when I knocked."

"You can't just barge in here. Get out or I'm calling security."

She advances on me and I back toward the door. "But I wanted to talk to you about the script."

Sasha grabs a handful of jelly beans and starts pelting me with them. "Get out!"

Realizing that she could snap at any moment, I turn and flee.

★   ★   ★

I've been studying the lunch table for ages, but I can't see anything that will purify my body after the jelly bean incident.

"Aren't there any healthy options here?" I ask the caterer.

"What do you mean?" she asks. "There's vegetarian curry, broccoli and snow pea stir fry, and scrambled tofu."

Who could resist a big plate of scrambled toxins? "Actually, I was looking for something where the enzymes are still intact."

"Ah, you've jumped on the 'raw' bandwagon," she says, rolling her eyes.

A star must rise above mockery of her habits. Someday, I will educate the caterer about raw philosophy. In the meantime, I pile spinach leaves and fruit onto my plate. It's not as interesting as yesterday's dinner, but as Dad would say, it fills the hole.

★   ★   ★

I bump into the costume designer on my way to set after lunch. Just the person I want to see. I have some ideas for Willow's wardrobe.

"Not now, Leigh," she says. "I have a fitting in five minutes."

She continues to walk and I keep up. A star doesn't allow people to dismiss her so easily. "Willow is becoming a media personality and she needs to start dressing for success. For starters, she should wear power heels. It would give her an edge."

"With 'power heels,' Willow would tower over every other character."

Is it my problem everyone else is short? "Jane can put them on apple boxes."

The designer reaches the wardrobe truck and disappears inside.

"I think Willow would wear more blazers too," I say, following her in. "How about I make some notes and get back to you?"

She slips into the back room and closes the door in my face. "You do that."

Was that tone? I give the woman some ideas that will show an audience that my character is growing and I get tone? That's because she didn't think of it first.

Jane had better give me a raise when she extends my contract.

If I have to keep thinking for everyone else around here, it would be nice to be paid extra for it.

★ ★ ★

I thought Annika would be in a good mood since she's seeing Jake for her tennis date tonight, but she picks another fight on the drive home.

"You don't sound happy that my role really is being extended," I say.

"You don't have a firm offer, Vivien," she says. "Don't count your chickens before they're hatched."

Those chickens are already crowing, and she'd hear them loud and clear if she stopped thinking about herself for a second. "The evidence is in the script: Willow is getting her own show."

"So much can change in a script before it tapes. You know that."

"This won't change. It's the perfect storyline for Willow."

Annika guns it across three lanes of traffic, honking at someone who's merely going the speed limit. "Even if Jane made an offer, darling, we'd have a lot to discuss."

"You mean about my wardrobe? I already spoke to the designer."

Annika laughs. "I meant something more serious: your father."

"Dad? Why? He'll be happy I have this opportunity."

She raises her sunglasses to give me an incredulous look. "This is Dennis Reid we're talking about. He barely trusts me to keep you in one piece for eight weeks."

"When he hears I plan to continue my education, he'll be fine," I assure her.

"Let's not cross that bridge until we come to it."

I notice she's willing to cross bridges early when Jake Cohen is standing on the other side. "Why don't you ask Jake about it tonight so that we can start making plans?"

"Darling, I can't use my personal relationship to further your career. That would compromise my integrity."

This from a woman who regularly has dinner—and maybe

more—with a married director in the hopes that he'll cast her in his movies. All I want is information. I suppose asking her to put in a good word for Gray is also out of the question.

When I lapse into frustrated silence, Annika pats my knee. "Cheer up, darling. I've left macaroni and cheese for your dinner."

"Why not just put a gun to my stomach and pull the trigger?" I ask. "Drop me at the health food store and I'll walk the rest of the way."

If there's one thing I've learned today, it's that I can't rely on other people to take care of my needs. So, once I've loaded up on organic produce, I stop in the drugstore to peruse the hair-color products. Bamboo Blonde . . . Butterscotch Blonde . . . California Blonde . . . Bingo.

What does Carla know? She probably said blond hair wouldn't suit me because she's too lazy to dye it. When it comes to hair color, Skippy is probably a far better judge.

fifteen

Annika screams when she sees me. It's not acting either. I've heard her scream in a dozen movies and this is coming from a different place. If she's drawing on an emotional memory, I'd hazard a guess at childbirth, which she said was "like passing a set of broken dishes." That's a graphic description for someone who's never proven she saw the inside of a delivery room, but whatever. I'm not interested in her pain today. I have problems of my own.

Last night, I overshot California Blonde and ended up with hair the color of a lawn after a really long dry spell. It's a burned-out yellow with a slight tinge of green. I washed it a few times, but it didn't help. Carla will have to do something when I'm on set tomorrow. Unfortunately, Rory arrives today.

Annika collapses into a chair. "What have you done?"

I pull things out of the refrigerator for my breakfast smoothie: wheat germ, bee pollen, brewer's yeast, ground flax, Omega 3 oil, and fruit. "Isn't it obvious?"

She picks up my script and fans herself with it. "It's awful. Horrible. A disaster."

I dump things into the blender at random to avoid looking at her. "Thanks. Your support really helps."

"But it's . . . green. How long did you leave it on?"

"Awhile." So I overcooked it a little. I was daydreaming about life as a blonde and lost track of time. "Carla will fix it."

"She may need to cut it all off and start over."

"Start over!"

"Vivien, it might be for the best. That color is just—"

"I know, I know—awful, horrible, a disaster." I push a button on the blender to drown out her next comment, but she just waits until I'm done.

"I hope the studio doesn't make a fuss about it," she says.

I turn and look at her. "The studio? Why would they?"

"Don't you remember *Felicity*, the show about the college student? She cut off her curly hair after the first season and the ratings *never recovered*." She whispers the last two words.

"*Diamond Heights* is not to going tank because I went blond. Sarah Jessica Parker had a different hair color every season on *Sex and the City*."

"Maybe I should call Jake and give him a heads-up." She stops and giggles. "Sorry, darling, poor choice of words."

I pour the smoothie into a glass and sit down at the table. She's become more animated since she managed to work Jake's name into the conversation. It's killing her that my hair has taken top billing over her date. "You just want an excuse to call him."

"I don't need an excuse to call him, we're friends." She gets up and pours what's left of the smoothie into another glass.

"You're actually ingesting food?"

"Tennis gave me an appetite." She giggles again.

There it is: the abrupt segue into the date debrief. "I don't want to hear about it."

"What's wrong? You said you didn't have a problem with my dating Jake."

"You said it was just a tennis game."

"It was just a tennis game."

She got home at one A.M. He must have really liked her backswing. "Are you seeing him again?"

"I don't know. I hope so. Darling, this—" She points to my head. "—isn't about Jake, is it?"

"I didn't do it because Jake likes blondes," I say, deliberately misunderstanding her. "Stealing boyfriends is your territory."

"If you want to chat about how you're really feeling, the door is open." Swallowing a mouthful of smoothie, she grimaces. "This is disgusting." She takes the glass out of my hand. "You're not drinking that."

I consider arguing the point but it is disgusting. "Then I'm not having anything."

★　★　★

I'm moving as fast as my three-inch heels allow, but Annika is just a blur in the distance. The way she's racing through LAX, you'd think it was her boyfriend arriving. Actually, Jake called her cell while we were en route; she got so excited that the Beetle practically lifted off and intercepted Rory's plane over the Rockies.

I finally catch up to her in the international arrivals area. "Thanks for waiting."

She glances at my pointy boots. "You don't even have a learner's permit for those. Where did they come from?"

"I borrowed them from wardrobe." I didn't bother getting permission, since no one else in the cast wears a size ten. "I wanted to practice. Heels are part of Willow's new, sophisticated look."

"I see. And the drugstore dye job?"

"It's not my fault I had to dye it myself. Carla was too lazy."

"Carla knew chartreuse wouldn't suit you."

I don't know what chartreuse is but I don't like the sound of it. "It's not that big a deal. You dye your hair."

"My hair is highlighted by a professional to bring out its natural luster."

To cover its natural gray, more like. I don't have time to point this out before the doors slide open and Rory emerges carrying an overstuffed backpack. My heart lurches in my chest and I'm relieved to find it's alive in there. Obviously, we still have some sort of connection.

It's not like I could forget what he looks like, given that I use his photo as my screensaver, but he seems different today. He is even paler than I remember, and the baggy black rocker T-shirt he's wearing makes his arms look like chopsticks.

Annika waves. "Rory! Yoo-hoo!"

He smiles and his eyes search the crowd around Annika. They widen when they light on my hair. "Howya, Leigh," he says, when he reaches us. He leans forward to give me a hug, and his heavy backpack slides off his shoulder and nearly knocks me off my heels. Steadying me with one hand, he says, "Sorry."

"It's okay." I notice that my eyes are on level with his forehead. It must be the boots because I remember him as being much taller than I am. I haven't grown.

"Deadly wig," he says. "I didn't even recognize you."

Annika has the decency to cover her smile.

"It's not a wig," I say, shoving my hair behind my ears. Now as coarse as straw, it bounces right back out.

"They made you dye it for the show, then?"

"No, I just wanted to try something different."

His smile fades and his green eyes scan my outfit. He doesn't look impressed.

Who is he to judge? His hair is too long and it's flattened on one side from sleeping on the plane. And while his smile is still nice, he has razor stubble.

No good ever comes of being *too* natural, if you ask me.

★   ★   ★

It's been a very long drive. Rory and I ran out of small talk about ten minutes outside the airport. I asked about his family (fine), his part-time job (boring), and his band (just cut their first CD single). He asked me about my acting course (not bad), Dad, Gran, and Millie (all fine), and *Diamond Heights* (great).

Annika has been trying to keep the conversation going ever since. "We're in the Hollywood Hills, now," she tells Rory. "Vivien can give you the grand tour. I'm lending her my car while you're here."

My head snaps sideways. "You are?"

"You'll want to show Rory around and I have appointments."

"You're not coming with us?" Mark this day in the history books: for the first time in her life, Leigh Reid actually wants her mother to stick around.

"I thought you might appreciate having some time alone."

I'd appreciate having someone to carry the conversation. "I have to work and—"

"Not all the time, darling." She smiles at Rory in the rearview mirror and gives my knee a playful little shake. Then she squeezes it. Hard. "You can show Rory around."

"Of course I can." If I'm able to walk again.

Annika releases my knee. "You can follow the same route you and Karis took. Did you tell Rory about Karis?"

"Yes." Annika's hand creeps back toward my knee tike a tarantula. I turn to Rory. "She's the girl I mentioned from my acting class."

"And . . . ?" Annika prompts.

"And . . . she surfs," I say. Talking about Karis makes me uncomfortable. We've hardly said a word to each other since she dropped me during the trust exercise.

"Karis's mother is Diana Russell," Annika supplies. "A lovely woman who's had far too much work done."

"Work?" he asks.

"Cosmetic surgery. It's an epidemic out here. Even girls Vivien's age are having it done."

"That's awful," Rory says, sounding appalled.

He has no idea what pressures an actor endures.

★ ★ ★

At the restaurant, I hold the seat back so that Rory can climb out of the Beetle.

"I've never seen you wear boots like those," he says.

Why can't he just say they look nice? Does he think I can't pull them off? "My character wears them on the show so I had to get used to them." Since Annika is handing her keys to the valet, I feel free to embellish the truth.

"They're really pointy," he says. "Do they hurt?"

"They're very comfortable," I say. Now that I've lost all feeling in my baby toes, they're not bad at all.

A valet rushes forward to open the door for me, confirming my belief that power heels bring respect. Rory will see that too. I am going to turn heads as I walk into the restaurant. I've learned how to make an entrance and it's time I put that skill to use. Holding my head high, I sail through the heavy glass doors and glide gracefully after the host toward our table. As we pass the open kitchen, my right boot connects with something slippery on the polished floor. I topple off my heel and clutch at another diner's shoulder. Startled, he clambers to his feet, sending me careening into a barstool. It falls on top of me.

From my position on the floor, I can see that I have indeed turned many heads.

★　★　★

Rory leans across the table. "Are you sure yer all right, Leigh?"

"Yes, I'm fine," I snap. I wish he'd stop going on about it.

"There's no need to be defensive, Vivien," Annika says. "Rory is concerned, and no wonder. I'm surprised you didn't crack your head open."

I review the menu carefully before ordering. "I'll have orange juice, if it's squeezed fresh on-site, and the house salad, but with avocado instead of goat's cheese, and raw pear slices instead of sautéed. Hold the dressing." I consult the menu again to make sure I haven't missed any toxins. "Hold the walnuts too, if they're roasted."

Rory and Annika are staring at me. "Vivien, you've had nothing to eat all day," Mom says. "You need more than salad for dinner." She tells the waiter, "I'll have the beet salad, please." To me she adds, "My bones aren't still growing."

"Mine had better not be either."

Rory asks, "Yer not trying to get skinny, are you?"

"No." How nice of him to point out that I'm not. "I'm just trying to improve my eating habits and there aren't a lot of options for me without a dehydrator."

"When you become an astronaut you can eat dehydrated food," Annika says.

"I heard Californians were crazy but I didn't know it was contagious," Rory says, laughing as he orders a cheeseburger and fries.

And I didn't realize the Irish were so disrespectful of other people's lifestyle choices.

★ ★ ★

The minute Annika is out of the room, Rory puts his scrawny arms around me and kisses me. I dreamed of this moment for six months and now all I can think about is getting it over with because I can totally smell the dead cow and greasy fries on him. Thankfully, Brando interrupts before I have to pull away in disgust and ask him to brush and gargle.

"I trust that isn't you licking my ankle?" Rory asks.

I lean over and scoop up my rescuer. "This is Brando. He's a Maltillon."

"Is that French for 'not a real dog'?"

"Very funny." I carry Brando to an armchair before Rory can get any big ideas about planting more beef particles on me. It's hard to believe I was scheming to get Dad out of the room at Christmas and now I am silently willing Annika to join us.

Rory squishes into the chair beside me and wraps his arm around my shoulder. He takes the remote control and flips around the dial. "You get so many channels here," he says. "Look, it's U2's latest video."

"Yeah, it's great, isn't it?"

He looks crestfallen. "I hate it." Then he brightens. "Hey, I brought my Game Boy. Want me to teach you Ace Combat Advance? It's brilliant."

"I'm not really into games," I say. "But if you want to play, I'll sit here and read." I reach for my copy of *A Streetcar Named Desire,* which I conveniently left on the coffee table to impress him. "I have to perform a scene in class next week."

He peeks at the cover. "Marlon Brando starred in the movie version, right?"

I figured that would grab his interest. Guys love Brando in this role. I nod. "It's such an amazing play."

"Depressing, though. Who are you playing, the wife Brando's character abuses or the delusional sister he rapes?"

Why did I think we had anything in common?

★　★　★

I'm at my computer complaining at great length to Abby when Annika knocks at my door. She opens it a crack and peers at me with one blue eye. "Where's Rory?"

"Hiding naked in my closet."

"Good, as long as he's comfortable," she says, coming in and settling, uninvited, on the bed. "We need to talk."

"Wait, don't tell me: you're engaged to Jake."

She smiles. "Let's save something for the second date."

I hate it when she refuses to be goaded. Fortunately, I also love it because it's a challenge. "If you were naked in *his* closet last night, I don't want to know."

Mission accomplished. The smile vanishes like magic. "You're obviously having some issues with my dating," she says.

"Not with your dating in general. With your dating Jake."

"You said you didn't mind."

"I don't mind," I say.

She throws up her hands in frustration. "Well, which is it?"

"Never mind."

What is it about relationships that turn otherwise smart people into crazies? Take Annika. For all her quirks, she's not an idiot. Yet something happened with Dad (also not an idiot) that led her to abandon him. Thirteen years later, he is still naming appliances after her and she spits out his name as if it were rancid.

If relationships worked, we wouldn't be having this conversation. She'd be busy teaching acting workshops in Seattle rather than telling me about her love life. It's unnatural. I am her daughter, not her friend. And it's especially harsh when my love life is in the Dumpster. I'm afraid that Rory is the second in a string of romantic failures.

Annika studies me. "What's really bothering you?"

"I've inherited your bad relationship genes. That's what's bothering me."

Her face spasms, as if she can't figure out whether to laugh or cry. "It's a little early to jump to that conclusion," she says.

I notice she isn't denying she has them. "It's obvious that I'm crap at this, just like you."

"Rory just got here. Give the dust a chance to settle."

"It's dead. So dead I can smell it." I turn and tap aimlessly on my keyboard. "Why does that happen?"

She sighs. "You're asking me? Like you said, I'm no expert."

"I thought he was perfect," I mutter.

"That's infatuation. Unfortunately, reality is often disappointing."

"We have nothing in common. He likes to play video games. It's so juvenile."

"He was playing a video game when you met him, so that hasn't changed," she says. "Maybe you've changed."

"Maybe I have." We've probably been drifting apart for months, but it's hard to tell with text messages and e-mails. "Maybe I've got more important things to worry about now, like my career."

"If you're so worried about your career, why are you on your computer instead of rehearsing?" she asks, using her warm up to a lecture voice.

"FYI, I'm going to rehearse after I send this e-mail to Abby."

"FYI, you better rehearse or you won't have a career to worry about." She gets up and crosses to the door. "Anyway, no matter how you feel about Poor Rory, he came out of his way to see you. He's a nice boy and you will treat him with respect while he's here."

I wait until she's halfway out the door before whispering, "Like you treated Dad."

She steps back into the room. "Pardon me?"

"Nothing."

"Good. Because I don't think you want to have that discussion again." She stares at the back of my head for ages before turning to go. "Rory is your guest so suck it up. And crack open that script."

When I'm finally able to continue my note to Abby, I see that I've unknowingly typed "hopeless" across the page a dozen times. I'm not sure whether that refers to Rory, Annika, or me.

★ ★ ★

As I hit SEND, my e-mail pings. It's Gray! He's asking permission to instant message, which I grant as fast as my fingers can click.

> Gray: Surprise.
> Leigh: How did U get my address?
> Gray: Class contact list. I'm inviting every1 2 a party at my
> beach house 2morrow nite. U in?
> Leigh: Definitely. Can I bring a guest?
> Gray: Sure. Who is it?

My fingers hover over the keys. I can hardly mention a boyfriend now, after holding Gray's hand the other night. It doesn't even feel like Rory is my boyfriend anymore. Yet at the same time, it feels like a betrayal to say he's anything else. Why does everything have to be so complicated?

> Gray: Still there? Who's the mystery guest?
> Leigh: A family friend.
> Gray: How was work yesterday?
> Leigh: Great. Looks like my contract will be Xtended. Will tell U
> about it at the party.
> Gray: Congratulations ☺ Did you get a chance to talk to Jake?

So much for hoping he'd forget about that.

Leigh: He wasn't on set.
Gray: Okay. Maybe tomorrow. I'll shoot you my address.
Leigh: CU there.

★ ★ ★

There's another knock on my door and I hastily pick up the script.

"It's upside down," Annika says. "And your father's on the phone."

"Tell him I'm rehearsing," I whisper.

"Isn't going to fly," she says, covering the receiver. "He's been talking to Abby's mother, and apparently she mentioned that you're staying in L.A. indefinitely."

That's what I get for bragging to Abby and not swearing her to silence. I wasn't going to tell Dad until I had the contract in hand.

He gets right to the point. "Tell me why I have to hear news of my daughter through the grapevine."

"I'm sorry, Dad. I was just waiting until I was sure. But it's a great opportunity. Willow may get her own series out of this."

"No," he says. "That's not part of the deal. You don't get to make these decisions without consulting me."

"But Mom—"

"—hasn't given you permission either. I've already spoken to her about it."

"But I'd finish school. The Academy has a tutoring program. Just one season on *Diamond Heights* would pay for my whole college education. Besides, it's the perfect way for me to learn whether this is what I really want to do with my life. Otherwise, I could spend years as a struggling actor, waiting tables and wishing for an opportunity like this, only to discover in my thirties that it wasn't my calling after all. Think of all the money and heartache this will save."

"You've been rehearsing that speech," he says, which is quite insightful of him.

"Can I stay, Dad, please?"

There's a long silence at the other end of the phone. "I'll think about it. Your mother says these things don't always work out. When there's an offer on the table, we'll have a family meeting."

What we have didn't qualify as a family last time I checked.

"You should have a verdict by the time I see you," he continues, referring to next week's *Danny Boy* premiere. "Is Rory coming to the premiere?"

Something about his tone suggests that a certain pair of collagen-plumped lips have been blabbing. "He's only staying with us a few days."

"He'd probably come back from San Francisco for something as important as this," Dad says. "Since he came all this way to see you, you should invite him."

Once I'm really famous, I'm going to declare my life a lecture-free zone.

★　★　★

Scene 19: Leigh Reigns Supreme

INTERIOR HOLLYWOOD HILLS MANSION

Leigh is lying on a white velvet divan admiring her three-hundred dollar highlights in a silver hand-held mirror. Annika enters, surrounded by a pack of teacup dogs.

ANNIKA
I've walked your dogs, Leigh. Will there be anything more?

LEIGH
Give Duncan Kirk a call, please. He's reviewing some scripts for me. You know, I

haven't made a single misstep since I hired that guy. I hope he lasts a few more years.

ANNIKA
That's a terrible thing to—

LEIGH
Uh-uh-uh.

ANNIKA
Right, no lectures. Sorry.

The door opens again and Dennis Reid and Gray Crowley step in, toweling themselves off.

DENNIS
Man, that wave was *sweet!*

GRAY
For an old dude, you're pretty cool.

LEIGH
Now Gray, too much flattery is bad for Dennis.

DENNIS
Sprout, I'll thank you to—

LEIGH
Uh-uh-uh. What did I say?

DENNIS
No lectures. Sorry, Leigh.

LEIGH
It's all right. Now, run away and invest
my millions for me.

*Leigh turns to Annika and notices that she looks
tired.*

LEIGH
Annika, call Dr. Gerrardi and book yourself a mini-lift on my tab.

*Annika exits and Gray reclines, shirtless, on another
divan.*

GRAY
What can I do for you, sweetie?

LEIGH
[joining him on the divan]
Not a thing, darling. Stay just as you
are. But tell me the truth: are you sticking to your raw diet?

GRAY
[kissing her]
What do you think?

LEIGH
I think—

"Vivien, for heaven's sake, stop daydreaming and run your
lines."

sixteen

I have traveled this stretch of freeway before, but the landscape looks different today, either because I'm behind the wheel, or because it's before dawn. Rory sits silently in the passenger seat, probably feeling sheepish about the early hour. Jetlagged, he awoke before four, and hearing him afoot, Annika appeared at my bedside in a white peignoir. She rattled the car keys like an irritable ghost until I agreed to take him to Santa Monica pier to watch the sunrise, which will occur at precisely two minutes after six. How she knows this, I have no idea. She tossed breakfast money onto my bed, ordered me to take Rory and Brando on to the studio, and flitted out of the room.

I maneuver the bug into a parking space (or two), and follow Rory to the ocean, where the light is beginning to glisten on the waves. The boardwalk is already alive with joggers, and several people are watching the sunrise from the benches.

"Look," one woman calls, pointing at the ocean. "Gray whales!"

I scan the water eagerly. Although whales are common in Seattle, it's a sight that never gets stale. Besides, the grays are usually long gone to Alaska by now.

An enormous, slate-colored back breaks the surface briefly. Moments later, it reappears with a companion. They shoot water four feet into the air. I can hear the *whoosh* from the shore.

"I've never seen a gray before," Rory says, clearly awestruck. There is gooseflesh on his arms. "They're huge."

"They're only half the size of a blue," I say. "A typical gray eats two thousand pounds of krill a day."

He laughs. "Krill, is it?"

"I am full of useless information," I say.

One of the whales is noticeably smaller than the other. Maybe it's a mother and a calf. She could have given birth so late in the season that she fell behind her comrades in their journey north. A whale mother would never abandon her young, even if it meant spending a lonely summer in Santa Monica.

We climb onto a bench and Rory puts his arm around me. It feels warm against the chill of the morning breeze. "What are you thinking?" he asks.

"I'm wondering if whale mothers communicate better than human ones."

"Annika isn't so bad," he says. "I like her."

"You are so misguided," I say. But I wrap my arm around his waist and we stand that way for nearly half an hour, until the whales are tiny black dots on the horizon.

"That was magical," Rory says, as we hop off the bench and stroll along the sand. "It was like someone opened a window onto another world." His face is flushed with excitement and his green eyes are shining. "I was lost in the moment, you know?"

I nod. "Me too."

"That usually just happens when I'm drumming. Hours can pass and it feels like I've only had the sticks in my hands for a moment."

"That's how it is when I'm acting," I say. "Sometimes I get so caught up with my character that I forget my real life."

"*Art washes away from the soul the dust of everyday life,*" Rory says. "Pablo Picasso."

I'd forgotten that the Irish are known for their poetic spirits. "I don't know if playing Willow Volume qualifies as art."

"It does because you inhabited her. I didn't see a trace of Leigh Reid in there."

"When did you see the show?" I ask, surprised.

"This morning. I was up early enough to see the first two episodes. I thought you were brilliant."

I don't know why I thought we had nothing in common. Our souls are still totally connected. I guess a bond like that doesn't break, no matter how far it stretches. This realization inspires me to tell Rory about my adventures as Willow and we become increasingly comfortable, until it feels like it did last summer.

"I can't wait to hear your CD," I say.

"We could listen to it in the car. It's just a single but I wrote the lyrics."

"So you're a poet too," I say.

"Not by half," he says, smiling at me. "You look grand this morning."

"That's a load of blarney." With Annika haunting me, I only had time to put my hair in a ponytail and throw on an old T-shirt and cargo pants.

"It's no blarney." He stops walking and wraps both arms around me and this time the kiss is everything I imagined it would be. There is no need for the gargling discussion after all.

★   ★   ★

I replay Rory's song so many times on the way to the studio that he finally begs me to stop.

"It's amazing," I tell him. "What's it called?"

" 'She Sees Me,' " he says.

I keep my eyes on the twisting road. "Is it autobiographical?"

"Maybe. Art always is in some way."

Now I'm really curious. I hit PLAY again, but the lead singer slurs and the words are hard to decipher. "Are the lyrics printed on the cover?"

"You'll have to check for yourself," he says.

'She Sees Me' . . . Is it possible that he's written about me?

That would be the most romantic thing in the whole world. 'She Sees Me' . . . And today, in the early morning L.A. smog, I do see him. He may not be buff and tan, but he is very cute. He's also kind and smart and interesting, which is so much more important. Meeting him in that Internet café really was fate.

I, Leigh Reid, have been immortalized in song.

I hope he didn't mention that I'm taller than he is.

★ ★ ★

Chaz presses a hand to his heart. "Oh my god. Where are my smelling salts?"

"Would you chill?" I say. "I updated my look, that's all."

"I'm so sorry Sasha isn't here to see this," he says. "It would make her day. You can't change your hair color smack in the middle of an episode, Veely—even if you choose something tasteful. Get over to hair and makeup and see what Carla can do."

"You are not my boss," I say.

"I speak for your boss," he says, throwing his chest out in combat stance.

As much as I'd like to stay and fight, the wardrobe designer is looming and I have some explaining to do about several missing pairs of size ten heels. Nudging Rory a little closer to Chaz, I say, "This is Rory. Can you get him set up to watch us shoot?"

"I don't have time to babysit your friends."

"Thanks, Chaz, I really appreciate it." I pass Rory the Juicy dog carrier. "Gotta run."

Rory holds the bag as if there's a bomb inside. "What am I supposed to do with this?"

"Just take him for a walk every couple of hours." I kiss his cheek and turn to go.

"I don't do froufrou," Rory calls after me.

★ ★ ★

"That wig looks ridiculous," Jane says.

It's also hot and itchy. "I told Carla but she wouldn't listen to

me," I say. I like Carla, but as an up-and-coming star of t
I can't afford to take the rap for people who don't do
properly. If Carla isn't up to scratch, she may have to go. Like Annika said, ratings depend on good hair.

"It looks nothing like your real hair," Jane says. "In fact, it
looks nothing like human hair."

"Maybe I should dump the wig until Carla has time to fix my
hair?"

"No, the dye job is even worse. There's only so much we can
do with lighting."

I'll remember this when I'm big and the network asks me to
recommend directors.

* * *

The designer finally corners me in my cast chair. "I need to talk
to you."

To preempt the lecture, I say, "Thanks for letting me try out
the heels. They're going to work out great for Willow." I hand her
a stack of magazine clippings. "I brought some pictures to give
you an idea of where I see her wardrobe going."

She flips through them quickly. "These are pretty high end. I
don't have anything like this in the trailer."

"We don't roll for another hour. If your buyer hurries, she
could make it down to Melrose and back."

Meeting my eyes coolly, she says, "I'll check with Jane and get
back to you."

Obviously, I'm going to have to start from scratch and build a
whole new crew.

* * *

INTERIOR VOLUME LIVING ROOM, NIGHT

*Willow is sitting in front of a roaring fire. Her
boyfriend Lake is massaging her shoulders when Max
and Sumac enter.*

"Cut. Leigh, you're wincing."

"Sorry, Jane. I think he broke my clavicle."

"Lake, ease up on Willow's shoulders, please."

                    MAX
          Your mother has some exciting news,
          Willow.

                    SUMAC
          I've come up with a plan to raise your
          father's profile in England. I'm going to
          produce a reality TV show—with you as
          the star!

                    LAKE
          Congratulations, babe!

Lake grabs Willow and kisses her.

"Cut. Leigh, try to look like you're enjoying this."

"Sorry, but someone had garlic last night." I offer Lake a genial smile; he doesn't return it.

"Carla!" Jane hollers. "Let's get some mouth spray in here, pronto!"

Lake grabs Willow and kisses her.

"Cut!"

"Leigh, that's my line," Jane says.

"He is kissing her in front of her parents. I hardly think he'd dive for her tonsils."

"Okay, tongues in your own mouths, please. Roll camera!"

>   WILLOW
>   I haven't agreed to anything. What's the
>   show about?

"Cut. Leigh, that line's not in *my* script."

"I added it."

"So you're a writer now?"

"No, but Willow's no fool and she wouldn't buy into a scheme her parents cooked up without asking a few questions." I run over to my chair and grab my script. "I highlighted some problem areas in pink and made suggestions in green."

Jane takes the script and tosses it aside. "I'm on a tight schedule."

"Jane, I feel very strongly about this."

"I hope you feel equally strongly about getting your lines right."

>   MAX
>   The show is called *Between a Rock & a
>   Hard Place*. You'll play yourself, slum-
>   ming it with an average family.

>   WILLOW
>   That's great, Dad.

"Cut. What's with the sarcasm, Leigh? Willow is thrilled about this gig."

"She'll be living like a pauper. Trust me, Willow wouldn't be thrilled about that."

"Trust me, she would be. Now do the line again and act happy."

I sigh. "Okay, but you're going to have to help with my motivation."

She steps onto set. "Here's your motivation," she says, counting off her points on one hand. "One: Willow is homesick for London and now she'll get to go back. Two: she's an egomaniac and is thrilled at having a show all about her. Three: she actually cares about her family and wants to help her father's career. Do I need to use my other finger?"

I notice that she's left the middle one folded. "No, I think I've got it."

It's disappointing when an actor can't have an intelligent discussion about character motivation without her director getting all huffy about it.

> WILLOW
> That's great, Dad.

"Cut. Leigh, you're not looking at Max and Sumac."

"I know, but the camera is getting too much of my profile. My nose looks better straight on. And listen, could I get an eye light?"

> MAX
> I'm announcing your show at my next con-
> cert. I'll introduce you to the crowd and
> give you a chance to show fifty thousand
> people your star power.

> WILLOW
> Daddy, that's fantastic! I'll...

"—'make you proud of me,'" Jane supplies.

"I'm sorry, but there's someone in my eye line and it's distracting me. Could you please clear the set?"

Jane grumbles as she gets out of her chair and walks into the darkness behind camera. Her voice drifts back to me. "I don't know how you and your little dog got in here, young man, but you'll have to go. You're distracting my actor."

★ ★ ★

"I'm so sorry, Rory," I say, leading him into the lunch room. "I had no idea it was you. It's impossible to see anything off the set with the light glaring in my eyes."

"You mean the light you demanded?" he asks.

"I didn't *demand* it, I simply pointed out what was missing."

Rory looks disgruntled. "Look, I'm going to do some sightseeing and catch up with you later."

"You want to leave? Why?" Most people would kill for a chance to hang around a film set all day.

"For starters, that weird guy you left me with ditched me. I sat around for hours watching you argue with your director and then your dog pissed on me."

"Oh, no. I told you to walk him."

"Leigh, you can't order me around the way you do every one else on set."

"I don't order people around. I make suggestions because I want *Diamond Heights* to be the best it can be." I can't believe I have to explain this to him.

The caterer interrupts to hand me a plate holding a brown and green triangle. "I made this avocado pie for you," she says.

I eye the bottom crust suspiciously. "Was it baked?"

"Just for a few minutes."

"At what temperature?"

"Three hundred and fifty degrees."

"I can't eat anything heated over one hundred and eighteen," I say, handing it back.

Rory intercepts the plate. "Yer woman made this especially for you. Try it."

"I'm sorry, but I can't." It's a slippery slope. One day it's a baked pie, the next it's force-fed calves.

Rory tells the caterer, "I'll eat it—and thank you."

Obviously, Rory hasn't tried living by his principles. Sometimes it involves making sacrifices.

★ ★ ★

Had I known Gray's beach house party would be held on the actual beach, I wouldn't have worn heels and a skirt. My progress across the sand is slow until Rory convinces me to kick off my shoes and continue barefoot.

Karis watches my approach with a smirk that penetrates the darkness. "I see your transformation into Paris Hilton is complete."

Pretending I don't hear this, I join her by the bonfire. "Hi, Karis. This is Rory Quinn."

She greets him pleasantly before resuming her taunts: "Mirror mirror on the wall, who's the blondest of them all?"

I could kill Carla. To punish me for taking matters into my own hands, she refused to work on my color, even though I offered to stay late.

Gray joins us at the fire and gives me a hug that lasts long enough for me to feel uncomfortable in front of Rory. "Welcome," he says. "That hair is really . . . sexy."

Far from being bothered, Rory looks bemused. And Karis actually laughs.

"What?" Gray asks, innocently. "I love blondes. Don't you, Skippy?"

"Oh yeah," Skippy says, nodding so vigorously his short pigtails pinwheel. "I told her she'd look like Kate Hudson and she does."

Karis snorts but before she can say anything, I hastily introduce Rory.

Gray shakes his hand. "Right, your mother's friend."

Rory looks at me quizzically. "Is that what I am?"

"I didn't say that," I say. "Rory is *my* friend."

"Cool accent," Gray says. "Leigh didn't mention you were Scottish."

"Maybe because I'm Irish," Rory says, raising a pierced eyebrow. Beside Gray's tanned and muscular body, he looks positively skeletal—and somehow very young.

Skippy says, "Same difference."

Rory doesn't smile. "Not really."

"Chill, dude, it's a party," Gray and Skippy chime in unison. They laugh and slap each other's shoulders.

"Losers," Karis says, shaking her head in disgust.

Skippy leans over to me and whispers loud enough that she can hear, "Poor Karis. She still wants me and it's killing her." Then he straightens up and says, "Hey, Rory, you've got a ton of tattoos. In California, you only see that much ink on bikers."

"That's interesting," Rory replies. "In Ireland, you only see pigtails on girls."

★　★　★

Gray leads me toward the picnic table and fills two plastic cups from a large jug of fruit juice. I take a sip and nearly choke. "How much alcohol is in here?"

"Just a bit to take the edge off," he says.

"I'm driving so that's it for me."

"You're an example to us all," he says. He smiles but I know he's really calling me a prude. "Can't your mother's uptight friend drive?"

Rory is deep in conversation beside the bonfire with Karis. "He's not uptight. And he'd drive if I asked him to, but he's used to driving on the other side of the road."

Asia and Blake join us and Gray tells them that my contract on *Diamond Heights* is being extended.

"Really?" Blake says, puckering as if she finds the fruit juice a little sour.

"Really," I say. "They're giving Willow a bigger story line."

"So you're not going back to . . . Where was it? Detroit?"

"Seattle. Not just yet."

Blake and Asia look at each other and shrug. I can almost see their thoughts merging in a bubble over their heads: *If this bad smell isn't going, I guess we'd better get used to it.*

Asia says, "Congratulations, Leigh. Any chance you could get me a job?"

"Back off," Gray says, draping an arm around my shoulders. "I asked first."

"But I'm prettier than you are," she tells him.

"And a natural blonde," Blake says.

★   ★   ★

I am sitting cross-legged on top of a picnic table beside Gray while the others sit on the benches or sprawl in the sand. We are holding court, the king and queen of the beach party. Gray encourages me to tell my stories about Sasha. Asia laughs until she topples off the bench into the sand. "Leigh, you're so funny," she says. Clearly she's been enjoying the spiked fruit juice.

"I'm just getting started," I say. "Wait until you hear about the Tabasco episode."

I reach for my plastic cup and find that it's still full. I could have sworn I drank most of it, but never mind. I feel completely sober, except for the fact that I'm having the best time in my life.

★   ★   ★

"Tell us more about Willow's story line," Asia says.

"I've said all I can without getting into trouble from the network," I say. "We sign a confidentiality clause."

I may be a little drunk on admiration, but I know better than to reveal insider information.

"Oh, come on," Blake urges. "You're among friends."

I look around at all the smiling faces and realize that I am. Thanks to Gray's backing, I've infiltrated the cool group. For once, they're laughing with me, not at me.

"Okay, just one more thing," I say, draining my drink. "There's a strong possibility of a spin-off series."

A murmur of excitement ripples through the group. Asia gets Skippy to help her to her feet and stands swaying beside the picnic table. "Seriously, Leigh, what would it take for you to recommend me?"

I think about that for a moment. Here's my chance to extract a promise that she won't diss my mother, my appearance, my personality, or my talent. But why put a damper on an otherwise wonderful evening? Instead, I say, "I'm pretty tight with my director, so if I get a chance I'll mention you." The rest of the crowd clamors to be included. "Okay, okay, I'll mention everyone, but you'd better start working on your English accents."

★ ★ ★

Gray looks over to Karis and Rory. "Well, those two are really hitting it off."

"Sure, why wouldn't they?" I ask, ignoring his insinuation.

"You're right, they're both kind of weird."

"They are not!"

Gray laughs. "Okay, relax. But Karis has never fit in, you know. At school she's a major loner. I'm surprised she even came tonight."

"Karis is brilliant and talented. And so is Rory."

"Then it's nice they've found each other," he says, taking my hand. "Isn't it nice when people find each other?" He gives me a significant look and I start blushing; fortunately, he can't see that in the dark.

Skippy lights up a joint and passes it around the group. Before it reaches me, I slip my hand out of Gray's and hop off the table. I'm not interested in expanding my horizons that far, but I don't want to invite mockery by refusing to either.

"Tired of the stage already?" Karis asks when I join them at the fire.

I will not bicker with her in front of Rory. "I just wanted to see how you two are doing."

"We're fine," she says. "How much have you had to drink?"

"Just one glass." It's true, but I feel light-headed. Either that juice was eighty percent vodka, or someone refilled my cup when I wasn't looking.

"Did you make sure the juice was fresh pressed on site?" Rory asks.

"Very funny." I take a swing at him and miss his shoulder completely. Uh-oh.

Karis clucks like a disapproving parent. "You can't drive like that. I'd better take you home. You can pick up the Beetle to-morrow."

And hand Annika my bleached-out head on a silver platter? I don't think so. "Would you drive, Rory?"

Karis speaks for him. "You can't ask him to do that. It's dark and he hasn't driven here."

"He can make his own decisions, Karis." Who is she to act so possessive? Last time I checked, he was still my boyfriend.

Rory says, "I'll be fine. Don't worry."

Glaring at me, Karis says, "I'll lead the way and Rory can follow."

I thank her politely, equally relieved and annoyed. After to-night, I won't need to worry about Karis's opinion again. I am in the cool crowd now.

★   ★   ★

When I go to say good-bye to Gray, he is standing at the shore with a blond girl I recognize from *Charmed*. Like him, she wears the invisible crown of Hollywood royalty, and when she slides an arm around his waist, I feel a savage pinch of jealousy.

"Leigh, wait!" Gray calls as I turn to go. He lopes across the beach and grabs my arm. "What's wrong?"

"Nothing. I just have to get going."

"Stay," he says, reaching for me with both hands.

I step backward and stumble over my heels. Gray steadies me and before I can register what's happening, his lips are on mine. As much as I want to stop him, I don't. Gray is a very good kisser—probably the best of the three guys I kissed today. Or maybe the music of the waves crashing behind us is clouding my judgment.

"So, that's what's taking so long," a voice says.

I jump away from Gray to find Karis watching me.

★ ★ ★

"Wait, don't tell me," Karis says, leading me up the path to the road. "You saved Gray from being swept out to sea and administered artificial respiration."

"He just kissed me good night, Karis. It's no big deal."

"Rory would definitely consider it a big deal."

"He's changed too," I say. "People grow apart."

She stops and turns. "When I met you, you seemed so cool and independent. But now you've gone off the deep end and you're no better than Asia or Blake."

So this is my reward for defending her earlier. She obviously resents that I'm more popular than she is, but I won't stoop to saying so. "That's so unfair. I'm just expanding my horizons, Karis."

I stride ahead of her up the path but she rattles on. "Rory is great, just like you said last month, before you got your head stuck so far up your own butt that you lost perspective. I can't even remember the last time a guy was more interested in hearing about *my* life than my mother's. We had the most amazing conversation."

I stop so suddenly that she runs into me. "How amazing?" Rory may not be right for me anymore but Karis isn't going to have him.

"What do you care?" she asks. "You just gave Gray Cowley the breath of life."

"Fine," I say, suddenly furious. "I'll break up with Rory and you can tell him all about your life until you're fed up with hearing your own voice. Like I am."

"Oh, get over yourself."

seventeen

Scene 23: Leigh Breaks Rory's Heart

INTERIOR LOS ANGELES AIRPORT,
EARLY MORNING

CLOSE-UP ON A MAROON CAR DOOR. The door opens and two stylish boots step onto the curb.

WIDEN OUT TO REVEAL Leigh Reid standing by as Rory scrambles out of the Beetle. In his no-name sweat-shirt and baggy jeans, he looks years younger than his girlfriend.

> LEIGH
> [leaning into the car]
> Would you mind waiting here, Annika? I
> need to speak to Rory alone.

> ANNIKA
> Take all the time you need, darling. I fi-
> nally understand that you've outgrown
> Poor Rory, but promise me you'll let him
> down easily.

LEIGH
Of course. A star must always be compas-
sionate.

*Leigh towers over Rory as they walk toward the
check-in desk. She's been waiting for the right moment to tell him it's over and the clock has run out.
Now she must say good-bye—and forever, because
they will never be able to be "just friends" after a
love like theirs. He would always be hoping for
more.*

*Rory takes his passport from the clerk, tosses his
knapsack onto the scale, and joins Leigh.*

RORY
This isn't really good-bye. I'll be back
next week for the *Danny Boy* premiere.

LEIGH
Actually, Rory, there's something we need
to talk about.

*CUE STRING ORCHESTRA. Leigh takes Rory's hand in
hers.*

LEIGH
[continuing]
This isn't easy for me to say, but—

UNKNOWN VOICE OFF CAMERA
Oh my god! It's Willow from *Diamond
Heights*!

MUSIC STOPS ABRUPTLY as a family wearing "Come Cut the Cheese in Wisconsin" T-shirts descends on Leigh.

> MOM
> You are such an asset to that show, Willow.

> DAD
> Especially in that bikini.

Mom slugs Dad.

> KID #1
> [displaying broken arm]
> Willow, will you sign my cast?

> LEIGH
> Actually, I'm sort of in the middle of something here.

> KID #2
> [yelling]
> Hey everybody! Willow Volume is just as mean in person as she is on TV! She won't sign my brother's cast!

Leigh hastily digs through her purse for a pen.

> MOM
> [corralling her family]
> Let's go, kids. There's nothing genuine about this one. Even that purse is a fake.

The family exits and Leigh slips on her shades to prevent being recognized again. She takes Rory's hand.

RE-CUE STRING ORCHESTRA.

> LEIGH
>
> Rory, as much as I've loved being your
> girlfriend, we've grown apart lately.

> RORY
>
> That's a load of old cobbler. We're great
> together.

> LEIGH
>
> We were great together, but now we want
> different things out of life. I need to ex-
> pand my horizons, experience new things.
> My career has become so important to me,
> whereas your priorities are video games
> and your band.

> RORY
>
> I can change. I *will* change—for you.

> LEIGH
>
> It wouldn't be fair to ask you to. You're
> beautiful just as you are. But it isn't
> enough for me anymore.

> RORY
> [voice cracking]
> Leigh, don't do this.

> LEIGH
>
> I must. I can't live a lie. It isn't you, it's
> me. You're fantastic and you're going to
> find someone better.

                    RORY
              [wracked by sobs]
        No...No...

                    LEIGH
              [eyes overflowing]
        I'm sorry, darling, our time together has
        come to an end.

Leigh brushes the tears from his cheek.

THE ORCHESTRA SWELLS as they embrace for the last time.

Rory's flight is called. Our heroes stand and the camera rises slowly into the air as the music soars. We continue to crane up, up, up until the orchestra reaches its crescendo. Leigh and Rory are but two tiny dots moving in opposite directions in the busy terminal.

★ ★ ★

"Leigh, don't cry. You know as well as I do that this is dead."

Rory's words shake me from my daydream and I realize that my eyes are streaming. "What's dead?"

"Our relationship. Weren't you listening to me?" Rory sets his knapsack on the floor of the busy terminal. "It's over."

I wipe my eyes and stare at him, stunned. "You're breaking up with me?"

"Yeah. I'm sorry but this isn't working for me anymore. You've become a completely different person."

"A different person? What do you mean?"

"I mean you've changed."

"Change is good, isn't it? I'm maturing, that's all."

He looks as if he has something snide to say, but he swallows it. "Well, we don't have much in common anymore."

I struggle to get my head around what this means. "But what about *Danny Boy*? You said you'd come back from San Francisco for the premiere."

"I don't think it's a good idea."

"Why not?" Something's gone very wrong, here. I'm practically begging Rory not to dump me, although I arrived fully planning to give him the axe. Maybe the Myers Phenomenon applies to me too: the less interest he shows, the more I show. Or maybe I was hoping he'd fight for me. Somewhere in the back of my mind, I figured we'd reunite one day, after he grew up a little and I got Gray out of my system.

Reading my mind, Rory says, "Take Gray to the premiere. You two seem tight."

Ah-ha. "Is this about Gray?"

He shakes his head. "I'm not jealous, if that's what you mean. If Gray's yer type, yer welcome to him."

"Then what is it about?" I look into his eyes, willing him to be honest with me. If I can't figure out exactly what went wrong, I can't prevent it from happening next time.

He thinks for a moment. "Did you ever read the lyrics to my song?"

"Not yet. We've been running around for four days." Four days in which he never held my hand or kissed me. Four days in which he asked about Karis six times.

"Well, the old Leigh would have."

"I'm sorry, but you can see I'm under a lot of pressure now that I'm a professional actor."

He shrugs. "Whatever. I was just trying to explain."

I reach for his sleeve. "So that's it?"

Rory pulls his arm away and picks up his knapsack. "Take care, Leigh."

★　★　★

"How did Poor Rory take the news?" Annika asks, starting the car.

"He dumped me first." I am still too stunned to put a spin on it. Her lip twitches and I turn on her because I have to turn on someone. "How can you laugh at me at a time like this?" I start crying again.

"What's with the drama?" she asks, surprised. "You told me before you walked into that terminal that you were going to break up with him."

I honk into a tissue. "I loved Rory."

She turns off the ignition and gives me her full attention. "I know you did, but what you're really upset about is that he beat you to the punch."

"He says I've changed—for the worse." I look at her, hoping she'll assure me he's wrong.

"Well," she says, choosing her words carefully, "change is inevitable at your age."

I replay the scene in my head, remembering how he shook off my hand. "He wouldn't even discuss it. He just wanted to get away."

She nods. "Boys are like that and it doesn't improve with age."

I fold my arms on the dashboard and put my head down. "It's so humiliating. This is the second time I've been dumped."

"And you will live to see a third," she says. "You're going to have plenty of relationships."

I peek at her. "Do you think so?"

She smiles. "I guarantee it."

Shoving myself upright, I say, "Next time I want to be the one making the dramatic Hollywood exit."

Annika starts the car again. "We'd better go or you'll be late for class. At least with these emotions roiling, you'll have lots to draw on for your performance today."

I clap a hand over my mouth.

"Vivien, tell me you didn't forget!" She cuts off a Park N' Fly bus and squeals out of the airport. "Your grade is riding on this."

"Hello? I just had my heart broken. A moment to adjust, please."

"You know the part, though, right? I didn't spend thousands of dollars on an elite program for you to blow it in one day."

"I know the part. I just hope Gray does too."

"You'd be confident of that if you'd rehearsed together."

"We ran our lines in class, but I couldn't see him after the party because Rory was jealous."

Annika reaches over and flicks me in the head with her index finger and thumb. "Pass the course, Vivien. Or else."

"Ouch! Stop it!" I shield my head. "I'm a professional actor now and I think can pass a simple class assignment."

★　★　★

I'm almost as nervous about seeing Gray as I am about doing the scene. He hasn't called or e-mailed since the party and even with my defective relationship genes, I know that's a bad sign. If only I could undo that kiss. Now he'll think I wanted him, when my heart is actually lying mangled on the grimy floor of LAX.

Outside the classroom, I grope in my bag for *A Streetcar Named Desire*. If I see the first line, it should trigger the rest of the scene. Stanley enters and says, *"Hey there! Stella baby!"* And I say, *"Don't holler at me like that."* Simple. I'm sure the scene is stored in my mental vault. If I can remember how many pounds of krill a gray whale eats, I can remember this.

I open the door and hear: *"Don't holler at me like that!"* It's my line but it's coming out of Asia's mouth. She is in the corner with Gray.

Joining them, I say, "Sorry I'm late. Thanks, Asia, I can take it from here."

"Didn't Gray tell you?" Asia asks, tossing her blond mane. "We're doing *Streetcar* together."

"But I'm Stella," I protest.

She grins. "Not anymore."

"Gray?" I say. "You promised."

"People make promises they can't keep all the time," he says.

"What do you mean?" I falter, knowing exactly what he means.

"You said you'd put in a good word for me with Jake Cohen and you didn't. I nailed the reading at the callback yesterday but he went with someone else."

"I'm sorry you didn't get the part but I didn't promise anything. I haven't even seen Jake."

He turns away abruptly and I sense I've seen the last of his six-pack. "Do you mind? We're busy."

Getting dumped by two guys in the space of an hour must set some kind of record. Especially since I was only dating one of them.

★   ★   ★

One slice of humble pie baked at 117 degrees, coming right up.

"Hi, Karis," I say. "How are you?"

She doesn't lift her eyes from her script. "Fine, thanks."

"Listen, I feel bad about what happened the other night. I haven't been myself lately." Not according to Rory, anyhow. "I want to make it up to you."

She looks up and her green eyes pin me to the wall like a specimen in a bug collection. "You mean you want to join my scene today."

"How did you—well, yes, if I could. I know there are three roles in it. But I also meant what I said."

"Everyone knows Gray dumped you for Asia."

There's that word again. "Dumped" is tattooed on one cheek, "loser" on the other.

Karis continues, "Did he mention that Asia's uncle is running open auditions for the lead in a new action flick?"

He didn't, but he didn't need to. "I get it, Karis: Gray used me, I'm an idiot. Is that what you want to hear? I'm desperate and I'm asking for your help here."

"I found a partner I could trust, Leigh. We adapted our scene for two characters."

She unpins me with her eyes and I feel the jolt in my chest as I hit the floor.

★ ★ ★

Professor Kirk is slumped over his desk. Although he often uses rehearsal time to nap, I don't hear snoring. I give his arm a shake, wondering if our CPR moment has finally come. He starts and lifts his head. "That arm is attached, Miss Reid."

"Sorry, sir. I thought you were . . . asleep."

"You mean you thought I was dead. Not yet, but today's performances may do the trick."

"Sir, I have to postpone my scene. Something's come up."

He shakes his head. "The show must go on. If you're not ready, you may accept a failing grade."

"That's unfair! My partner ditched me."

"Your personal problems are no concern of mine. You should have chosen someone more trustworthy." He raises his bushy eyebrows to remind me that he picks up more during his siestas than he lets on.

"Can I do the same scene he's doing?" I ask.

"Surely a talented soap opera star like you has another part up her sleeve. And no," he adds, as my face lights up, "a scene from *Diamond Heights* won't do."

I get a sudden inspiration: real people might let me down, but Scarlett O'Hara never has. "I'll do something from *Gone with the Wind*."

Nodding wearily, he pulls the screenplay off the shelf and offers it to me.

I could take the easy way out and do the jail scene that I used for my audition, but the dramatic climax of the movie would make a far bigger impression. Scarlett tells Rhett Butler that she loves him after spending most of their marriage pursuing the spineless Ashley Wilkes. Already packing to leave, Rhett tells her it's too late and she collapses on the stairs, sobbing.

I can totally relate to how Scarlett felt. Now that Gray has shown his true colors, I realize even more clearly what I lost in Rory. But Scarlett rises again in the end and so will I. Leigh Reid does not fail. She channels her emotions into her performance. Desperation, humiliation, remorse . . . No need to dig, they're all right there.

"Professor? I need someone to play Rhett Butler. Would you do me the honor?"

His head is already back on his arms and his only response is a faint snore.

★   ★   ★

Everything hinges on the cape and the apple box.

Running into the classroom in the long violet cape I found in the wardrobe room, I break out my best Southern belle accent. "Rhett, wait!"

I step up and down on the apple box to simulate ascending stairs before shedding the cape and throwing myself into a nearby chair to answer the empty apple box in a deep voice. A ripple of laughter spreads through the class as people realize I am playing the parts of both Scarlett and Rhett. Heaving myself off the chair, I hop back on the box and fling the cape around my shoulders to deliver Scarlett's next line. Then back to the chair for Rhett. And so it goes, up and down and back and forth, until Scarlett's voice is breathy and Rhett's accent starts slipping. When I accidentally deliver one of Scarlett's lines in Rhett's voice, the class explodes. Karis doubles over in her chair, and Asia and Blake lean on Gray for support. I glance at Professor Kirk and discover that he is very much awake, though nearly incapacitated by laughter.

There is nothing for it but to turn the drama into slapstick. Giving up my pretensions, I go for camp, swishing and swaggering and chasing myself down the apple box stairs. I mop at invisible tears with an invisible handkerchief and ultimately demand of Rhett, "Where shall I go, what shall I do?"

Then, squaring my manly shoulders and striding to the door,

I summon the deepest voice I can muster and deliver the famous line: "Frankly, my dear, I don't give a damn."

I slam the door behind me and collapse on a bench outside the classroom. They can laugh their butts off for all I care because I gave that scene everything I've got and I am moving on. I don't need this class. I have a thriving acting career.

At last, I got the perfect Hollywood exit I craved.

If only I hadn't left my purse in the classroom.

eighteen

I grab Carla's wrist as she dangles the paintbrush over my scalp. "That dye is awfully dark. I thought you were going to do highlights or something."

"Jane told me to take it back to its original color," Carla says.

I squirm out of reach. "But blonde symbolizes Willow's transformation to a TV personality and celebrity in her own right. Give me a chance to explain to Jane. For now, I'll wear the wig."

Carla shakes her head. "No wig. Jane's worried it'll fall off during the stunt."

"What stunt?" I ask. I'm not in again until the big concert scene and it doesn't feature a stunt. "Even if there was a stunt, they'd have a stunt double for me."

"All I was told is that there's a stunt and there isn't a double. They're rewriting the script today."

It's a good thing I know that Jake Cohen really likes my mother. Otherwise, I might have a bad feeling about this.

★   ★   ★

Chaz hands me a stack of mustard colored script pages with a flourish. "Hot off the presses," he says.

I fan through the paper. "That's a major rewrite."

"Isn't it? The story department has been working around the clock."

Chaz is so excited that he's dancing like a popcorn kernel in a hot pot. It can only mean trouble for Willow. The stunt Carla mentioned must be worse than I feared.

"Go ahead," he encourages me. "Take a look."

A little voice in my head tells me to review the script in the privacy of my own cubbyhole, but I can't resist. I flip through it until I come to Willow's story line.

Interior Diamond Dome, Max Volume concert...Max introduces Willow to the screaming fans... blah, blah, blah . . . *Willow walks on stage in high heels and designer togs...* excellent, they're listening to my advice . . . *Max announces Willow's new show...* So far so good . . . *Bright spotlight on Willow...* Must speak to the cinematographer about flattering diffusion . . . *Willow walks to the front of stage to take a bow...* Like it, like it . . . *Willow is blinded by the spotlight...* Huh? . . . *misses the edge of the stage and topples off...*

I look up at Chaz. "Willow falls off a stage? She could get hurt."

"She could," he agrees. "Keep reading."

Paramedics arrive...Willow loaded onto a gurney... On the bright side, this could be a good dramatic opportunity . . . *Max and Sumac hover beside her...Willow utters her last words...* Last words? Last words before what? *She dies.*

"She dies? *Noooo!*" It's a howl of anguish.

"I'm afraid so," Chaz says. "Internal hemorrhage. Tragic."

"She can't die. It's so—"

"—permanent?" Chaz supplies.

"Well yes. Wouldn't that mean I'm—"

"—finished?" He smiles broadly, confirming the awful truth.

"I can't be finished," I say. "What about the reality show? They've been building towards that story line for two weeks. How can they drop it now?"

"You skipped that part." He reaches over and flips back a couple of pages.

"Willow's dying wish is for her parents to give the show to Fallon?"

"She was a sweet girl underneath, our dearly departed Willow," he says.

"Maybe they'll resuscitate her in the next episode. They do that sometimes."

"Not this time. But you will be back."

"I will?" Hope surges in my heart. "As an angel?"

"Just a coffin shot for the funeral."

The script drops out of my hand and hits the floor with a dull thud.

Chaz dusts it off and hands it back to me. "Buck up, kid. That's Hollywood."

★ ★ ★

I've been sitting on the stairs of the honey wagon for nearly an hour, my belongings heaped into a cardboard box. Crew members step around me silently as they come and go to the restrooms. No one loves you when your career is in the toilet.

Eventually, nature calls Jane, as well. "Are you okay?" she asks.

"Yes." My voice sounds faint and faraway.

"I'm sorry Chaz got to you first, Leigh. I was scouting locations or I would have fired you myself."

The word makes me flinch. If she's tossing it around so freely, it means I have to stop hiding behind fantasies of Willow coming back to Diamond Heights as a vampire or a nearly identical cousin. I truly have been dropped from the show.

"I thought you were going to extend my contract," I say.

"I was until you let me down. With the tight timelines on this show, I decided I couldn't afford someone like you."

"Someone like me?" I echo.

"You haven't been rehearsing and you've turned into quite a little diva."

I tackle the easier issue first. "I only flubbed my lines a couple of times."

"More than a couple. Instead of learning them, you've been

wasting your time rewriting them and meddling with things that aren't your concern."

"I was trying to be helpful. I want this show to do well."

"The best way to help any show succeed is to do your job as an actor. I pay professionals to worry about wardrobe and hair and lighting."

"I can change." I sound even more pathetic than I did with Rory.

"It's too late. You've crossed a line and there's no going back."

"But you're giving my role to Sasha and I'm the better actor."

Jane smiles. "I see this hasn't completely decimated your confidence."

"But it's true," I insist. "And she's just as difficult as I am."

"Maybe so, but when I can't manage Sasha, her father can." She leans against the railing and forces me to meet her eyes. "Why do you think I hired you, Leigh?"

"Because of my knack with accents?"

"No, because of your attitude. You were so eager to please that I thought you'd work hard for me. And you did, for about two weeks. Then you started to get cocky."

I stare at the ground, trying not to cry. I must salvage what little pride I can here.

"I think you do have a raw talent," she continues, her voice softening a little. "It could amount to something with the right training—and a big dose of maturity. But the sooner you understand that you can't coast in this business, the better. There are thousands of attractive girls with the same talent waiting to take your place."

I search her face through a haze of tears but there's no sign of relenting.

Jane turns to go. "If you really think about what I've said, you'll learn something. In the meantime, make sure you get some rest before your last scene."

The least she could have done was let me go out as a blonde.

★   ★   ★

Annika careens into the studio parking lot and screeches to a stop beside me. Turning off the ignition, she jumps out with Brando under one arm. She's been letting him sit on her lap while she drives, although I outlawed it.

"Go get changed, darling," she says, handing me my Puma bag and smoothing her low-cut dress.

"Changed? Why?"

"We're hitting the town, that's why."

"I just want to go home, Mom. I've had a bad day." I reach out to pat Brando and he rears away, wrinkling his little black nose at the stench of failure.

"I know," she says. "Jake told me. That's why I brought the rescue kit." She pats the Puma bag. "Everything you'll need is right in there."

"Everything I'll need for what?"

"There comes a time in every Hollywood mother's life when she has to lead the Fire Drill."

"The Fire Drill?" My senses aren't working at full capacity right now, so it takes me a few seconds to smell the smoke. "You mean you've been fired before too?"

Annika gives me a little shove. "Go get ready. This is going to be better than months of therapy, trust me."

★   ★   ★

If I could feel enthusiasm for anything, I'd be excited about getting my hands on Annika's black and white Narciso Rodriguez dress, something she's refused to let me touch all summer. But of course, I can't. I'm so depressed that it takes all my energy to squirm into it and cover up the evidence of my crying jag. Annika thoughtfully included eye drops in the rescue kit, as well as a new fuchsia handbag. The card says, *"Everything looks better when you've got the right purse. Love, Mom."*

If I could feel enthusiasm for anything, it would probably make me feel good that a couple of guys whistle as I walk back to the parking lot. Even so, something gives a little kick inside. I may

be an unemployed actor with mousy brown hair and a bad attitude, but I can still get a whistle.

Annika has laid out a hair brush and clips on the hood of
the car, and with a few deft moves, she sweeps my hair up and
secures it. Then she offers me the car keys. I shake my head,
but she insists: "Driving will help take your mind off your trou-
bles."

"Nothing will do that," I assure her. But I climb behind the
wheel anyway. Soon, I will be going home to Seattle in disgrace
and will rarely be allowed to drive. I might as well take the chance
while I have it. And somehow, as I accelerate up the ramp and
onto the freeway, my mood does lift slightly.

Annika directs me to a small, dingy movie theater. After I park,
she slings Brando's bag over one shoulder and commands, "Shades."

I open the fuchsia bag to find she has stashed my shades inside. She puts hers on too and strides ahead of me to the ticket
booth. The young guy at the cash takes one look at Annika and
falls into a slack-jawed stupor that prevents him from noticing the
dog. He gives us two tickets for the price of one and presses his
face to the Plexiglas to watch us go.

Annika chooses a row in the center of the theater and leads
me in. Brando gets a seat all his own beside her. When did she
hijack my dog, I wonder? The lights go down before I can ask her
and the credits roll for *Attack of the Killer Tomatoes*.

"This is a classic," she says. "You're going to love it."

I highly doubt that. I am incapable of feeling enthusiasm for
anything again. My spirit has been crushed. I have been fired. I
have failed. And my failure will soon become public knowledge.
My only comfort is in knowing that Gran will be overjoyed about
Willow's death. Dad may pretend he's not, but he'll leave a stack
of college brochures on my bed in which he's flagged the veterinary programs. And in two short weeks, I will retreat gratefully to
the cloistered walls of the Nerd Academy, where no one has heard
of *Diamond Heights*.

★　★　★

"Shades," Annika commands again as we exit the theater.

I slide my D & Gs over cheeks that ache from laughing. Not that I was laughing from the heart; it was more like an involuntary spasm. "That was so bad," I say.

"So bad it was great, right?"

I nod. "Everything about it was totally lame, especially the acting."

"That's my point. Do you think you could ever do any worse than that?" Without waiting for a response, she pushes me toward the driver's seat. "Next stop, the Beverly Hills Hotel."

I drive up the curved driveway under the palm trees. The sun is setting on another perfect L.A. day that is an insult to my current mood. The cloud and rain of Seattle will suit me far better.

Again, Annika leads the way through the front door, Brando's bag over her shoulder. She sails up the stairs and into the lounge of the grand old hotel.

"Mom," I whisper. "They're going to card me."

"They're not going to card you," she assures me. "You look twenty-five—that's why I put your hair up. Just keep your shades on and don't show them the whites of your eyes."

She pulls out a chair for me and sits down opposite. Even though it's a weeknight, the Polo lounge is humming. A waiter hurries over, staring at Annika as he tries to figure out if she's "anyone."

"Two glasses of Dom Perignon," she says, treating the waiter to a dazzling smile. She leans forward, perhaps to offer a glimpse of cleavage. It's entirely unnecessary, as he does not so much as glance in my direction. Moments later, he returns with two tall, ice cold flutes.

I wait until he is out of earshot. "Are you really going to let me drink this?"

She nods. "Providing you promise not to tell your father. This is a momentous day in the life of any young actor."

"Mom, getting fired isn't something to celebrate."

"Maybe not but recovering from it is. Almost every actor I know has been fired at some point—including Diana Russell."

"Really? What about Geoff Cowley?"

"Oh, yes," she says, waving dismissively. "Twice that I know of, probably more."

"How many times for you?"

"Three, although only one I actually earned."

I take an educated guess. "For being a diva?"

"Of course not," she says. "Well, it might have factored into that one. With the others I was innocent. Treat Williams had me fired because we didn't have chemistry, if you can believe it. The other time, I got cut because I refused an affair with the director."

"Something you got over by the time you met Roger," I say. I must be bouncing back if I can get a shot in.

She lets it go. "My point is that it's quite common, Vivien. Rejection is part of an actor's life."

If I could feel any enthusiasm for anything, it would be the champagne. I can't, but I chug it anyway in case she changes her mind.

"Don't gulp, darling," she says. "It's champagne, not Sprite."

Finally, I explode. "It was so unfair," I wail. "I am a better actor than Sasha. You said so yourself."

"You are," she confirms. "But I also told you that talent isn't enough." She taps my arm with one red talon. "You took your eye off the ball, didn't you?"

I ponder this for a few moments before nodding. "I was so sure that new contract was mine that I stopped trying. Jane says I turned into a diva and I guess she's right."

Obviously, I've inherited more than Annika's bad relationship genes. But the first step toward recovery is admitting I have a problem.

"I'm proud of you, darling," she says, lifting her glass to propose a toast. "To self-knowledge." She clinks her glass against mine. "You've gained some new skills and learned some hard lessons this summer. This is a difficult profession and if you're going to make it, you'll have to toughen up."

I stare at my empty glass, wondering how it all disappeared so soon. "I don't want to make it. I just want to go home."

"I suspect you'll be back at some point. And Jake thinks so too."

"He does? I thought he'd be thrilled that his daughter got the part."

She shakes her head. "He's not sure Sasha has what it takes to succeed in this business, but he thinks you might."

"Oh, Mother, he's just trying to get into your—"

"Don't go there," she warns.

"Fine, he *likes* you and he's not going to tell you what he really thinks about me. If I had such potential, he and Jane would give me a second chance."

"They might, down the road. At least you'll have an opportunity to leave a lasting impression. Go in prepared, be a professional, and die a great death."

I let my head drop onto the table with a clunk. "This is so humiliating. I bragged to my class about getting my own story line. I just wanted to be the cool kid for once. The worst thing is, I don't even like any of them, except Karis."

"Darling, your hair," she says, forcing me to lift my head again. "Don't dwell on that. Focus on your death instead." She laughs at the sound of this. "Make it something people remember. And just think, your father will be there to see it."

I groan. "I forgot Dad was coming." He's flying in early for the premiere so that he can see *Diamond Heights* shoot. "I can't die in front of my own father."

Annika tips the last of her champagne down her throat. "It could be worse. You could have to do a love scene in front of him."

"That's true." I giggle in spite of myself.

"That's more like it," she says. "Now, what are you doing to do tomorrow?"

"Die well."

"And?"

"Show them what they're going to miss when I'm gone."

"Exactly. Now, let's get a bite to eat. If you want, we can go to a raw restaurant."

"Are you kidding? If I have to die, I want pizza for my last meal."

"As you wish," she says, holding out her hand for the car keys. "Now that you're smiling, I'm taking those back."

★　★　★

After dinner at Mulberry Street Pizza, we go on to Kate Mantilini's for a sundae. I'm chasing a cherry around the empty bowl when I hear a familiar voice. "If it isn't the lovely Willow Volume."

I drop the spoon into the bowl with a clatter. It's Adam Brody.

"Hi," I say, my voice so loud the table rocks. I yank off my shades, lest he think I'm a poseur.

"I'm a big fan of the show," he says, grinning.

Noticing that I'm at a loss for words, Annika steps in. "That's lovely of you to say, Seth."

I decide to speak up before she does any more damage. "Do you really watch *Diamond Heights?*"

"Sure, when I'm not shooting. What's next for Willow?"

I bow my head in shame. "Well, I'm afraid—"

"—that she can't say a word," Annika interrupts smoothly. "You know how it is with confidentiality clauses, Seth."

"How about I give you something about *The OC* in exchange," he teases.

I smile. "Maybe next time I see you."

"Fair enough." As he turns to go, he says, "You look a lot older today."

"Thank you," I say. What a sweet guy. If I could feel any enthusiasm for anything, it would be him.

I lean backward to watch him walk out the door. A moment

later, a waitress arrives with two flutes of champagne, compliments of Adam.

It's enough to make me want to outlive Willow.

Even though Annika confiscates my glass after one sip.

nineteen

INTERIOR DIAMOND DOME, NIGHT

Fifty thousand fans scream and stamp their feet until Max Volume reappears from the wings leading his wife, Sumac.

> MAX
> Thank you, Diamond Heights! Before I do my final song, I want to make a special announcement. My lovely wife Sumac is producing a fantastic reality series called *Between a Rock and a Hard Place.* It's going to be the hottest show on television—and I'm not saying that just because my daughter stars in it. And speaking of my daughter, I'd like to introduce her now: Willow Volume!

The lights dim and a single spotlight lands on Willow. She is wearing a black Versace mini dress and over-the-knee Prada boots. After posing for a moment, she teeters toward the audience on four-inch heels, hand raised in a salute.

Blinded by the spotlight, Willow misses the yellow tape marking the safety zone and accidentally kicks a footlight. She stumbles, arms thrashing wildly as she tries to regain her balance. Max rushes forward to help, but before he can reach her, Willow topples off the edge of the stage.

"Cut!" Jane's voice booms through the speakers. She's using a microphone because we're working in a large space today. "Leigh, I need you to sell the fall. Pump up the drama, okay?"

I clamber off the thick mat that cushioned my fall and climb the stage stairs. Although I didn't enjoy the twelve-foot plummet, I am proud to be doing a real stunt.

"Cut," Jane calls after take two. "Better but I'm still not buying it."

Willow topples off the edge of the stage.

"Cut. You're going over too quickly. Build suspense. Let the audience think you might find your balance."

Willow topples off the edge of the stage.

"Cut. Really swing those arms, Leigh. Fight it!"

Willow topples off the edge of the stage.

"Cut. Stop thrashing and freeze for a second before you fall. Let your expression register the shock."

Willow topples off the edge of the stage.

"Cut. Keep your face to the camera as you fall."

Willow topples off the edge of the stage.

"Cut. You forgot to trip over the footlight."

Willow topples off the edge of the stage.

"Cut! Excellent! We've got it." Chaz whispers something in Jane's ear at the monitor. "Sorry, Leigh, one more time."

The stunt coordinator helps me to my feet. "How are you holding up?" he asks. "If you've had enough, I'll insist that we move on right now."

"I'm fine," I say. I'm actually dizzy and sore, but I'm not giving up. "What's a few bumps and bruises? Willow's bikini days are over."

Jane booms over the mike again, "Leigh, can you pull down your skirt as you fall? I don't want any complaints about indecent exposure."

Obviously, I flashed the goods the first eight takes. "No problem," I call.

"You got it all straight?"

"Sure. You want me to wobble more, kick the footlight, flail bigger, freeze, register shock, fall naturally, keep my face to the camera, and land with my skirt down."

She nods. "Exactly."

I look down at the stunt coordinator and smile. "Piece of cake."

★   ★   ★

Max Volume races down the stairs, screaming Willow's name. His microphone picks up fractured conversation.

MAX
[to security staff]
Don't touch her! Wait for the paramedics!

Willow's eyes open as her father takes her hand. Sumac joins them, already weeping.

                         MAX
          You're going to be fine, sweet pea.

Paramedics push through the crowd and lift Willow
gently onto a gurney. Max and Sumac walk on either
side of the gurney, holding their daughter's hands.

                        WILLOW
          Daddy, I'm so sorry.

                         MAX
          Sorry? For what?

                        WILLOW
          The TV show...It was supposed to revive
          your career.

                        SUMAC
          We'll make the show when you're better. It
          doesn't matter.

                        WILLOW
                    [voice weakening]
          It does matter. Dad needs this show. You
          have to make it anyway—no matter what
          happens, Mum.

                        SUMAC
          There can't be a show without you. You're
          the star.

                        WILLOW
          Fallon can do it—she has the attitude.
          As long as Dad is the host, it will still
          help his ratings.

SUMAC
But you hate Fallon and she'd become an
instant celebrity.

WILLOW
I don't hate her anymore. Promise me
you'll give her the part if I don't make it.

Sumac begins to sob as she realizes the severity of
Willow's condition. She turns to a paramedic.

PARAMEDIC
There's nothing we can do, ma'am. She's
hemorrhaging internally.

WILLOW
[wincing as she hoists herself onto her elbow]
Promise me.

SUMAC
[sobbing uncontrollably]
I promise.

WILLOW
[falling back onto the gurney]
Don't be sad, Mum. I'm going to a better
place. Maybe I'll have my own show
there…My own fans…

Willow's words carry throughout the silent stadium
and someone begins to clap. Others join in and soon
the applause is deafening.

Tears roll down Willow's cheek, but she smiles.

                        WILLOW
        Don't forget me.

She dies.

                    ★ ★ ★

Someone slides the sheet over my face and I lie motionless, holding my breath, until Jane finally yells, "Cut! Print! That's the one!"

To my surprise, the applause continues to grow. Jessica pulls the sheet back before starting to clap herself. The entire crew joins in, with the notable exception of a certain skinny blond man who deliberately crosses his arms over his clipboard.

"That's for you," Jessica says. "You were incredible."

I sit up on the gurney. "I was?"

Jane comes over to shake my hand. "Now that was the girl I hired. Well done."

Sliding off the gurney, I ask, "How about a resurrection?"

She laughs. "Nope, you're still fired."

A commotion at the cameras prevents me from ruining the moment with begging.

Chaz's voice drifts our way. "This is a hot set. You can't just waltz in here—"

"I'll waltz where I like, Chuck," Annika's voice replies. "Out of my way or I'll tap dance on your pedicure. Vivien, darling! Bravo!"

"Thanks, Mom," I say. "Did Dad make it in time?"

"He was right behind me." Annika doubles back to yank Dad from Chaz's clutches. "For heaven's sake, Dennis, ignore the annoying little man."

My father hugs me wordlessly until I break away, embarrassed. "What did you think?" I ask.

Annika answers for him. "He was bawling like a baby."

"I was not bawling," Dad says.

"He used all my tissues."

"I was overwhelmed by her talent, that's all."

"That comes from *my* side of the family," Annika notes.

"Well, she has *my* hair," he says.

Mom glances at me pointedly. "Today, maybe."

I haven't seen my parents banter like this since . . . well, forever. They obviously had some chemistry once and maybe there's still hope for them yet:

> *Daughter's dazzling death scene mends thirteen-year rift between B-movie Scream Queen Annika Anderson and her estranged husband.*

Sounds far-fetched, even with my imagination.

"Look," I interrupt. "Since you're getting along so well, would you mind if I take off for a while? I have some unfinished business."

Annika offers me the car keys. "Your father can take me home."

"She can't drive on her own in L.A.," Dad says. "The traffic here is insane."

I glance at her pointedly. "You have no idea, Dad." Wait until he sees Annika in action, one hand on the wheel, the other plucking her eyebrows.

★   ★   ★

Sasha is climbing out of her Mini Cooper when I reach the parking lot. She pretends she doesn't see me, but I'm having none of it. I intend to take the high road. Even in the face of disgrace, Leigh Reid has class.

"Congratulations on your promotion," I say.

"Congratulations on your death," she says.

"Sorry you missed it. I got a standing ovation."

"Probably your last."

I hurl myself off the high road and into the gutter. "One more than you'll ever have."

"Well, your career's already peaked."

"You should be nicer to me. Our parents are dating and we may end up sisters one day."

She swallows hard. "Don't even joke about that. It will never happen."

"Wish I could stay and chat, but I have so much to do before the premiere of my first feature film tonight. And you've got new scenes to memorize."

"What do you mean?" she asks, blanching.

"I don't envy you those last-minute changes," I say, continuing on to the Beetle. "Especially with your memory."

"Better luck with your next career," she calls after me.

"I'm available to coach you anytime, Sasha. See you at the wedding."

If you ask me, class is highly overrated.

★　★　★

Karis stands in the doorway of her parent's mansion, taking in my mousy hair, Gap khakis, and T-shirt. "You look just like someone I used to know," she says.

"Yeah, I've had a makeunder," I say. "May I come in?"

The foyer alone has the square footage of Annika's entire house. Obviously, Diana Russell bounced back quite nicely from being fired. There is hope for me yet.

Karis leads me to the poolside terrace, saying, "What's up? I haven't seen you since your stunning performance as both leads in *Gone with the Wind*."

I would have thought I was beyond embarrassment at this point, but my face is still capable of a rolling boil. "Not one of my finer moments."

"Actually, it was hilarious," she says. "In a good way. Professor Kirk thought so too. He said you'd make a fine comic actor one day."

"He did?" That's the best news I've had in ages. "But I'm sure he still failed me."

"Nope. If you'd come to the last class, you'd know everyone passed except Gray and Asia. Kirk failed them for dumping their partners at the last moment. It's the ultimate breach of trust, he said."

"Worse than dropping someone on her head?" I ask.

Karis flushes this time. "I didn't *drop* you. Asia pushed you too hard and Blake deliberately let you slip. When I tried to catch you, my wrist gave out. I would have explained at the time, but I was mad that you thought I was even capable of it."

I sigh. "Too bad the fall didn't knock some sense into me before I got in bigger trouble."

"What do you mean?"

"Brace yourself, Karis: Willow is dead."

"Dead?"

"Deceased. Dusted. The hearse just pulled out of Diamond Heights."

I expect her to laugh but she doesn't. "What happened?"

There's no point in sugarcoating it. "I got fired."

"I'm sorry."

It sounds like she means it, so there may be some hope for this friendship yet. "I'm here to apologize," I say, presenting Karis with a small box. "I know I lost perspective for a while."

"That's an understatement," she says, holding the gift out of reach so that I can't snatch it back.

"Look," I begin soberly. "You know what I've gone through, Karis: abandoned by my diva mother, repressed by an authoritarian father, scarred by the Nerd Academy . . ." I stop and smile. "Are you buying it?"

"Hardly. I've got my own problems, remember?" After a moment's silence she adds, "You were right, you know. I am afraid of my mother. And thanks to your comment, I just landed a one-line part on *All My Children*."

I give her a hug. "I suppose your mom tried to beat you with her Oscar?"

"She wouldn't risk scratching the veneer," she says. "Besides, I haven't told her yet."

Karis opens the gift and laughs when she finds a gold charm in the shape of a soybean pod. "I want you to remember me prediva," I say.

She slides the charm onto her necklace. "What happened with Rory?"

"Dumped me. I guess I pushed him into it, but I've regretted it ever since."

"So what are you going to do about it?" she asks.

"Learn from it and move on, I guess. It's too late to go back."

"Don't be so sure about that. He was pretty crazy about you."

"*Was.* Past tense. As in dead, deceased, dusted."

"Don't order the hearse just yet."

★   ★   ★

Annika stands in my bedroom doorway. "What are you doing?"

I crumple another sheet of paper and hurl it at the wastebasket. "Nothing." She doesn't need to know everything.

"Well, finish getting ready," she says, turning so that I can zip up her red Oscar de la Renta gown. "You can grovel to Rory tomorrow."

"You think you're so smart."

"Not to mention easy on the eyes."

I laugh. "You do look great."

"Do you think Jake will like it?" she asks.

My stomach lurches. "You invited him to the premiere? What about Dad?"

"He won't be shocked, darling. We've been divorced a long time. Now put on some makeup."

"I already did."

"Put more on. There will be cameras."

"Mother, I've already cremated the diva."

"There's a time and a place to show off and your film premiere is one of them."

After she leaves, I take another stab at my letter to Rory, struggling to strike the right balance between pathos and dignity. I thank him for the beautiful song, but I don't tell him that it makes me cry to the point where I washed away some of the print on the lyrics. (I've got them memorized anyway.) I do tell him about Willow and that I am going back to Seattle with my tail between my legs. When I am finally satisfied, I slide it into an envelope with the charm I bought for him: a silver whale. If he doesn't despise me, he can wear it as an earring.

The third charm I bought already dangles from my bracelet. It's a tiny pair of sunglasses. Whenever I look at my Hollywood shades I'll remember my nasty collision with my own vanity, as well as the Fire Drill that helped me bounce back.

★　★　★

I've had a lot of humiliating experiences this summer, but seeing myself blubbering on a one hundred-foot-high screen ranks right up there. Why on Earth would Roger give me a close-up? I am red, blotchy, soggy, and hiccupping. It's the closing sequence of *Danny Boy* and my character, Sinead, is wracked with sorrow over her brother's impending departure. Couldn't she show some restraint? It's not like he's her boyfriend or anything. And as Roger once said, *"Less is more."* He probably included the close-up to illustrate his point.

Although I had reconciled myself to my mole on the small screen, I'm alarmed to see that it is roughly the size of Mom's Volkswagen Beetle tonight. As for the nose, all I can say is that it's a good thing I have decided to focus on a veterinary career again. Sick animals won't care how I look.

I sink lower and lower in my seat until Annika hisses, "Sit up, Vivien, your dress is wrinkling."

Her eyes snap back to the screen at the sound of her own voice, however. Now there is a face worthy of a close-up. Two perfect tears shine like diamonds in her huge blue eyes. They spill out and roll gracefully down her cheeks without disturbing her makeup. Somehow she manages to convey sadness while looking positively radiant.

The camera lingers on Annika's face as the first faint strains of U2's "Walk On" begin. Then it passes through the window and soars over Ireland's soft green hills into the sunset. The audience bursts into applause as the credits roll. When my name appears, I lean forward, wishing I could hold it on the screen a little longer. Dad, whose eyes glitter suspiciously in the darkness, whistles and claps louder than anyone.

Roger steps to the front of the theater to acknowledge the entire cast and crew. He presents my mother with an enormous bouquet of her favorite, yellow gladioli. This time it is Jake Cohen who whistles and claps louder than anyone. I stop clapping to glare at him.

He must feel it because he turns quickly and asks, "Wasn't she magnificent?"

"Totally," I say, scowling. "What do you think, Dad?"

"Annie did all right," he says. "But you, Sprout, were magnificent."

I wasn't magnificent, but Annika has proven what she's said all along: she is more than just a pretty face.

★   ★   ★

I wrap my arms behind my back. "No way. I am not your bridesmaid."

"Darling, please," Mom says, trying to thrust three dozen gladioli upon me. "How am I going to shake hands with my fans?"

"YP, not MP," I say. It's a great expression. Too bad I have to think of Chaz every time I use it.

"Vivien, I insist."

"Insist all you like. Better yet, browbeat your groom."

"Just like old times," a male voice says. "The girls are still milling."

Sean Finlay wraps one arm around Annika and the other around me. He's even better looking than last year, thanks to a funky haircut and some newfound muscle.

"I'm secure enough in my manhood to carry your flowers, Annie," he says. "You're going to have a lot of hands to shake after that performance. I smell an Oscar."

I smell something else—and it isn't an Academy Award.

"Oh thank you, Sean," Annika gushes. "I guess I did all right."

"That's exactly what Dad said," I offer.

Annika narrows her eyes and Sean hastily adds, "You're even more beautiful than I remember, Annie. Absolutely stunning."

"Oh, stop," she says, giggling so hard that she nearly inhales a gladioli petal. "I played your mother, Sean."

I open my mouth to make another observation and Sean says, "Keep it civil, kid, it's a fancy dress affair. And by the way, you look gorgeous too."

I am wearing the pink dress I loved from *Diamond Heights*. Annika pressured the designer into letting me keep it. She gives me a smug smile before excusing herself to speak to the entertainment reporters.

"You were so great as Danny," I tell Sean.

"And you did well for a greenhorn," he says. "I heard you've also got a role on a soap opera."

"Not anymore," I say, ruefully sharing the story of my meteoric rise and fall in the fictional town of Diamond Heights.

Sean laughs until he sputters when I get to the part about my untimely death. "Consumed by your own smoke at fifteen," he says.

"Sixteen."

"Let me tell you a secret," he says. "I was a regular on *Ballykissangel* for a while. Then I got a little too big for my britches. Next thing you know, *sacked*."

"You got fired too?"

He nods. "I took some time off to lick my wounds and then tried again. Now, I work hard and keep a level head."

"I think I'm going to stick with academics from now on. It's a lot safer."

"Safe is boring," he says, winking at me. "So you've had a little stumble. Get up, dust yourself off, and remember where the potholes are next time around."

★ ★ ★

Roger's eyes are the size of tennis balls behind his thick, dark-rimmed glasses. "You blew it, Verna," he says.

When you're a director, tact is optional. But I learned last year that fancy footwork only annoys Roger more. "Yeah, I blew it."

"What the hell happened? Jane said you had attitude. You never gave me any attitude."

I wouldn't be alive today if I'd given Roger attitude. Shrugging, I mumble something incoherent to my size tens.

"Speak up, kid. I recommended you for that audition and I want to know how you could possibly stink enough to deserve firing."

"I didn't *stink*," I say. "I just got too big for my britches."

He stares at me so long that I drop my eyes again. "It doesn't matter how talented you are if you've got a bad attitude," he says. "Lose it. Then come back and make me proud of you." He turns to walk away. "For what it's worth, Viola, I heard your death was something to see. Jane expects a ratings spike because of it."

★　★　★

Dad and I stand waiting to walk down the red carpet to the row of limos.

"I hate him," I say, nodding at Jake Cohen, who is carrying Annika's bouquet.

"Jake?" Dad asks. "Why? He seems like a good guy."

"For starters, he spawned a viper," I say. "And I don't think he and Annika are good together."

"Well, she seems happy, Leigh, and that's all that matters."

I happen to disagree, but I recognize that the red carpet is not the place to discuss it. Still, Dad's lack of concern bugs me. "I have another dog, you know."

"I saw that sad excuse for a canine," he says. "It's a good thing he's staying with your mother because Millie would make short work of him."

"Mom can't have him, he's mine. Besides, she hates dogs."

"Did you see them today? Her bracelet matched his collar."

"Excuse me, Mr. Reid," Sean says, joining us. "Would you mind if I borrowed your date?"

"Not at all," Dad says. "As long as it's just a walk to the car."

"Dad. Mom's given me a lot more freedom this summer."

He gives me a little shove toward the red carpet. "Enjoy it while it lasts. You'll be back in the convent soon enough."

The photo flashes are almost blinding as Sean and I follow Annika and Jake down the red carpet.

"Annika!" the photographers shout. "Over here!"

My mother's head swivels left and right, her lips locked in a smile. Her right hand rises in a regal wave.

Beyond the velvet rope, a gaggle of girls screams. "Sean! We love you! Who's your girlfriend?"

A dozen camera shutters whir as their lenses swing toward us. Sean says, "This is my costar, Leigh Reid."

"Vivien Leigh Reid," I say. This is a professional event, after all.

"Hey, Vivien," a reporter says. "What was it like to be plucked out of obscurity to act in a major motion picture?"

Heads turn to catch my reply, but with so many microphones pointing at me, I freeze. "Uh . . . awesome," I finally manage.

Another reporter calls my name. "Love you on *Diamond Heights*. What's next for Willow Volume?"

Annika magically appears at my side. "The plot is under lock and key," she says. "If she told you, they'd have to kill her."

The reporters laugh. "How about a mother-daughter photo?"

Annika wraps an arm around me and tilts her head to make sure the cameras capture her best angle. I shift awkwardly, not knowing which camera to target.

Someone points a microphone at me. "What was it like working with your mother?"

"How much time do you have?" I ask.

The reporters laugh but Annika's smile keeps stretching until the ends meet at the back of her head. She pinches my ribcage until I squeak. "It was a wonderful experience for both of us," she says. "Right, darling?"

Without waiting for an answer, she fields new questions and poses for more photos, somehow keeping track of everything, flirting and bantering and making each reporter feel important. Being a diva is more work than I realized.

A photographer says, "Could we get another shot of Annika alone, please?"

My mother hesitates but I'm happy to yield the spotlight. She's used to the heat and the glare, and I'm not interested in getting burned. My horizons have expanded quite enough for one summer.

Someday I might step out of the shadows again. For now, the light is squarely on Annika, where it belongs.